ALPHA *hole*

ANN GRECH

Edited by: Hot Tree Editing
Cover Model: Brandon M
Photographer: Wander Aguiar
Cover design: CT Cover Creations
ISBN: 978-0-6457813-8-0

Blurb

An eye for an eye—her identity, their lives.

Vengeance will be sweet. And I *will* have it. My mother's and brother's killers will suffer.

Ryder, my brother's best friend, is by my side. He's ready to help exact retribution.

Together we will destroy the earth to find the culprits.

But I want more. I want Ryder.

I want *us*. All of us.

I'm not the only one either. My guys want Ryder as much as I do. My professorhole, my bosshole, and my cinnamon bun are all secretly in love with him too.

If only convincing Ryder to try out this unconventional relationship was easy. He's a loner, the alpha, and his walls are iron clad.

But I am Queen, and I want him as one of my kings.

I won't let anything stand in my way.

Billionaire Boss Girl is a contemporary why choose/polyamorous series. There is no need for the leading lady (or her men) to choose in order to find their HEA.

Alphahole is the FINAL book in this slow-build, high-heat new adult romantic suspense series and should be read after Professorhole and Bosshole.

There are some difficult themes in this book and the overarching series that as author, I wanted to make you aware of. They include, but are not limited to:

- On and off page death (including a parent and sibling);
- References to suicide (off page and in the past); and
- Grief and mental health struggles.

DISCLAIMER

This story refers to the Australian Federal Police throughout. The events in the story involving the AFP do not follow police procedure. This was an intentional decision by the author. All deviations from procedure, ethics, and laws are purely for entertainment purposes only. The author holds both the AFP and the state police forces in the highest respect, and any artistic decisions should not be taken as a reflection on any of those police agencies.

For Dad
We should have had more time with you. But we cherished every moment we had and every memory we made. You'll always be in our hearts.

In Bosshole I said people told me that losing someone and grieving is a process that apparently gets easier. As I'm sitting down to write this it's been thirteen months since we lost Dad. Some days are easier than others. The first anniversary of losing him was not one of those days. But, Dad, we're trying to do you proud and we're working hard to live and love each other without you. But I know you're not really gone. I see the signs every day that you're still with us. That's growth, I suppose.

This story has been a challenge at every turn for me to write. You'll know the chapter that was most challenging when you read it. It nearly broke me. But getting to the end of the story and writing about Zali's dad was good for me. He's much like mine was—always there for the people he loves, and for everyone else too. I was so privileged to have been raised by him and Mum. They were and are the best parents my sister, brother, and I could ever have asked for. We should have had decades longer with Dad, but when he was alive, he taught us love, kindness, and the unwavering belief that if you can help, you should. Dad left behind a gaping void in our world. But it just proves how important he was to all of us.

I'm so very grateful for the people in my life who make my stories possible. My family—my gorgeous husband and kids, Mum, my cousin (who was also my IT advisor – all embellishments, and there are a lot, are my own), my beautiful sister-in-law (who was my financial/auditing/insolvency advisor genius on this – and there are fewer embellishments than you'd imagine here), my best friend (who I count as a sister), and my girlfriends in my MM DreaMMers author group. Thank you for always being there. I'm grateful every day for you being in my life. Words will never be enough.

McKinley Krantz and the team at Hot Tree Editing, thank you for weaving your magic, your encouragement and enthusiasm. I adored working with you and can't wait for the next one!

To Amber, thank you for the work you've done to keep me in line and organized and all the support you give me. I appreciate it, always.

Wander Aguiar and your fabulous team, thank you for the gorgeous photographs of your guys. A massive thank you also goes to Clarise Tan from CT Cover Creations. You worked your magic and both the photographic and discreet covers are stunning. Absolutely gorgeous. Your talent is incredible.

Jaye Pratt, your formatting of all the hard covers is just gorgeous. Thank you for indulging my dreams and making them come true!

Linda Russell from Foreword PR, my friend, you are amazing. I love working with you. Thank you for all the work you've done and always do behind the scenes for every one of my releases. It's truly appreciated.

To my A-Teamers, I love you guys and girls. You're my safe space to fall and you've been there for me every time I hit rock bottom. Thank you.

Last and most certainly not least, thank you to you, the readers and bloggers, for your unending love and support. Sharing, reviews, general shout outs and, importantly, reading our words means the world to every author. I never dreamed it would be possible to make a career out of my childhood dream, but you've made it a reality. I'll forever be grateful.

Ann xx

Mum, this book is all levels of spicy. For the love of all things holy, please stop reading now!

ONE

Zali

The sky was crystalline, such a vivid blue that it was impossible to describe its beauty. A lone sea hawk circled high up, riding the wind currents as it searched for its next meal. Dolphins had been swimming alongside the yacht as Ry had navigated us north along the coastline to Jumpinpin. They should still be around somewhere, but I couldn't see them. I couldn't see much of anything except the sky as I floated in the waters of the quiet cove.

I needed this. I was desperate to disconnect from the stress and the reality of the world bearing down on me. It had built up to breaking point over the last few weeks. I was like a volcano, pressure building up until I was hissing noxious steam, a fissure cracking open in my chest, and my very soul bleeding out in red rivers.

This moment of peace, the chance to get back to who I really was at my core, was almost as essential to me as breathing. My eyes drifted closed. The late summer sun warmed my naked skin as the hum of the ever-moving waters filled my ears. When I lifted my head, I could hear the waves crashing against the eastern side of the sand dune sheltering us, the squawking of the gulls, and the splashes when birds dived, or a fish broke the surface.

The tension in my muscles melted in the balmy water as my hair drifted around me like a halo. A cool breeze peaked my nipples, and I sighed happily. The contrast of the two existing so harmoniously was a reminder that I had to manage the push and pull on my emotions too. The research was heavy. The subject matter even more dire. I needed to know the truth. That meant finding out exactly who had stolen my mother's identity and what they'd done in her name since. But I was coming up short. I couldn't find anything that suggested her identity had been used for more than the bank accounts I'd found on our trip to Monaco. The gaps in my knowledge terrified me the most.

What was I missing?

Finding out could mean discovering who was responsible for my mum's and brother's deaths. It was the only way I could get justice for them.

No, that wasn't quite right.

I wasn't seeking justice.

I wanted revenge.

Vengeance.

Retribution.

I would tear apart the person who took their lives. They would bleed. They'd regret ever crossing my path.

I would revel in their destruction. I would gouge away at their very being, torturing their body and soul one piece at a time. I would force them to endure every moment of agony.

Just so I could watch them suffer.

They would regret ever being born once I got my hands on them.

And I *would* get them. Nothing would stand in my way.

Water rushed up around my face, and I sucked in a breath before sinking under. I opened my eyes, focussing on the shafts of sunlight piercing the surface, casting spots of shimmering light straight onto the white sandy bottom. A couple of bait fish scattered as my foot touched the soft-as-silk sand, my toes digging into the fine grains.

I tread water, keeping myself under. It was another world down here. It wasn't the deep hole or any of my favourite diving spots, and I didn't have my spear gun or my mask and air tank, but I had everything I needed. I had peace. The water was my sanctuary, my escape.

Unclenching my jaw, I exhaled slowly, letting the tension bleed out of me. Bubbles floated lazily to the surface. With my muscles strung tight, I mentally catalogued every part of my body, forcing each muscle to relax. Beginning at the frown between my brows all the way to my curled toes, I relaxed every one of them, slowly shaking off the stress and the tautness.

Time became meaningless. It was probably less than a minute, but I stayed under until my lungs burned, the instinct to breathe screaming at me to inhale. Instead, I pushed off the shallow bottom, my face breaking the surface barely a second later. I heard Flynn's relieved "There she is," and warmth filled my chest.

Turning to the yacht, I smiled and waved at my guys. Flynn stood on the marlin board, wringing a towel in his hands while Ry had his shirt half off and was wearing only one shoe. My guys were looking out for me, and like a watchful sentinel, Flynn had summoned my knight the moment he'd sensed danger.

I went back to floating, but I couldn't get lost again. I couldn't zone out and just be. My favourite place in the world, the little corner of the Broadwater far from the Gold Coast's hustle and bustle, wasn't cutting it today.

I couldn't get the weighty thoughts out of my head. ReimagINC's downfall, my mother's and brother's boating accident deaths, the podcast that Tristan was producing on her, our trip to Monaco to get a retinal scan—the key to breaking the so-called "unhackable" security measures of the Grande Banque Unie—and the results of that hack— bore down on me like I was Atlas carrying the world on his shoulders. Sighing, I flipped onto my stomach, swam back to the yacht, and climbed the ladder. Water flowed in rivu- lets down my body, the chill of the ocean breeze making me shiver. Gooseflesh appeared on my skin, my nipples puck- ering and the fine hairs on my arms standing on end.

Flynn wrapped me in a thick white towel the moment I straightened and tugged me against him. His warmth in- stantly surrounded me, seeping into my bones as he rubbed up and down my back, drying me. He gave me a concerned smile, the furrow in his brow not lessening despite the slight upward tilt of his lips. "You look... a little more relaxed."

"You're a bad liar," I teased. Then I sighed and cuddled into him, resting my head on his shoulder. "I couldn't switch off."

"Yeah, I get it." He pressed a kiss to my hair and squeezed me tighter, his way of encouraging me to open up in my own time.

"I've got the same thought running over and over in my head."

He stroked down my wet hair, careful not to get his fingers tangled in any knots. "What thought?"

"What else have they done? They wouldn't have just kept a bank account or two open in her name. There has to be more."

"I was wondering that too. I think we all are." Flynn pulled back and gestured to the stairs up to the main deck. "Why don't you come upstairs? The guys want to talk."

I sighed, not wanting to leave his arms just yet. But I'd known it was coming. It'd been a whirlwind of emotion and activity since I'd downloaded the data a few days ago in Monaco. I couldn't even say how long ago it was. We'd gotten the data, and the boys distracted me with food and sleep, threatening to tie me to the bed without the happy ending if I dared do any more work. I'd woken later in the day and wandered out into the living room, wrapped only in the white bedding, to a murmured conversation.

"We need to get the glasses back." Ezra rubbed his temples. His hair stood up on end as if he'd run his hands through it over and over.

"How?" Ry asked. "You're not seriously talking about breaking in—"

Tristan vetoed the idea before Ry even had a chance to finish the sentence. "Absolutely not."

I smirked at my guys. My professorhole had come a long way in a very short period of time, but that cautious, protective streak of his was still very much a part of who he was.

"I can do it," I interrupted from the doorway. Four sets of eyes turned to me, each with varying degrees of concern, disbelief, and outright disapproval painted on their faces. I huffed out a laugh. "Relax. I'm not talking about breaking in anywhere." I crossed the room and planted my butt on Ry's lap. I batted my lashes at him when he raised an eyebrow in an "Are you comfortable there?" kind of expression, and then I grinned when he wrapped an arm around my hips to hold me steady.

"Moragreiga gave me his card. Told me to look him up for a good time. How about I invite him over—"

Tristan's growl was hot as hell, but it was Ezra and Ry who made me bark out a laugh. Their simultaneous "Fuck, no" had me giggling and holding my hands up in a stopping gesture before they tore Moragreiga's sleazy but innocent head off.

"Just to talk business," I clarified. "I wouldn't sleep with him if he was the last person on earth. But if I can get him here to talk business, he'll hopefully show me some *opportunities, chat about what the bank has to offer if he thinks I'm qualified, and once we're finished, he'll take his glasses off—"*

Flynn narrowed his eyes, but I knew it wasn't in annoyance with me. He'd confessed as I was lying in bed, being forced to nap that he'd hated feeling powerless to protect me when Moragreiga had felt me up.

"If he gets any ideas about taking anything else off—"

He balled his hands into fists, his knuckles turning white. I reached for him, closing my hand over his, and replied, "I give you permission to cut it off."

"It could work," Ezra mused. "We just have to do the swap exactly like we did at the ball."

"But it can't be you or Ry. He can't see or hear either one of you. If he does, he'll know something's up," I warned.

"So, Tristan?" Flynn asked.

"I was thinking you, actually." I bit down on my lip and let myself linger on his sexy, lithe body. "Sex clearly distracts him. If he thinks I'm easy and he has a chance, he'll be focussed on that not on his glasses." I flicked my attention to Tristan and hummed happily when his intense gaze seared my insides, want coiling low in my belly.

"I'm sure I've got something that will show a little too much tit. If he gets an eyeful after he takes his glasses off, it'd give Flynn the perfect opportunity to swap them over while his attention is snagged."

Flynn growled and fell to his knees. As he moved over to us, he said, "Business associates don't flash each other."

I shrugged, pursing my lips. I'd used sex as a weapon in the past. What difference was there using it now?

I had my answer when Flynn narrowed his eyes at me and spread my knees open, reaching for the feather down duvet and tugging on it until my naked body was on display for them. "These breasts are ours. This pussy is ours."

He pressed a kiss to my mound before licking my slit and letting his fingers drift down to circle my pucker.

"This arse—ours. He doesn't get a single part of you."

"Never," I promised breathily, my clit pulsing as Flynn flicked his tongue over it while he spread my juices from my aching cunt down to my hole.

Ry shifted underneath me, his hard cock pressing against my back, and I moaned, spreading myself open and inviting them to take. Flynn obliged, sliding the tip of his thumb into my arse. He brushed his fingers against my cunt before he pressed inside, licking and sucking on my clit. I moaned.

He hummed, the vibration shooting sensation straight through me. My channels gripped him tight, trying to keep him in place as my body started its climb to nirvana. Being naked in front of them all ramped me up, but Flynn's touch had me racing to the finish line.

"Tristan, Ez," Ry growled. "Give your girl what she needs." I nearly came apart at his words, my cunt clenching as I cried out. Flynn's moan against my clit sent a shivery kind of electricity through my veins. My nipples peaked and my hips thrust up, seeking more as my body reacted.

Ry hadn't claimed me, but he wasn't shying away from group sex either.

"Take my arse," I begged Ry, reaching up and threading my fingers through his hair. He sucked a mark onto my throat and growled, but said nothing more as Tristan strode over and claimed my lips in a bruising kiss. My nerve endings went haywire, the sensation of three mouths on me over-whelming.

A hand brushed against my nipple. Rough fingers teased the bud until it was taut. Ry. I cried out again, my back arch-ing as I tried to pull him closer.

Hands under my arse lifted me. The covers that I'd had wrapped around me were quickly whisked away, tossed to the side of the sofa.

There was nothing between us except my guys' clothes.

It was a problem that had an easy solution, one that could fix it in a hurry.

I reached for Tristan's buckle, trying to tug open his belt. But Ezra was already there, flicking it open and pushing his jeans down his hips without ceremony. I moaned. Need washed over me. I wanted to taste him, for them to fill me up.

When Tristan pulled back, I chased his lips. But Ry held me tight, keeping me in place. "Fuck her face, Tris," Ry or-dered. I whimpered, my cunt clenching hard.

"I need inside you, Zee," Flynn groaned, his voice filled with pained restraint.

Ezra shoved a travel-sized bottle of lube into Flynn's hand. "For Ry," he murmured. "Help get him undressed so he can fuck our girl too."

Flynn didn't hesitate, slipping his fingers out of me and lifting my butt back up.

I was bereft. Empty. I hated it. I wanted to be stretched. Filled. Consumed by them.

But it was a means to an end. Ry shifted his hands, brushing them against my back as he fought to undo and push down his cargo pants. I moaned when his heated skin branded me, his hard cock slapping me at the juncture of my spread legs.

It turned into a frustrated cry when Ry froze, the snick of the bottle top halting his movements.

Dicks surrounded me, but no one was touching me. Not a single one was buried inside me, and I needed that. Stat.

"When were you tested, Ry?" Flynn asked, and I groaned. I loved him and yet hated him for always checking. He'd done it three times now, and each time I'd just wanted to be fucked. But I couldn't be mad. He was a sweetheart to look out for my welfare.

"A month ago. Got the all clear last week," Ry rasped, and I preened.

A grin lit up Flynn's face, and he bit his lip holding in his words. But it was as if the question was bubbling up, fizzing out of him like a Mentos in a bottle of Diet Coke. "Been planning this for a while, Ry-Ry?"

"Shut it," he growled, and I bit my tongue, unsuccessfully stopping my grin. I managed to hold back my cheer. Barely.

Instead, I turned to Tristan and Ezra, sharing a private grin with them as Ry gave us a small insight into his psyche. But Flynn didn't hesitate. He barked out a laugh before responding, "Lube up, Ry, and fuck our girl nice and deep."

I shivered, want spiralling through me, and gasped as Ry gripped my hips, stopping me from trying to wriggle free of Flynn's grip and grind against him.

"Please," I begged, my voice breathy and dripping with need.

Ry tightened his fingers on my hips, and I heard the grind of his teeth as he fought with himself. Bugger that.

I reached for him, sliding my palm over his veiny cock and spreading the lube down his length. Ry groaned, the sound so pained that I stopped.

"Don't stop," he rasped, his voice as rough as sandpaper.

He let go of me, and Flynn lowered my hips so I was once more lying on Ry, who was holding his slicked-up cock so that it prodded my entrance. I slid lower, letting his cockhead press against my ring. I wanted Ry to make the next move, but I wasn't above using dirty tactics to persuade him.

"Ry," I pleaded.

He tilted his hips forward, breaching my arse with just his cockhead. I cried out, loving the burn. He wasn't all the way in, and I needed him to be. I needed him to push past my resistance—the final barrier stopping him from burying himself deep. My cry was borne of frustration, desperate for all of him.

I spread my legs wide in a silent invitation to Ry—to all of them—to use me, to fuck me in any way they wanted. I was theirs. Their possession. Their fuck toy. Like Flynn had said, they owned me, body and soul. My heart was theirs too, and I needed this connection, this moment of being filled to bursting with them.

Ry growled, his teeth closing on my shoulder as his body vibrated under mine. "Fuck me, Ry," I begged. "Own me like the others do."

In a single motion, he slammed his hips up and pressed me down onto him, bottoming out in one smooth glide. I shouted out, my orgasm rushing at me just from the stretch of my channel around his thick cock.

Then Flynn was at my cunt, nudging my clit with his cockhead. I moaned, incoherent sounds coming from my throat as Ry withdrew and surged forward again. It was overwhelming. Their dicks set me on fire, my nerve endings electrifying and shooting bullets of bliss through me.

Flynn pushed in when Ry pulled back, and I cried out again. I was stretched tight around them, Flynn's piercings caressing my sensitive inner walls as he moved in me. Ry grunted as his dick slid up against Flynn's through my thin barrier. It was heady.

My cunt rippled around Flynn, my orgasm racing at me like a freight train. He moaned, shuddering as my core tightened around him, readying to detonate.

Ry moaned and punched his hips forward, both of them filling me. The buzz started in my veins, and I cried out, wanton and needy. Arching up, I writhed on their cocks, needing everything.

Tristan knew what I needed. He pressed his cock to my mouth, and I greedily sucked, his taste bursting on my tongue as I lapped at him. He threaded his fingers through my hair and guided me down his shaft, fucking my face in long slow strokes, his hips moving fluidly like the crashing waves of the Mediterranean only a stone's throw away.

Ezra twisted my nipple between two fingers, cupping my face and opening my mouth wider with his other hand. I knew what he wanted, and damn, did I want that too.

Tristan pulled back, his cock falling from my mouth and slapping against his flat belly as Ezra guided his dick into me. His movements were slower but deeper as he pushed into my throat on his first thrust. I moaned around him, and his fingers tightened on my nipple.

Tristan gripped my hair harder, forcing my head back, and then he pressed his cock in alongside Ezra's. I couldn't take them as deep, but it didn't matter. They were all inside me, stuffing me full.

This was what I'd wanted, what I'd craved.

Being filled by as many dicks as I could take, stretched to the brink and fucked senseless. I wanted their cum inside me, all over me, until it was dripping from me. I wanted them to own me, to use me, to fuck me until I couldn't stand.

I wanted to come again and again.

Flynn ground the barbell at the base of his dick against my clit, and Ry slammed up into me once again. I cried out, my shout muffled by the cocks lodged in my mouth.

My orgasm ripped through me, blinding me with its intensity. White heat suffused my very core as my guys' movements turned frantic, and my body, wracked with shudders and pulsing with ecstasy, contracted around them.

Ry's cock hardened, thickening inside me. I cried out again, loving how the stretch bordered on painful. He was huge. So fucking thick.

That bite, the sting, renewed my orgasm, my body tightening once more. The flood of his cum inside me was like a drug pumping through my veins and lighting me up. I moaned, never wanting the rush to end.

Only a second later, Flynn shouted out, his cock pulsing inside me. My greedy cunt spasmed, wanting all of it. But Flynn didn't linger, pulling out as soon as the final pulse painted my walls. I whimpered, frantically reaching for him as Ezra pulled away too.

"No," I sobbed around Tristan's dick. But the sound was incoherent as he threaded his second hand into my hair and pumped forward, his cock sliding straight into my throat. I gagged, and Tristan groaned, pulling back only far enough to let me steal a breath before he pushed forward again.

My shout burst out of me when another cock filled me. Ezra. He slid into my cunt, punching his hips forward hard and fast.

"Fuck me, you're so wet. Flynn drenched you, little jailbird. He filled you so good. I'm gonna do the same. Pump you full of cum until it's dripping from you."

I moaned, and Tristan withdrew once more, letting me breathe again before sliding deep and holding my face against his groin, his trimmed pubes tickling my nose. "She loves being our cum slut," he ground out. "Going to pump you full of it too."

Flynn sucked on my nipple, biting down and sending a lightning bolt of paint/pleasure straight to my clit. Another set of fingers—I wasn't sure whose—teased my clit, and I was gone, every nerve ending obliterated by the storm being unleashed inside me. Ecstasy rippled like waves through me, and a cacophony of moans and grunts sounded as my vision blacked out. I went limp in their arms.

Every sensation was happening in slow motion. I could feel Ry's dick bucking inside my arse, still half hard even though he'd already come. His fingers tightened around my waist, and he started moving again, fucking into me slowly.

Ezra's cock flexed, thickening and hardening as if he was riding the knife's edge and experiencing sensation overload like me. His harsh cry as he flooded me with pulse after pulse was enough to renew my flagging orgasm, extending it. Heat rippled through my sweat-slicked body, and I gasped a breath as Tristan withdrew before plunging forward again, his salty essence hitting the back of my throat as he moaned long and low.

My guys collapsed in a pile of sated, noodle-like limbs and fast breaths as I floated on cloud nine, trapped between them, my skin still tingling.

I snapped back to reality when Tristan asked, "Kitten?"

I shook my head, pulling myself out of my X-rated stupor and saw Ezra and Tristan sitting opposite each other, both pairs of feet up on the table. They were working, their laptops out and sheaths of paper trapped underneath weights. Ry was nowhere to be seen, but he'd been about to dive in after me only a moment earlier.

"Sorry, I was away with the fairies. What did you say?"

Tristan patted the empty spot next to him and repeated, "Come and sit."

I slipped onto the seat, and he tugged me to his side, his arm anchoring me against his body as Flynn stretched out next to me. "Did you enjoy your swim?"

I shrugged. "I was just telling Flynn that I can't switch off. Even when I'm out there, I still have a million things going through my head."

Ry placed a glass of iced water in front of me and slid into the empty armchair next to Ezra. "Thank you," I whispered, then I guzzled the cool liquid.

"That's what we wanted to talk about," Ezra continued, running with Flynn's earlier comment. It didn't sound ominous, but my heart was in my throat when I nodded. *What had they found?* Someone saying, "Let's talk" was never a good sign.

"We're worried about you," Flynn explained, his voice soft and soothing like he was speaking to a cornered animal. Ezra sat up, dropping his feet to the deck and resting his elbows on his knees.

"You aren't sleeping or eating properly," Ry added, pursing his lips, his gaze zeroed in on me.

"Neither are you," I retorted with a raised brow. Most nights the tossing and turning got so bad that I would get up, scared of waking whoever was sharing my bed. When

I'd stumble out of my cabin, more often than not, I'd run into Ry sitting at the table working on something or another.

"Maybe it'll help if we were all a little more open with one another. You know, try to avoid the mistakes I made," Ezra replied, clasping his hands as he looked between us.

"I know a little of what you're going through, baby girl," Ry started, his head hanging low. His voice was rough, filled with emotion. When he looked up at me, his eyes were glassy, his mouth set in a frown. "We're here for you."

"I just don't know what else they did. I need to know. I need to fix it." I sounded helpless even to myself, and I hated that. I was fucking Queen. I wasn't powerless or some damsel in distress. I should be able to find the information I needed to put this to bed.

To find the people who did this. To take them down.

"We don't want you to lose sight of the important things," Tristan murmured, his voice rumbling through me.

"They stole her identity. I'll never forgive those fuckers for it."

Ry blew out a breath before he shook his head and continued. "But you have something they'll never be able to take. Their memories and their spirits live on in you."

I nodded slowly. I knew what he was saying—don't let what they did tarnish the memories. He was right. But that's not what I was doing. My memories were locked away safely. They were protected. They were cherished.

The fire running through my veins, the worry keeping me up at night, was something a lot darker. I wanted revenge. I wanted to punish them, to make them experience pain like Mum, Ash, Dad, and I had felt. Ry and Flynn too. They were going to pay. I'd make sure of it.

Two

Zali

I picked up the glasses we'd taken back from Moragreiga and fingered the arms. The plan had gone off even better than we'd hoped. I'd invited him over to talk business. He'd accepted, but before we got into the details, he received a telephone call and excused himself to take it. He'd walked out onto the patio overlooking the bay, leaving his glasses on the table. I'd simply swapped them over. He was never the wiser. Once we'd spoken, it was clear I didn't meet the bank's requirements. He'd excused himself, wished me all the best, and my tits stayed safely covered by my dress.

Now I had some answers, but the information I had raised even more questions. Sighing, I ruminated on the pep talk my guys had given me half an hour earlier. They hadn't tried to get me to back off or to walk away. But they were worried about me. They wanted me to pace myself. Apparently, I didn't need to know everything yesterday.

But that's where they were wrong.

On the face of it, the only thing those bastards had done was open a few bank accounts in Mum's name. But I knew there was more. I had no doubt that they'd threatened Tristan. They were the ones who stood to lose the most if we found them out.

Tristan had his podcast. He didn't want to walk away from it. So, letting sleeping dogs lie wasn't an option. As long as he was pushing ahead with it, his life was at risk.

The only way I could keep him safe was to hunt down the arseholes who'd killed Mum and Ash and put them in body bags.

Losing Tristan wasn't an option. I'd only just found him, he and Ezra had only just reconnected, and something beautiful was developing between Tristan and Flynn. I would burn the world down to protect them.

Vengeance would be sweet, but keeping my guys safe was my priority.

Dropping the glasses with the inbuilt retinal scanner on my desk, I focussed back on the paperwork in front of me.

My phone vibrated, the screen lighting up with a text from Cara.

Hi lovely, saw these and thought of you. They'd look super cute on you!

A photo of a pair of Jimmy Choo stiletto heels with a matching handbag in a buttery yellow was attached. They'd go perfectly with my frilly yellow top.

They're gorgeous! I want, I replied, then picked up the phone to call her.

"You need these shoes and the bag," Cara gushed the moment she picked up the phone. "They're so you."

I groaned playfully. "I think I'm in love, and I don't have yellow accessories."

"Gosh, if I had the money…. You should get them."

My hum was more of a weighted sigh. The distraction was good, but guilt and fear were eating me alive even for stopping long enough to make a call.

"Hey, are you okay?" Cara asked, the noise in the background disappearing. "Did I catch you at a bad time?"

"No," I reassured her. "I'm just stressed out. I have this research to get done for class, and I'm worried about what it means."

"Doesn't make it easier when Professor Reid seems to ride you harder than the other students."

I bit back a snort of laughter at her unintended pun. She was absolutely right; he did ride me harder.

"It sucks that he expects a higher standard of work from you."

"I don't mind it," I murmured, playing with Moragreiga's glasses again. "That's the kind of research I do for a living, so it makes sense he expects more of me."

"What *do* you do?" she asked curiously. "Your shoes are too pretty for you to be a broke student." Her laugh had a pretty tinkle to it, feminine and a little nervous.

I huffed out a laugh, hating that I had to use my cover employment with Cara. I couldn't explain it, but I really liked her. She put me at ease, and her friendship wasn't contrived. She was genuine. "I'm actually a cyber investigator for the Federal Police. Ezra is technically my boss."

"Oh."

There was a momentary pause, and my gut twisted. Did that put her off being friends? I'd never been worried about that kind of thing before, but I found myself wanting to open up and talk to her.

"Oh, sugar!" she exclaimed. "I yelled at your boss? I mean, he shouldn't be mean to you, especially outside of work—or during work for that matter. But you should have told me! I didn't put your job at risk, did I—"

She cut herself off, and I couldn't help my snort of laughter. Ezra was acting like anything but my boss the night Cara had met him at the pub. He was grumpy and fighting himself, wanting to join our relationship but holding back because of his friendship with my dad.

"It's okay; you didn't put my job at risk. He actually apologized afterward, so even he acknowledged that he was wrong."

"I'm glad to hear you laughing again, Zali. I like it when you do that. It makes me happy too," she said.

Her comment hit me square on in the chest, and I wished that I was right there next to her so I could hug her.

"Thank you," I said quietly, unsure of what else to say. I hadn't had a girlfriend before. Flynn had been my best friend since we were kids, but I'd never connected with a girl like I had with Cara.

"Get back to what you were doing and take a break in an hour. I'm going to put these shoes and bag on hold for you. Call back during your next break and pay for them. Then, call me when you've done that, and if I'm still here, I'll pick them up for you."

My chest squeezed and I grinned. "Sounds like a plan." We said our goodbyes, and I turned my attention back to the screen.

Transaction data allowed me to follow the digital trail left behind. But for two out of the three accounts, the trail was cold. Some of the ISPs had shut down. The IP addresses used were dynamic, changing frequently, and every one I checked out was long gone.

The transactions on the third account—the one used more recently—kept resisting my attempt to trace it. The VPN used was CIA quality. I could crack the codes—it wouldn't be any harder than getting into the Grande Banque Uni—but I wanted a faster option than chasing my tail for weeks.

There had to be another way.

Pushing my fingers into my hair, I massaged my scalp and tried to stretch out the kinks in my neck. I needed to come up with a different approach. But what?

Time slowed as my mind ticked over all the options. Every one of them ended the same way—at a dead end.

Except one.

If I couldn't follow them, maybe I needed to lure them out. Get them to do the chasing. They'd threatened Tristan. They had some knowledge of what he was doing. They were keeping tabs on him in some way.

That was it. Tristan was the key.

Wrapping up in 2021, the Federal Police ran Special Operation Ironside. They had developed an app with an encoded messaging function that was accessible only on stripped back phones—ones that weren't capable of making calls or sending emails. The app resulted in smashing more organized criminal activities than perhaps any other on record.

The app had undergone a complete overhaul. It had been expanded into a dark web marketplace, that part of the internet that wasn't traceable and gave users complete anonymity. Except only the gateway to the site was on the dark web. Once users gained access, the site cloned itself. User interfaces, and even the underlying code, matched those on the dark web, but the marketplace actually operated on the deep web. The site whisked away data on users, creating a trail for law enforcement agencies to follow. Cyber investigators creamed their pants over it.

I fucking loved it.

The marketplace had exploded in popularity after Special Operation Ironside. Crims were looking for the next "safe" option. Seeds of doubt had been planted. There were questions. Were some of the other big marketplaces really anonymous? The answer was no. They were very much monitored by law enforcement agencies, but that was a tightly held secret. The FBI had closed down one of the sites in spectacular fashion, arresting a few high-profile mafia targets and making the charges stick. A different marketplace had resulted in the downfall of the head of a Russian organized crime syndicate. She'd been taken into custody by Interpol but had never made it to trial, her own people shooting her in the head just as she was about to step into an armoured police truck.

Hopefully, whoever was after Tristan had placed their trust in a marketplace I could monitor.

With my fingers crossed, I accessed the back end of the site using my Federal Police credentials and searched, narrowing down the wanted ads seeking out criminals for hire to reveal the threats against Tristan.

Nothing even closely relevant appeared. Sure, there were invitations to issue threats but none close to the dates of the previous notes and none that reflected a note being left. Revenge porn featured heavily. One was a threat against a teacher, but not in the same geographic location. I flagged that threat and sent it to Ezra to refer to the state police for follow-up.

Drumming my fingers on the desk, I navigated to the closed chat section of the site. It was a lot like Facebook marketplace—advertisements could be placed for services available or required and interested parties could privately message the poster for further information without disclosing any form of identification to the other. My access allowed me to monitor those posts and conversations, giving me unfettered access to everything on the site, especially the clandestine back-end data collected by the site and funnelled into databases concealed by multiple layers of obfuscation.

Keyword searches narrowed down chats to the relevant ones, allowing me to discard anything irrelevant and sift through the remaining results.

Hours passed, the sun dipping on the horizon and plunging behind the low mountain range in the west as I whittled down the results. My guys dragged me out of my office for dinner, but I was back at it straight after I'd finished.

Then I saw it.

A message from one supposedly anonymous person to another.

The message was stark. My chest seized, the breath catching in my lungs. Right there in black and white. A few keystrokes by some random arsehole and Tristan's life had been endangered.

My hands shook and my gut bottomed out, the floor seemingly falling away from me. It was as if I'd been dropped from my jet without a parachute and was plummeting down, the earth racing up to meet me with devastating consequences.

My throat burned, bile crawling up it as the words in front of me blurred. But there were no tears. There was no panic. Instead, hatred as violent as a Category 5 cyclone was devastating, boiled inside me.

I paced the room, trapped like a wild animal in a cage. I clenched my hands into fists, squeezing them until the crescents left by my nails stung and my fingertips came away red with my own blood. My nostrils flared as I sucked in a breath, and my teeth cracked as I ground my teeth together.

"Ezra," I barked, and immediately heard footsteps rushing toward me.

He slid to a halt in the doorway, and his eyes widened a fraction before he reached for me. I shook my head, warning him to stay away, but he was undeterred.

"Hey," he whispered, coming closer and brushing his thumb along my cheek. "What's happened?"

"I found the threat against Tris," I ground out in a voice I didn't recognize as my own.

He froze, the only movement in his body a slow blink. Colour drained from his face, and he sucked in a shuddery breath. "Show me."

I pointed at the screen and his gaze followed my outstretched arm. But he didn't step closer. Instead, he grasped my hand and peeled open my fingers, exposing my bloody palm. His eyes softened, and he held my hands gently. I didn't need his care and compassion though. I needed ruthlessness and anger.

But despite Tristan being the man he loved above anyone else in the world, I hadn't fully comprehended how incapable of cruel vengeance Ezra truly was until that moment.

"Ry, can you please bring me the first aid kit?" he called out.

"Never mind," I muttered, pulling my hands free of his gentle hold. "Just... stay out of my way."

Ezra tugged me close, holding on as I struggled against him, trying to push him away. He sat on my chair, pulled me onto his lap, and locked his arms in place around my waist. I could either elbow him in the nose or sit still.

Tears formed in my eyes, my hands shaking as the enormity of what I had in front of me registered. Tristan—my guy—a man I loved was at risk. Threats had been made against him. Someone had tried to scare him into backing away.

What would happen if he didn't? There was no doubt in my mind that they'd simply escalate. Threats would become actions. Actions would turn deadly.

"It's okay. We're going to fix this," he murmured against my hair, his deep voice lulling me into a sense of peace.

But it evaporated in a fizz the moment I lifted my gaze to the screen. Tristan's name and address were front and centre. The content of the most recent note was written out with instructions to deliver it to Tristan's door. Payment details and a price were set out below. Under it, written by the original poster was, "Accepted." Below that, "Executed."

"Can you trace it?" Ezra asked carefully.

"Yes. It's the AFP's marketplace."

"Do it."

I looked at Ezra, searching his gaze for any doubt, for any uncertainty. He was crossing a line that he might not be able to come back from. This wasn't going to end with me finding out information like we'd done in Monaco. He knew the score. He knew what I would do when I found out who was responsible for Mum's and Asher's deaths.

But there was no hesitation.

Ry arrived a moment later and took in the state of my hands with a shake of his head. He wiped them, smirking when I hissed at the sting, and wrapped a gauzy bandage around each of my palms. "I'll check them again before you go to bed."

Ezra gave me back my chair and moved in behind me, sighing as he massaged my shoulders. "I'll go and talk to Tristan. Can I get you anything?"

"Cuppa?"

"I'll get it," Ry offered. He playfully tugged on a piece of my hair and gave me a small smile before he walked out.

"He seems to be opening up," Ezra mused.

"A little, but then in some ways he's even more closed off." I dropped my gaze to the floor. "He's avoiding me."

"He'll come around." Ezra dropped a chaste kiss on my hair and pressed his forehead to my head.

"Maybe." I blew out a breath. "But first, I need to find who did this."

* * * * *

Finding the IP address was easy. But it was a shared one, the user's data hidden by a VPN. At least it gave me a direction. Hours passed with me locked in a brute-force attack with the VPN, trying to get past its protections and into the programming interface. While I worked, Ezra read the technical specifications and user agreement, intermittently asking me questions.

The leak protections the VPN had in place were top quality. That system acted like a reinforced seal on a pipe. If the seal failed, even for a split second, the backup kicked in, preventing the true IP address from being revealed. There was also a kill switch that cut all access to the internet if the VPN dropped out altogether.

But those weren't the features I was interested in.

I needed to know whether the VPN kept logs. If they did, I had a chance at nailing these bastards to the wall. If not, my job would get immeasurably harder. I'd be relying on failures of their leak protection systems and kill switch protocols for any chance at identifying the anonymous user on the marketplace.

"Bingo!" Ezra laughed delightedly.

"No fucking way," I breathed as he turned the laptop around so I could see the screen. He was on page forty-five, the font absolutely tiny if the zoom on the screen was anything to go by. Clear as day, the VPN's terms announced that activity logs and connection details were recorded and used for analysis to ensure the VPN was operating at its declared standards. I shook my head, huffing in disgust. They'd compromised the security of their entire system for performance data that they could use in their marketing.

"Are you in?" he asked, pointing at my screen.

"Not yet." I sighed, frustration bubbling in my veins.

But another two hours later, as the sun rose over the sandbank to our east, I did it.

I was in and looking at the result of the search.

Mauritius.

That was as specific as it got. A whole country.

I scrubbed my hands over my face and groaned. I'd been hoping for a small city. Better yet, a town. But narrowing it down from one and a half million people was doable. At least not all of them were internet users.

My eyes were raw and gritty. Exhaustion swept over me, and I yawned. Ezra was asleep on the couch in my office. Ry had paced the hallway for hours until I ordered him into bed. Tristan had stayed with Flynn after he and Ezra had spoken, needing Flynn's eternal optimism to stop him drowning in fear. The last time I'd checked on them, they were curled up together, Tristan's head on Flynn's chest, my guy's fingers tangled in our professor's hair, holding him close as they slept.

I stumbled into the galley and set the kettle to boil, and then I rested my head against the cupboard. I needed to close my eyes just for a moment.

I jumped when strong arms slipped around my waist and a soft kiss landed on the sensitive spot below my ear. "Morning, kitten," Tristan rasped. "Did you get any sleep?"

"Haven't been to bed yet."

"You need sleep," he scolded, but there was no bite to his words.

I turned in his arms and met his gaze. Playing with the soft cotton of his open button-down shirt, I responded, "I've got a country. Now I just need an address."

"Can you get it?"

I nodded, tentative but hopeful. "I think I can. It's a bit of guesswork, but with a bit of luck, I'll find them."

He shook his head and cupped my face, dropping a soft kiss to my forehead. "You don't need luck, love. You astound me with your skills. You've got this." He smirked and patted me on the butt. "Now get out of the kitchen. I'm cooking breakfast this morning. Go take a nap while I burn everything and we end up eating Ry's food anyway."

I wandered outside and stretched out on the lounger. It was already warm. Even an hour after dawn, the late summer sun still packed a punch. Closing my eyes, I napped until the smell of sizzling bacon and coffee filled my senses.

Tristan and Flynn were in the galley, dishing up plates for Ezra and Ry. Their conversation was hushed until Flynn spotted me and came over to kiss me good morning. "Glad to see you got some sleep."

I smiled, but it was an effort. Exhaustion still held me under, my movements slow and my thoughts even slower. But I was hungry, and that ruled my movements for the moment. "Yeah. Food."

My guys shared a look, and Flynn passed me to Tristan, ushering us out of the galley.

"Come on, let's get you comfortable," Tristan murmured against my temple as he wrapped his arm around my shoulder and walked me to the sofa outside. I curled into him, using his chest as a pillow. Holding a plate of food, Flynn joined us, and he fed me bites of scrambled egg and pieces of bacon while I lay there. Ezra sat on the coffee table next to Flynn. He held a cup of green tea up to my lips, letting me drink from it without having to hold the cup. Ry was with us a moment later, carrying sunscreen, a gauzy sheet that he laid over my bare legs, sunglasses that he slipped onto my face, and a hat for Tristan.

We were quiet, the guys letting me eat and drink my fill until I couldn't keep my eyes open anymore.

I forced myself to move though. I still had work to do. I had a whole country to whittle down.

"Stay," Tristan ordered gently, holding me in place.

"Need to find out who it was." I was almost delirious. But I was determined too.

"Let us help," Flynn coaxed. "We know where to look. It's just a matter of finding them now."

"I'll stay," Ry offered. "You're all better at investigations than me."

I was shuffled around. Tristan stood up, and Ry slipped into his place, tugging me against him once he was settled. He stretched his feet out, propping them on the table, and ran his fingers through my hair, massaging my scalp. I groaned, my world going dark as I slipped into sleep once more.

THREE

Tristan

"How do you want to tackle this?" Ezra asked us as we sat down in Zali's office, Ezra next to me on the couch and Flynn on the coffee table in front of us.

Hooking my foot around Flynn's, I smiled at him and shifted closer to Ezra, my shin pressed against his thigh as I leaned my side against the back of the couch.

"Zali narrowed the location of the online activity to Mauritius. Starting there is obvious, but we don't have the same skills that she does to attack it from an IT perspective. We need to better utilize the information we already have. If we approach it differently, we'll be able to see what shakes out." I paused, thinking through my approach. Ezra was as skilled in investigations as I was. It was a nice change being able to spitball ideas with him rather than having to keep secrets between us, and Flynn had proven himself a keen study.

"What information do we have?" Flynn asked, but it was a rhetorical question. He didn't give either of us a chance to answer before he began listing items on his fingers, first holding out his thumb. "We have the bank transactions. We know from Zee that we're looking at Mauritius." He held out his index finger. "We have… is that it?"

"We have a timeline," Ezra supplied. "We know when the accounts were opened and when transactions have happened." He ran his fingers through his hair, pushing it off his forehead, but it flopped straight back into place in front of his eyes.

I reached out, fingering the strands and then tucking them behind his ear. I wanted to pinch myself. I couldn't believe I could do that—just reach out and touch him like a lover would do. He bit his lip, smiling shyly at me, a flush rising in his cheeks as he laid a hand on my thigh. Warmth spread through me at his touch, and I threaded our fingers together, squeezing his hand.

"You two are so stinking cute together," Flynn quipped with a grin.

I narrowed my eyes playfully at him, and he barked out a laugh.

Ezra rolled his eyes and huffed before adding, "We've considered the transactions in each account individually. But if one person was pulling the strings, the three accounts can't be considered in isolation from one another. Let's see if there are any regular transactions being made or any pattern within dates or amounts. There's got to be something there."

"I can do that," Flynn offered. "The statements are all spreadsheets. It's just a matter of re-ordering them."

He hopped onto his laptop and plugged in the portable hard drive we'd saved the raw research to.

"What else have we got?" I asked Ezra.

He squeezed my hand. "The threat. There was more than one note sent to you. I'll see if I can find the messages and give Zali something to look at when she wakes up. If you can work with Flynn to cross reference the dates when you got the threats against the transaction records, we might be able to definitively tie them to the case."

Flynn stilled. He turned slowly, his gaze bouncing between us. "What case?" His voice was devoid of its usual happiness, that bubbly feistiness that I loved so much. "This isn't an investigation that the police will take to court, Ez. You realize that don't you?"

I ached seeing the frown line on Flynn's forehead and his downturned lips. I wanted my cinnamon bun back, the man who had comforted me the night before when my reality had crashed into me like a ten-tonne wrecking ball. I still couldn't get my mind around the fact that someone was actually after me. I couldn't compute that it wasn't just some sick joke.

"Yeah. I know, Flynn—"

"Do you? Really?" He returned to his perch on the table and closed his hand over our entwined ones. "Whoever did this isn't going to survive to be prosecuted. Either Zee or Ry is going to end them."

Flynn sighed heavily, and I could see the weight he was carrying, the internal struggle that he was coming to terms with in the downturn of his shoulders and the dullness in his normally electric eyes.

"You both need to be prepared that whoever is guilty will die. You need to make peace with that happening at Ry's or Zee's hands. I know it's going to be hard—you're in law enforcement—" He gestured to Ezra with a tilt of his chin, then to me. "—and you've built a career, a life, on criminal investigative journalism. I get how important the law and following it is to both of you… but they stole Zee's family."

"You're right," I answered, a pit forming in my stomach. Logically, I knew he was, but it was an entirely different thing to be faced with the reality of it. Even now, talking about it wouldn't hold a candle to the real thing. I looked at Ezra, exhaling in a rush when I saw a similar resignation in the tight lines around his eyes.

"It's even more important that we make 100 percent certain that this is the person responsible," Ezra stated after a moment. "I won't risk either one of them having to live with the knowledge that they'd taken the wrong life."

I swallowed hard. Jesus, how hadn't he balked at the idea? He'd barely batted an eyelid. How could he be okay with this? They could get hurt. Worse, what if they died? What if someone retaliated and put out a hit on them?

What if the guilt ate them alive? Would they become shadows of themselves? It would kill me to see them struggle, to watch them lose their battle.

Fuck me.

I didn't have a problem with them ending a person's life. My feelings for Zali and Ryder wouldn't change. That didn't even come into it.

I was frightened that they wouldn't be able to live with it.

I was terrified that it could destroy them.

Whoever did this to Zee's mum and brother deserved the shitstorm that karma and my girl would bring down on them. If they suffered because of it, all the better.

But I drew the line at hurting Zali and Ry. If anything happened to them, those bastards would have me to contend with.

And I'd make them wish they were never born.

I ground my teeth together. The determination to defend my kitten and her lion protector welled up inside me with a ferocity that surprised even me. My nod was short and sharp, my muscles vibrating with coiled restraint. We needed to get this done. I needed to figure out who it was. Protecting Zali and Ry from ever having to live with ending a life became my top priority.

Even if I had to do it myself.

"Let's get this done," I growled.

Flynn pressed his lips together in a thin line, worry furrowing his brows. "We make certain we have the right person. Then we stand with Zee and Ry. We support them unconditionally."

I nodded, and Flynn shot me a small smile. "I should keep going," he said.

He went back to work and Ezra turned to me. "You look like you want to go on a murderous rampage."

"You have no idea."

"When the time comes…." Ez paused, seemingly mulling over his words. He took both my hands in his and met my gaze. I could see the same iron-clad determination in them that was thrumming through my veins. He leaned in, his lips brushing my ear as he murmured, "We need to know who it was for sure. I'm trying to stop this, Tris, but I'm so far out of my jurisdiction, and I have so little legally obtained evidence that it's going to be almost impossible to pull off." Ezra rested his forehead against mine, his eyelids fluttering closed. He exhaled, the gravity of this situation clearly weighing on him heavily.

"But I can't stand by and watch them take a life—not when it could irreparably harm Zali or Ry. I've seen what it does to a person, and I can't let them become shells of themselves like my colleagues have."

"We protect them," I agreed. It was a promise to do whatever was necessary. And I would, without hesitation.

That meant finding out who did this. We likely had video footage of at least one person connected with them. Getting an identification on them was a decent first step.

I pulled up my building manager's contacts, then I hit her number and waited for her to answer. After exchanging hurried pleasantries, I cut to the chase. "So, Laura, reason for my call is that I've had a few notes left on my door, and I was wondering who delivered them."

"Oh, I remember that," she said with a smile in her voice. "A few months ago, a guy came in and said he was your boyfriend. He wanted me to let him up to your apartment so he could surprise you. He had a wicker basket and a blanket. It was so romantic." She sighed, then cleared her throat. "I'm sorry if I ruined your surprise, but I couldn't let him up—as lovely as a surprise date is, I hadn't seen him before, so I didn't want to breach security. I told him that, and he shrugged it off. He took out a note and laughed, telling me that he was prepared. He asked me to stick it to your door. I would have put it in your mailbox, but he begged me to put it on your door in case you didn't check your mailbox and inadvertently stood him up."

The whole scenario—the story, the actor, the props—made my skin crawl. With a shudder, I replied, "He wasn't my boyfriend. I don't know him."

Her horrified gasp was a comfort in some respects. It meant that I wasn't overreacting. But if they thought for one moment that she was disposable, if killing her was a means to get to me, then what? Laura had done me a solid by not letting him up. We were lucky that they hadn't pushed things further. But what if we weren't as lucky next time?

"Would the security cameras in the lobby have picked up the exchange? I'm trying to confirm who he was."

"Yes, but we only keep footage for thirty days." The slight shake in her voice made my gut twist. I needed to calm her down, or she'd call the police the next time he came in, and who knew whether he'd retaliate. "The most recent times he came in might still be on the system."

"Okay, here's what we'll do." I pulled up the dates I'd received the threats and instructed her to check the footage for me. I made her promise that if he came in again, she would do exactly the same thing she'd done in the past—take the note and deliver it to my door as promised. Then she needed to clip the footage and send it to me.

"You should call the police, Professor Reid," she advised. "Stalking is serious."

"It's being handled… by ah… the university," I bluffed, hoping that my spur-of-the-moment lie didn't bite me in the arse later. "I think one of my students got my address and is playing a joke on me. I'm having it investigated, and the university will apply sanctions if necessary."

She hesitated for a moment. "I mean, obviously you know what you're doing, but if he's coming to your home…."

"Yeah, it's not ideal. But like I said, don't worry about it. I've got it under control." We said our goodbyes, an anvil sitting in my gut at the knowledge my building manager was the first line of defence against this person. How the hell could I protect her too?

"Ah, guys," Flynn called. "I'm seeing a pattern here."

I moved over to Flynn, a blanket of worry wrapping around me. Fear sank its claws into me, ratcheting up the tension in my spine until my head was pounding. Rubbing my temples, I looked at how Flynn had organized the transactions. He'd set them out based on date order rather than by the account numbers. Each line was highlighted in yellow, green, or aqua, a dizzying combination, but it was clear that each of the accounts was being used in turn, likely spacing the transactions out between them.

Flynn indicated a series of three entries, each in a different colour. They'd occurred within two days of each other and totalled over eight million dollars. Better still, the transfers were all to the same recipient. There was no doubt in my mind that the accounts were being operated by the same person.

"Someone bought something big," Flynn explained.

"That was just before Rosa and Ash went missing." Ezra sighed, scrubbing his hands over his face and running his fingers through his hair.

"A hit?" I asked.

"Nah, it's too much money. You can get someone killed here for fifty grand. Fake passports and even full identities aren't anywhere near that much either. I agree with Flynn. I think they were buying something."

That didn't make me any more comfortable.

Flynn hummed thoughtfully. "So we're looking for an asset. What can you buy for eight mil? The possibilities are almost endless."

"Given the recent transactions from the open account were from Mauritius, I think we should start there," Ezra recommended.

I agreed, but had nothing—no suggestions, not even an idea of where to start.

"Yeah, I agree," Flynn stated, opening an internet browser as he spoke. With just a few clicks, he had found a list of luxury properties in Mauritius for sale. "My money is on a beachfront mansion. It'd be the perfect place to disappear to."

"Or a yacht. That gives them mobility."

"Could have been crypto," Flynn bounced back. "Bitcoin started around then, but it was worthless. No one in their right mind would have invested that amount of money in it. And if they did, the market for it would have exploded way earlier than it did." He sat back in his chair and rubbed his smooth chin, his moves short and sharp. He was clearly frustrated. But what he'd said had triggered an idea.

He continued, oblivious to the cogs in my mind clicking into place. "Heck, they could have bought people for that amount of money. Who knows what these sick—" He exhaled harshly, pressing his fingers against the bridge of his nose and cutting his own words off. "Who knows what they're capable of."

"The databases," I murmured as it hit me. My heart pounded in my chest, beating at a frenetic pace. My breath caught, and nerves borne of possibility and dread coursed through me. That was it. The key.

And I had it at my fingertips.

"What are you thinking?" Flynn asked as I flipped open my laptop and logged onto the university library. It had a treasure trove of rarely accessed databases that contained exactly the kind of obscure data I needed.

"If this was a multi-million-dollar property purchase right when the GFC was sending markets toppling, it would have made the news."

"So…," Ezra prompted, dragging out the vowel.

"The university has access to news databases around the world, and they go back decades. If there was a newspaper article written about it, we might be able to narrow down a whole island to a handful of potential addresses."

"Are yacht purchases recorded the same way property purchases are?" Flynn asked. "Because we shouldn't pin all our hopes on that and disregard the other possibilities. And let's face it, someone who was trying to hide probably wouldn't splash that much cash on a house."

"No, you're right," Ezra agreed. "It would cause a hell of a lot of speculation if some rich landowner moved in right when the world was going to shit. But a yacht sailing in might just look like a tourist. They could keep moving around too."

"What could you get for eight mil back then?" I asked.

"Nothing like this," Ezra said. "But that'd probably work in their favour. We found Zali that quickly because the yacht is so recognizable. Something a lot more toned down would have been cheaper as well as less conspicuous."

"Would Rosa's yacht have been capable of making it to Mauritius?" Flynn asked, his words quiet. Wide-eyed, his gaze bounced between Ezra and me. "Her yacht was never found. What if they were killed the weekend they went missing, and their murderers stole the yacht, changed the registration markings, and left the country? Could they have made it there?"

I looked at Ezra, but his face was carefully blank, the kind that only detectives could pull. My gut twisted and nausea washed over me. I'd suspected at the beginning of this project that Rosa Weatherall was guilty of stealing a shitload of cash from her investors, only to commit suicide when the house of cards she'd built was starting to tumble. The results of our research had led me to lean toward an alternative—that Rosa was innocent and someone else in the company had defrauded their clients of the money. The threats against me were real. The liquidator being connected to a crime family was real. The fact that most of the high-level employees were no longer working, many having just disappeared from professional networks altogether after ReimagINC went under, hadn't been manufactured. But the simplest explanation here was undeniable. Had Rosa faked her death and disappeared? Had she simply sailed on out of the country and moved halfway across the world with padded bank accounts in an international bank known for its discretion and security?

"Could Rosa have sailed it there?" I asked.

"No," Ry answered from the doorway behind us. "The yacht wasn't built for long, international open-water trips like that."

"Oh, hey, Ry," Flynn greeted him with a smile. "Zee still asleep?"

"Yeah, but she's in bed. She didn't want to get sunburnt." He gestured at our computers. "How's it going?"

"We're working on theories. Why do you say it wasn't built for those trips?" I asked, curious to hear his opinion.

"The fuel tanks weren't big enough to make that kind of journey. Even if it was broken up and the pilot skirted the Australian, Asian, Middle Eastern, and African coastlines to get there, that length of journey would have been incredibly difficult to pull off. There are a lot of remote areas not set up to receive yachts, so sourcing fuel would have been a problem. It's not like you can fill a jerry can and pop it in the tank to get you to the next fuel station if you're in the middle of the ocean or on some deserted beach. You'd need tens of thousands of litres of diesel."

"Okay, so that's out," I conceded. Whoever stole the money would have had enough to pay for fuel, but getting it onto the yacht would have proven prohibitive.

"But someone could definitely have bought a yacht over there with eight mil," Ezra agreed. "I'll take a look and see if I can find anything. I'm not sure if I can search the international databases the same way I can for the Aussie ones. I might need something more solid to go off."

"You guys yell out if I can help, yeah?" Ry gestured upstairs. "I'll be in my office."

We went back to our tasks, each of us going quiet as we worked. Database after database turned up nothing, the news records of the tiny island nation off the African coast almost impossible to find. The newspaper archives were there; I just had to find them.

Finally, I stumbled on the right database, immediately getting hits to my search terms. Narrowing it to the three-month period on either side of the date of the transfers, it condensed the results even further, leaving me with only a handful of results. Two were irrelevant—land deals funded by the British in Rwanda and land management grants being issued in Senegal—but the third article had me sitting up straighter.

I blinked in disbelief. The words were right in front of me in black and white. But they seemed too easy. I read the article, then read it again.

"Fuck me, listen to this," I gushed. Ezra's and Flynn's heads snapped up, their undivided attention immediately on me. "'*Foreign Investors in Mauritius Real Estate Boom.*

"'*Record high prices have been paid for five secluded luxury estates along the Mauritius coastline, buoying market confidence in land investments in the region in recent months. Local real estate agent, Marie Bundhoo, listed three of the properties sold in the past sixty days.*

"'*Our agency prides itself on representing the best of the luxury real estate market in Mauritius.*

"'*Despite the uncertain state of the international economy, investors are still flocking to Mauritius.*' There are pictures too."

I spun my laptop around and showed my guys the grainy images of mansions to rival the ones in Beverley Hills slotted between lush rainforest gardens and pristine beaches.

"I can work with that," Flynn said with a sense of urgency that had me moving to see what he was up to. "Download that article and send it to me so I can pull it up on Zali's screen."

"What are you doing?" I asked.

"A Google Earth satellite search. We know they're waterfront. We know they're not in the middle of town and they're big. How hard can they be to find? It's an island. Once I narrow it down, I can look it up on Google maps and hopefully find a few addresses."

"They could be holiday houses too," I pondered, bringing up a travel website.

"Hide in plain sight," Ezra agreed. "What better way to get the locals onside than contribute to the local economy. People aren't likely to look too hard into your past if they're earning money from you."

"Exactly."

Ezra scrubbed his hands over his face and groaned.

"How are you going with the yacht info?" I asked.

"I've got nothing on yachts. Without knowing more information, I can't narrow down the search," Ezra huffed, his frustration clear.

"Search for holiday accommodation," I suggested. "I'll check how property ownership is recorded over there. We might just be able to do an online search to find who the owners are once we narrow them down."

At one point Mauritius was a British colony. Systems of land ownership were often one of the things the good ol' Brits foisted upon their colonized lands. How else would the king demonstrate ultimate dominion over them than by creating a land ownership system to reinforce it? It was a feudal system of ownership that reflected centuries of in-built oppression and inequality. Then Robert Torrens came along and revolutionized how ownership was recorded, streamlining Australia's systems, and soon after that, much of the Commonwealth. If Mauritius was one of those countries, we'd be able to search the records.

* * * * *

"Okay, so Ezra realized that one person might have been operating the accounts. Flynn figured out that they bought something big with eight million dollars, give or take." Zali looked between us, and we each nodded. She quirked her lips, biting back a smirk, no doubt at our almost identical reactions.

"Based on the location of the transactions I identified, you're guessing it's in Mauritius. Tristan, you found some articles, so you think it could be property there, and Flynn has narrowed down which properties it could be, using Google Earth."

"In a nutshell," I responded.

"Okay, then." Zali slumped in her seat and yawned. She hadn't had much sleep, but she did look more rested than before.

"I've matched a few of the properties in the article with holiday accommodation. Tris has figured out how they keep a record of property owners and how to search it too," Ezra added.

She shook her head and lifted her palms up in a shrug. "I can't believe how much progress you've made. It's more than I've done in weeks."

"No, not true. You laid the path. We're still kind of guessing," Flynn challenged.

I agreed and said, "We don't know whether the money was paid to a real estate agent or not. We're assuming it was. We're also assuming that it was one of the ones mentioned in that article. I could be completely off base. We had a hunch, and we're finding evidence to support that hunch, not letting the evidence lead us to its logical conclusion."

"It's possible that we're completely wrong," Ezra warned her.

"Well, let's find out, shall we?" Zali ushered Flynn off her executive chair and brought up a search engine. "Tristan, can you find me the website for the government organization that registers property owners? Flynn, I need those addresses."

I entered the website I'd found, and Flynn handed her a piece of paper.

She typed like her fingers were on fire, command prompts popping up on the screen and disappearing as she swapped between them, issuing orders to do her bidding.

"Zali, please don't cause an international incident," Ezra begged. "This is another country's government records. It's espionage."

"Have faith, boss." She smirked and tossed him a wink that had Ezra chuckling as he pressed a kiss to her forehead.

"Behave, jailbird."

The others went back to work, Ezra looking for the messages that put out the threat against me, and Flynn checking transaction data. Headache raging, I needed a break.

I also needed to speak with Ry.

FOUR

Ryder

"**K**nock, knock," Tristan said from the open doorway. My office was a broom cupboard compared to Zali's, but she'd made it clear that it was my space, just like my cabin was, and I appreciated Tristan treating it the same way.

"What can I help with?" I asked. They'd been at it for hours, researching and theorizing, trying to come up with the who and the why. I wanted to be there with them, but it got suffocating. Knowing that Rosa's company collapsing was the cause of my dad's death made it hard to be sympathetic to her death. But that fucked me up even more. How could I not be sympathetic when it was Asher's mum who'd died?

Asher was my best friend. He'd been my light during the darkest time of my life, and I'd lost him too. In some ways I was still grieving for him. I didn't think I would ever fully accept that I'd never see him again. There were days when a memory hit me, or I got such a strong sense of déjà vu that

I turned around, expecting him to walk around the corner or call out to me.

I sometimes wondered what Asher would be like if he were alive. We'd still be friends—I'd make sure of that—and I knew he'd be larger than life. He would have been the most popular guy at work, and I had no doubt that he'd be doing something extraordinary. I could picture him on a research vessel somewhere off Western Australia, searching for new species of shark or something like that. He was obsessed with the predators and fanatical about scuba diving. He would have ended up a marine biologist or ecologist with just as much personality as Steve Irwin.

I missed him—more than I cared to admit most days.

But as much as it killed me that we'd lost him, I couldn't muster up the same emotion for Zali's mum. I wasn't sad for Rosa's life being cut short. It probably made me a shitty person, but her incompetence had robbed my parents of everything, including my dad's life. Mum was set up financially again. I'd made sure she had enough for her retirement—the ridiculous salary that Zali paid me on top of all my living expenses took care of that—but Dad had blamed himself. He couldn't forgive himself for putting his faith in someone he should have been able to trust.

So yeah, helping Zali and her guys find out what happened to my best friend was so fucking important to me, but Zali's mum complicated things. My emotions were loaded, my dad's death muddying the way I felt about her. But I'd do it for Zali and for Ash to give them justice and get Zali and Roe the closure they deserved.

"Actually, I was checking in on you," Tristan said, interrupting my train of thought. "We're all rallying around Zali, but I know how much Asher meant to you. Going over everything again can dredge up ghosts, and that's not easy to go through. I wanted you to know I was here if you ever wanted to talk...."

His words hit me like a gut punch, except the fluttery kind that warmed me up and left me off balance. I had people in my corner, I knew that, but being the focus of his energy and having all that charisma zeroed in on me was like being under a shaft of sunlight that was warming me up from the inside out. There was no laughter in his eyes, no sparkle of humour. He was serious, and that genuineness was as disarming as it was comforting. He set me at ease at the same time as making every molecule in my body vibrate. He was captivating.

It didn't matter that I hadn't known him for long; I knew he'd be there if I needed him. He was reliable and there for the people he considered important. He'd proven that to me when Ezra had been forced to arrest us. Tristan didn't need to, but he'd organized a lawyer for us.

He was the kind of man my uncle and Dad's mates had taught me to be.

My throat closed over, a lump forming that I couldn't swallow past. I choked out, "Thanks, but I'm okay."

"Okay." He lingered in the doorway, waiting for something else, but I didn't know what. My breath was shuddery, and I laced my hands on my lap to hide the shake. Somehow, I knew he wanted more. I knew he wanted me to speak to him. But I didn't—I couldn't get past that damn lump. He visibly swallowed as if he was attuned to my predicament and opened his mouth to speak before snapping it closed again.

After a moment, he asked, "I might be stepping out of line here, but can we talk about your dad?"

"No," I said, extending out the vowel and shaking my head. I didn't want to go there. It was uncanny that our thoughts were so aligned, my dad and Asher already at the forefront of my mind, but that was a place I didn't want to go with Tristan. Not now, and possibly not ever.

"Right. Well, as I said, I'm here if you ever want to talk about any of this. Whether it's as a sounding board or just to vent, I'm here." He shrugged, but the casual gesture didn't fool me for a second. He was trying to look nonchalant and failing miserably.

"Why?"

"Why am I offering?" he countered, his brow creasing as he spoke. I nodded, and he turned his lips upward in a hint of a smile before he continued, "Because I'm a nice guy?"

I barked out a laugh, and he sobered, adding, "Because I know what it's like to experience something that has affected you so profoundly that it changes your life. I don't know loss like you and Zali do, but I can empathize. Believe it or not, I'm a half decent listener too. And if that's not enough, you're important to—" He sucked in a breath, a sharp intake that cut his words off. It was as if he'd caught himself about to say something, then changed his mind.

Eventually he continued, saying, "You're important to Zali, Flynn and Ez, which makes you important to me."

"You aren't half bad yourself," I conceded with a chuckle. I was trying to play off just how much his words meant, and as much as I didn't want to talk, I kind of needed to. It wasn't just the research—it was him. He was making me see things that I hadn't seen before. Same with Ezra.

But I wasn't ready to talk about that, and if I had to choose, I'd speak about the shit in my past every day of the week over choosing to deal with the quagmire of thoughts plaguing me now.

My leg bounced as I gathered up the fortitude to speak about those dark days. "My dad committed suicide. My pops died of a heart attack really young. At first, we thought it might have been the same thing. But the autopsy found otherwise. He'd taken pills." I closed my eyes and tried to block out the memories that hit me.

I sensed rather than saw Tristan move further into the room and lean against my desk within reaching distance of me. He squeezed my forearm tight, letting me know without words that he was there. I needed the contact, needed the strength that he was lending me to keep talking, and when he let go, I immediately missed his touch.

I inhaled slowly, and his scent enveloped me. He smelled good—he always did.

He was throwing out calming vibes, warmth and concern covering me like a warm blanket on a winter's night. I soaked in it. I hadn't been cared for in a long time.

I was the one who was there for everyone else.

When Dad died, the role reversal from kid to caretaker had happened quickly. I'd been thrust into it by the expectations my uncle and Dad's mates had placed on me, expectations that had settled heavily on me. I bore the burden willingly, but giving in and letting Tristan be there for me in the same way I tried to be there for everyone else—Zali, Flynn, and Mum—was a relief.

"Mum and Dad had been saving forever to buy a house. They both worked normal jobs. We weren't well off or anything, so it was hard for them. They were talking to Rosa, trying to figure out how to bump up their savings, and she suggested they invest in her company." Tristan squeezed my arm again and didn't let go this time. I closed my hand over his, needing to keep him where he was.

Pain crashed over me, the wounds I'd tried to bury deep opening again. My heart hurt, my eyes stung, and my breath hitched.

"They fought over it," I said, my voice cracking. Clearing my throat, I added, "I think in the end, Dad might have just transferred their savings without telling Mum. But Mum was adamant that he get the money back. Then everything turned to shit. Rosa didn't return it. She always had an excuse. All I remember was the yelling—Mum and Dad, Dad on the phone, Dad at me. He was lost and angry for those last few months. He died shortly after. Mum never saw the money again."

"I'm so sorry, Ry."

"Me too." I nodded, wishing that my life, just like I did Zali's and Roe's, had turned out differently. "But it is what it is."

"Still not fair." He squeezed my arm again, and this time I let him release me. "I read about your parents when I was doing my research, but I didn't know their names—I talked about them to Zali, taunted her with their story. I'm sorry I did that. It was shitty of me."

I shrugged, not knowing how to respond. It was shitty, but he didn't know me then. He still didn't, not really, but I appreciated his apology.

"I didn't put it together at first—the interview transcript had names redacted—but then Flynn recognized your dad's name on Zali's wall. He said that he'd died suddenly." Tristan looked around my office, taking in his surroundings without comment. His voice was melancholy when he finished his thoughts. "I'd hoped it was natural causes, knowing it was anything but."

We were quiet for a time, both of us processing our thoughts. I broke the silence, asking, "Do you think she could have saved the company if she hadn't died?" I didn't know what difference it made now—probably some misplaced hope that if the cards had fallen a different way, we might not have lost them. But I needed to know.

He didn't answer straight away, and the longer he delayed, the more I knew what his conclusion was. "She would have needed a miracle," he finally murmured, his voice full of regret. "There was a lot of money embezzled. To make it back during a period of economic growth would have been difficult, but to do it when the world markets were collapsing was nigh on impossible."

"Those bastards took my parents' money. They have a fuckton of blood on their hands." My blood boiled whenever I thought about them living the high life while Mum had struggled both financially and emotionally. Dad's life insurance payout had never been forthcoming. Apparently, he'd changed it just before he died, thinking that the new policy offered more coverage. It would have if the exclusion period had passed. Suicide wasn't covered in the first twelve months of a policy, so Mum got nothing.

"I want them dead, Tris," I seethed, my hands now shaking from blind fury instead of sadness. "I want to make them suffer."

"I know. But there's something I need you to do first."

My gaze shot to his as he stepped closer, and his scent filled my lungs. My eyelids fluttered, and I mentally kicked myself. I couldn't get into this again. Yeah, he smelled good. So what? It wasn't like I wanted to jump his bones or anything. Jesus, talking made my walls crumble, and I hated it. I needed distance between us.

I'd managed to separate myself enough that I avoided coming face to face with a fuck fest on most days. But it was getting harder. I'd allowed myself to indulge two times too many, three if I counted Zali's plane in Sydney. Monaco was a mistake, something that should never have happened if I had any hope of keeping my defences intact. I knew that if I let myself get any closer to Zali, I wouldn't be able to resist the others either. Tristan was too damn charismatic for his own good, Flynn was adorable but in a sexy excitable puppy turned demanding and confident kind of way, and Ezra was sex on legs. It didn't take a genius to spot how attractive they all were, and all four of them together was too much of a temptation for me to resist.

"Yeah?" I asked, my voice more of a squeak than my normal baritone.

"Yeah." He nodded with a smile that bordered on wicked. His emerald eyes sparked, daring me to react. "I need you to man up—"

His words were like a slap to the face. A bucket of ice-cold water dousing me. My chest squeezed tight, and disappointment in myself flattened me with the force of a steamroller. But he was wrong. It's all I'd ever done. I'd worked so hard to make them proud. I'd focussed all my energy into becoming the man they wanted me to be, one Dad would be proud of.

Anger surged through me, and I reacted on instinct, pushing up out of my chair so fast that it skittered across the small room and bounced off the wall.

"What the fuck?" I barked.

I crowded Tristan, grasping his button-down shirt in my fists and shoving him against the desk. I loomed over him and clenched my jaw, my lips turned up in a sneer.

Who the fuck did he think he was?

He didn't know me.

I'd stepped up from the moment Dad died. I'd been there for everyone. I'd taken care of Mum, my grandma, and pop. I'd been there for them, the shoulder to cry on and the person who helped pick up the pieces when they needed to be put back together again. I'd started a part-time job so I could help pay the bills and take the stress off Mum. I'd become the man of the house just like Uncle Kev and Tom and Chris, Dad's mates, had told me over and over.

I'd done it for Dad.

I'd done it for Mum.

When I wanted to cry, when I wanted to be held and rocked and told that it'd all be okay, I shoved it down. I buried it. I held my head up and my arms out so Mum could lean on me.

Only Ash had seen me fall apart.

Then I'd lost him too, and I'd stepped up again. I'd erected walls around the shattered remains of my heart and held my arms out wider. I'd pulled Zali and Flynn into my embrace. When Roe was barely holding on, I'd made sure he knew that his daughter was safe in my hands to take the stress off him.

I'd watched out for Zali, protected her. I'd made sure that the fuckers who wanted her body didn't take more than she was willing to give. I'd made sure she got home every night and that the worst of the guys never got anywhere near her. I'd kept the drugs and alcohol away and made sure she ate properly and rested enough. I'd checked in with Ezra, making sure he knew he'd have to answer to me if he didn't look after her too.

Then after all that, when Roe was still struggling, I'd helped Mum reach out to him so they could hold onto each other, grieve, and slowly heal together.

Tristan didn't know the first fucking thing about me. If he thought he could walk in here and tell me that I needed to man up, he had another thing coming. My nostrils flared as I sucked in a breath, cocking my fist back.

"Settle down, Ry," he coaxed, resting his hands on my chest. His touch was soothing—strong and confident. Warm. I shook him off, fighting that wave of calm he threw out, blanketing me with it and trying to draw me under. He was like a wizard casting a spell.

But I wasn't an idiot.

I wasn't falling for that. He reached out again, and I lifted my chin, proving to him that he didn't affect me. His eyes softened. It wasn't pity I saw in them, though, but rather the same genuineness I'd seen earlier. I gripped his shirt again, shoving him back until he was practically sitting on my desk, his legs spreading to make room for my hips as I forced him off balance.

It wasn't until I pushed my weight onto him, pinning him in place, that I realized my cock was raging hard. I swallowed back the groan at the heat of his body pressed up against mine.

His pupils flared and his jaw ticked, his breath coming harder. I liked him like that, trepidation making his heart beat faster.

I didn't want genuineness or caring.

I wanted to pound it out of him.

Flashes of hot and sweaty naked bodies writhing together exploded in my mind's eye. Tattoos and muscles, masculine grunts, and deep gravelly groans. Tongues tangling together, hands and mouths against bare skin.

I ground my teeth again, fighting my body's reaction to him.

I channelled my anger, my pulse spiking and throbbing in my veins.

He brushed his thumbs over my nipples, and my hips punched forward without any conscious thought on my part. My fucking body was betraying me no matter how much I tried to convince myself that I was angry, not turned on.

Tristan ran his hands down my naked chest and around my hips, clutching me tightly. He pulled me harder against him, and I gasped at the perfect way our erections nestled together, our hips trapping them in place.

He growled, "I want you to man up and take what you want." Dropping his gaze to my lips, he licked his own and ground against me, his fingertips digging into my arse. "Get your shit together, Ry." He rolled his hips again, slowly thrusting against me, and my eyes fluttered closed. My breath caught, and my cock pulsed.

"Admit to Zali that you want her. Admit it to yourself."

He leaned forward and ran his nose up my throat, stopping me in my tracks. My body went haywire, every one of my nerve endings on overload. Like I'd been struck by lightning, I was electrified. Every instinct in me screamed at me to do something. Anything. I should shove him away, but I wanted to pull him closer. I wanted to pin him to the desk and rub myself all over him until we were both completely sated. Jesus Christ, if I didn't back the fuck off right now, I'd come in my pants if he so much as breathed on me again.

Tristan dug his fingers into the meaty part of my hips and held me steady, staring into my eyes as he said, "The ball's in your court—she wants you, and we want you with her too. You just need to reach for her."

"No," I growled, fighting him. This right here was the very reason why I couldn't give in and reach for Zali.

I tried to pull away, to put some distance between me and his dizzying scent that burrowed inside me and gnawed away at the walls I'd carefully erected. Instinctively, I knew that I could lower them and be safe with him.

But that wasn't what I was put on earth to do. I was there to support everyone else. I didn't get the luxury of being anything other than the strongest in the room, the one who was there for everyone.

Dropping that drawbridge and letting him pass through would utterly destroy the man I'd tried to become.

For them.

I'd done everything asked of me. I'd taken every responsibility placed on me seriously. I'd fucked up more than once, but everything I did was to make them proud of me, to show Mum, Uncle Kev, Chris, and Tom that they could rely on me to be a man, to be the man they all needed. To step into Dad's place just like he should have been here to do.

That was my job, my responsibility.

But I would fail if I gave in.

If I stopped resisting and reached out for what I really wanted, it would be the end of things. They wouldn't recognize me as the man they'd once been proud of.

It would disappoint them, and I'd never risk that. I'd idolized them as a kid. Now, as an adult, I saw that some of their views were toxic. But I couldn't shake that need, the desperation, for their approval.

It was better to stay on the path than risk veering off into the unknown and disappoint, and probably lose, the people I had left.

"Don't be a stubborn arse," Tristan snapped, fighting back against my feeble attempt to pull away.

He pushed off the desk and stepped forward, shoving me against the wall. He stood in my personal space, his chest pressing against mine with every breath I sucked in. My pulse rocketed through my veins, thrumming in my ears as I clutched his shirt tighter.

Gentling his voice, he added, "You love her, I know you do."

"And what, I get her and all of you too?" I sneered, my defences on high alert. I couldn't want them, and because of that, I didn't want to be anywhere near them. If I let them get too close, temptation would overwhelm me.

I'd cave.

I'd want things I shouldn't.

I'd be weak for them.

They were dangerous, and I needed to be strong.

I couldn't let it happen. There couldn't be anything between Zali and me because of them. Because of me.

"Is that so bad?" he asked quietly. "You love Flynn, and you and Ez were friends not so long ago. Why is it so bad to share her with us?"

He didn't understand. He couldn't. He was free to get it on with anyone. But they had expectations. My family put pressure on me without even knowing it. The weight of my father's loss and the risk of my family's disappointment were heavy burdens to carry.

I couldn't cave. I couldn't give in. I couldn't want it.

I couldn't want them.

I stepped back, let go of his shirt, and smoothed it down, my attempt at removing the creases utterly futile. "You need to leave," I rasped.

"Ry—"

"Please leave." My shoulders fell, slumping under the weight. I couldn't look at him. If I did, the outcome would be inevitable.

He nodded and stepped out of the door, hovering with his hand on the frame. With his back to me, he spoke softly, barely loud enough for me to hear. "If it's me—if it's us—don't let it stop you from being happy with Zali. You have a real shot, Ry, and I want that for you. For both of you. I won't give her up. But I'll give up time with her so she can be with you."

I didn't answer him. What was there to say? Thank you? Yeah, no.

"Aren't you tired of denying it, Ry? Denying yourself?" I stayed still and quiet, and he sighed. "Fall. We'll catch you."

I huffed out a laugh that held no humour. My falling and their catching me were the two things that I just couldn't allow. He tapped the frame with his knuckles and added, "Just… think about it," before he walked away.

Ryder

I tasted blood and swiped my tongue over my lip. I'd been worrying it from the moment Tristan walked out of my office. I'd wanted to call to him to come back. I'd wanted to talk. But what could I say?

Now hours had passed, and darkness had descended over the yacht. Zali's Noble Steed. Fuck, I wished I could ride the thing right the hell on out of here. I needed a break. I needed to be able to steal a breath without going under, water filling my lungs and drowning me.

I *was* tired.

Exhausted.

The fatigue was bone deep. Tristan was right. I was spent.

But what choice did I have? The baggage was mine to carry. I couldn't just pass it off to someone else.

Uncle Kev, Tom, and Chris believed in me. They saw me as the kind of man they could clap on the back and say, "Well done, mate," to. They were proud of me. I'd done that. I'd made them proud.

I'd dragged myself out of the depths of despair and made sure that the people closest to me were right there with me. I was strong enough to do it, to be a real man. My shoulders were broad enough to carry the weight of expectation.

I was the alpha of the pack. But that didn't make me one of those chest-beating dickheads. I knew what I needed to do, and I did it. I'd proved to them they could trust me. I always tried to lead by example—be a good person, care for the people around me, and be kind to them. I kept my family safe. I wasn't aggressive to them in some need to show off my masculinity, but I would defend them to the death if they needed my protection.

It wasn't all a hardship. I got to play with the most fantastic toys—cars, yachts, planes. Who could complain?

But I was a fraud too. They saw me as a man they were proud of. Would they feel the same if they knew the truth? Would they even still like me? Out of fear, I'd buried my sexuality a long time ago. I didn't think I could cope with losing anyone else. Mum's disappointment would gut me with a rusty knife. Disappointing Uncle Kev, Tom, or Chris would be like losing the last remaining piece of Dad all over again.

I'd worked fucking hard to get where I was, to be seen by them as their equal. It'd been drilled into me that a real man steps up when needed. They'd turned me into a man who would make Dad proud. But if they knew the truth, would they still think that? Or would their disappointment in me, in what I craved, be the end?

I couldn't risk doing something just for me when the outcome could hurt them. And them being disappointed in me would hurt them.

So I sacrificed that part of me to keep them safe and happy because that's what a real man does.

I'd watched Uncle Kev, Tom, and Chris with Dad over the years. They watched sport and knew every team's stats. They knew every player; they could recite their height and weight, tackles, or how many hundredths of a second they'd driven the lap faster or slower than their competitors. They kept team photos and copies of signed memorabilia up on the wall, and their favourites were obvious.

But they were always manly about it. That manliness was as much a lifestyle as a mindset.

They told me to find the prettiest girl and marry her. A round arse, perky tits, kissable lips, and a tight pussy in the one woman made her a keeper. My stomach had rolled when they'd told me that, but I'd nodded, taking it in and knowing that my sexuality would give me nothing but problems. Being pansexual at least gave me options, though, and I thanked God for not making me gay.

It was easier to pretend I was straight.

Chris had sat me down to talk just after the funeral. We hadn't even moved to the wake. I was spaced out, staring at the place where the hearse had driven Dad's coffin away from the chapel. He'd told me to go and find a party that weekend. If I got my dick sucked, it'd make me feel better. He'd said that at my age, he was already fucking the girls in his year level. If I did that, it'd pep me up, help me feel better.

But I wasn't even remotely interested in sex. I'd just wanted to fish and swim with Ash. I was a kid, for fuck's sake, but he'd treated me like a man.

It had clicked then. He considered me one of the guys. Uncle Kev had done the same, trying to show me what a man did. He'd hammered it into me—don't cry. Don't be weak. Men were strong. Men supported their women, and Mum was my responsibility now.

Tom talked to me about doing what was best for his family. Now I looked back on that conversation and my gut lurched, nausea washing over me. He'd held himself up as an example. He'd let his piece of arse on the side go. He'd sacrificed a hell of a good time in the sack with her because getting busted fucking a wild woman would hurt his wife.

But even though their examples weren't stellar, they were my family. Uncle Kev was Mum's brother. He still looked out for her, renting the other half of his duplex to Mum at a reduced rate. Tom and Chris were Dad's childhood friends. The four of them, Uncle Kev included, were the awesome foursome, completely inseparable. They made me feel important. They taught me how Dad would have wanted me to grow up and how to make them proud.

And they were proud of me.

I sighed and banged my head against the desk. Fuck me, I was tired.

There was a *thunk*, and I looked up to see that my phone had slipped off the book I'd had it propped on. I palmed it and exhaled, dialling Mum before I could stop myself.

"Hi, honey, how are you?" she greeted me. Mum was a ray of sunshine, and my chest warmed immediately on hearing her voice.

"I'm good, Mum," I lied. "I'm just checking in."

"Everything is good here, but it's been too long since you've popped over," she chastised me.

"I know," I sighed.

"Come for dinner soon."

"I will." I agreed. Awkwardness settled over me. I didn't do awkward—or silences with Mum for that matter. I could always talk to her. What the hell was wrong with me?

I asked, "Do you need anything done around the house?"

I could almost see her waving off my concern. "One of the lights is out in the kitchen, but I can't reach it. If you could bring a ladder with you, I'd appreciate it. What's happening in your world, Ry? It's unlike you to be so quiet."

"I've just been working. Zali's doing a big project at the moment, so it's taking up a lot of time. I'm trying to support her."

"You work too hard. You deserve a break. Zali should see that. The hours she has you working are ridiculous."

"Mum," I warned, my voice holding an edge. "It's literally my job." This wasn't helping. I bit back my frustrated groan. I didn't want to argue with her, but that's where it was heading.

Her voice was gentle when she said, "I want you happy, Ry. I want you to meet a lovely girl and have a family. You're only young, but the longer you wait to start looking, the longer it'll take to find her."

How could I be mad at her when all she wanted for me was the thing she wanted for Dad? How could I break her heart by telling her that kids were a definite no, but I'd trade them for three other guys?

I huffed out a silent laugh that held no humour.

I settled on, "There's time." But I knew better than most that time was the one thing we didn't know if we had.

"Are you happy, Ryder? Really happy?" Mum asked, surprising me. She was so damn perceptive. She'd seen straight through my poor excuse for calling her and knew exactly when I was fobbing her off because I didn't like the direction our conversation was headed.

I sighed, unable to keep it in, the weight on my chest paralysing. When I boiled things down, I wasn't happy. I was lonely. I wanted more than what I had. I wanted what Zali and Flynn had found in each other. I wanted friendship and love. I wanted hot-as-fuck sex.

I didn't want to be Tristan and Ezra, or even Zali and Flynn, wasting years they could have been together.

But that's exactly what I'd done. I'd wanted Flynn and Zali, so I'd put both in the friend zone to protect myself. I couldn't in good conscience wish that things had been different. If I'd been with Zali, she and Flynn might never have gotten together. I certainly wouldn't have understood her wanting to be with multiple men without having seen it work first. We probably would have imploded spectacularly, and I would have lost them both.

Now, with Ezra and Tristan added too, it was even more complicated.

That was the problem in a nutshell—a poly five-way relationship was so fucking uncertain. Was the risk worth taking? Should I try for something more and disappoint everyone around me? And it would be a disappointment. If it worked out, I wouldn't be able to keep up the barrier between myself and the other guys—I'd cave—and my family, the men I looked up to, wouldn't be able to look at me again in the same way. If it didn't work out, I'd lose all of them anyway.

I finally settled on, "I don't know, Mum. In some ways, yes. But not in others." I shrugged even though she couldn't see me. "But it's one of those things. I've got lots of things to keep me busy." I laughed, and it sounded forced, even to my ears. "After all, when would I get time to change your lightbulbs if I had a girl breathing down my neck, wanting babies?"

Mum was quiet for a long time, so much so that I checked to see if the line was still connected. "Ryder Beckett, you listen to me," she growled. "I am a grown woman. I don't need you to be alone and unhappy to be available to change a lightbulb or do any other chores around the house for me. I'm perfectly capable of doing them myself." There was a pop and a glugging sound—Mum pouring herself a glass of wine. "I'm not an obligation to you. I'm not a responsibility—"

"I know that, Mum—"

"Well, stop acting like you need to be my hero." Her voice softened when she added, "You already are." She paused so her comment could sink in, and I closed my eyes, letting the sentiment wrap around me. "Ask Zali out, Ryder. Don't let more time pass without knowing whether she feels the same way as you do."

"How do you…," I groaned. I'd opened my fucking mouth and had just given myself away. Instead of denying it, I'd basically admitted my feelings to her, and Mum was relentless. She wouldn't accept the excuse that I should stay the hell away without dropping all the juicy details on her lap, and there was no way I could do that.

"Be the brave man I know you are, Ry. Being scared is okay—it means it's important to you."

"Mum, I can't," I mumbled, knowing it was futile to try to explain.

"No, Ryder, you can." She paused, and I heard her breath hitch, her voice wobbling when she spoke again. "You dad was a bit of a dick when he asked me out."

I blinked and barked out a laugh. She'd never told me how Dad had asked her out. I knew that they got together just after Mum had finished school, but I didn't know the full story, and clearly this one was half decent.

"Tom and Chris were egging him on, and Kev was ready to kill him. He was three sheets to the wind and slurring his words. But he sidled up to me in front of all my friends, all suave and full of himself, and he asked me to go bowling with him." She chuckled, her laugh soft and a little melancholy.

"I told him yes after he'd pestered me for an hour, and we agreed to meet. But he was drunk enough that he didn't remember our conversation and stood me up. I called Kev to tell him his friend was a dick, and by the time I got home, he was waiting on our doorstep with a bunch of service station flowers and an apology."

I could hear the smile in her voice, and it loosened the vice-like grip that had closed around my heart.

"We only got a few years together, but they were worth every bit of heartbreak when he died. Don't hold back, Ry. If she's the one you want, ask her out." Then after a moment, she tacked on, "While you're sober."

I laughed again and nodded. Yeah, I wanted that. I wanted what they'd had. Maybe I could make it work. Maybe if I took up Tristan on his offer, I could get part of Zali and keep enough distance with the guys that I got the best of both worlds. I could have her and keep the other parts of me buried like I'd always planned. It was no different to dating any other woman—except that she was the one I wanted.

I bit my lip and hissed, the sting and fresh tang of blood oozing into my mouth reminding me that I'd worried my lip until I'd made it bleed. Could I do it? Could I keep the walls in place and get some of what I wanted?

There's only one way to find out.

Six

Zali

A knock on my office door had me turning my head and smiling at my interruption—until I got a good look at him. His lip was split and swollen as if he'd copped a fist to the face.

"Hey," Ry greeted me as he hovered in the doorway. "Can we talk?"

"Always." My heart lodged in my throat, my gut twisting. What had happened? I hadn't heard any fighting. The yacht had been as quiet as a tomb for hours.

He stepped inside, shut the door softly, and sat down on the couch. I joined him there and reached up to touch his cheek, his stubble soft against my fingers. "What happened?"

"Tristan came to see me before. We had words." He didn't seem angry, not even a little pissed. If anything he seemed kind of anxious. What the hell had happened?

I was trying not to jump to conclusions and overreact, but the butterflies in my belly were swooping, and not in a good way. It was as if I was in one of those mining carts on rail tracks you see in the movies, ready to be thrown out on a particularly gnarly turn.

Instinct told me to yell out for Tristan and demand that they sort their shit out like adults, not rowdy teenagers. But I held off. They were both stubborn shits. What if they wouldn't work it out? I needed both Tristan and Ry. I had no idea how to make things work between us if they didn't get along. How would Tristan ever feel comfortable spending time on the yacht if he and Ry clashed? I couldn't ask Ry to leave—this was his home as much as it was mine. But that meant me visiting them in their apartments—and yeah, that wasn't going to happen.

Maybe they both needed a little attitude readjustment. A spanking administered by the other. I bit back my smile—inappropriate as it was—and asked, "What kind of words?"

"He, um, told me to man up."

I snapped my head up, my eyes wide. What in the actual fuck? Why the hell would Tristan say that? What was it even in relation to? And seriously, why would Ry react in a way that resulted in Tristan hitting him? What were they, thirteen?

Ry huffed out a laugh and shook his head. "This is me manning up."

I was lost, and my confusion must have been etched onto my face if Ry's eyeroll was anything to go by. Or maybe he thought the whole concept was ridiculous. I had no idea.

"What are you manning up about?" I asked, my confusion turning into frustration. We'd finally managed to reach some sort of silent understanding between us—Ry seemed to be letting down his walls and was at least slowly getting closer. Why was Tristan rocking the boat? Why was he stirring up trouble? Especially now.

It had to be about Monaco. Ry and I hadn't spoken about what had gone down there. The sex had been incredible—his practically dumping me off his lap and walking away immediately after, not so much. But I knew we'd eventually talk. Even if the outcome wasn't the one I wanted, we would sort things out. I respected Ry too much, and loved him more, to risk pushing him away.

After all, he wasn't just considering dating me.

I had a whole lot of baggage in the form of three other boyfriends that he had to contend with.

I thought we'd shown one another that we could make it work, that we respected one another's boundaries. But maybe I'd been wrong.

The silence stretched out between us as he fiddled. It was so unlike Ry that it had my anxiety ramping up. Why had Tristan told him to man up?

Ry rested his elbows on his knees and clasped his hands together. He exhaled slowly, his knuckles turning white as he squeezed his fingers together, then he said in a rush, "Tristan told me that I needed to get my shit together and admit that I wanted you. Mum told me to ask you out."

Shock held me immobile. My mouth opened and closed like a goldfish's. I didn't know where to begin to process either nugget of information—and I didn't mean the one that Ry was attracted to me. We'd pretty well established that. It was the part where Tristan and Ry were speaking about feelings, or the one where Ry went to his mum for advice. He was so buttoned up. He was happy to listen to any problem presented to him, but he never reciprocated. He never opened up about anything. Hearing that Ry was speaking about anything like that, and Tristan was encouraging him to be open, blew my mind.

"Ah—"

"He told me to stop backing away because of the three of them." His smile was tight, and it didn't come close to reaching his eyes. The tension around them remained clear to see in the crease in his brow. "Apparently, he's prepared to give up time with you so I can have some of it." He sounded relieved, sending a stab of disappointment through me, but I was still stuck on the part where he'd spoken with Tristan.

"Oh—"

"So, yeah." He swiped his tongue over his swollen lip before standing up.

"Wait, where are you going?" I asked, panic infusing my tone. I lunged forward and gripped his wrist, tugging him back to the couch. "You can't just say shit like that, then up and leave, Ry. Are you going to give me a chance to speak?"

"You just did. You said, 'Oh.' I figured that was your response." He clenched his jaw and diverted his gaze, staring out at the starlit water just outside the window.

I shifted to sit on the coffee table in front of him and tried to reach for his chin to turn his face toward me. But he wrenched out of my grip. "Turn around, Ry," I begged, resting my hand on his knee and cupping his cheek with the other. When he finally turned, my heart melted at the vulnerability shining in his eyes. "I have feelings for you too, you stubborn man. You shocked me—"

"How do you not know that I want you?"

"Not that." I grinned and held my finger and thumb a centimetre apart. "Well, maybe a little given we've never actually talked about it, but it's more that you and Tristan spoke about us and that you called your mum. You're so closed off, but then you come in here with a split lip, and I'm thinking that you're gonna tell me you dragged him off the yacht. Instead, you tell me that you've had a heart-to-heart with not one but two people and somehow manage to get a split lip in the process. I'm confused as fuck."

Ry chuckled and shook his head, closing his hand around the one I had cupping his cheek and then turning it to kiss my palm. "He didn't hit me. This is me pacing my office for hours, chewing on my lip until it was fucking bleeding, then doing it again outside your office while I worked up the courage to come in here and talk to you."

"Oh, Ry." I crawled onto his lap and snuggled into him, kissing his temple and brushing my fingers on his chest right over his heart.

He kissed my cheek and down my face, nipping my jaw gently. His warm breath ghosted over my throat, and my heart beat harder, gooseflesh breaking out over my skin as he kept going. His lips tilted up in a smile when I gripped his biceps and moaned quietly.

Ry angled my head up and nibbled on my lobe before sucking gently on the skin below it. He was different like this, quieter, and while in control, he wasn't being his usual bossy self. He was savouring me, leisurely tasting me as he teased me with sensual, barely there touches.

My cunt clenched, and my nipples peaked as he brushed his thumb across the buds. When I moaned, Ry sucked harder. I loved that he was marking me as he leisurely swept his hand down to my hip.

Everything tilted sideways in a split second, and he was lifting me, stretching me out below him. He tugged my legs open and crawled between them, hovering over me with his heated gaze trained on my body. I was splayed out on my back, my knees apart and my oversized T-shirt riding up to expose all of me. He licked his lips, and the move lit me up like an inferno. When he reached the juncture of my thighs and focussed on my naked cunt, he groaned.

"Fuck, baby girl, you test my restraint," he growled. The rasp in his voice was so damn sexy. I squirmed, and my core clenched again, wetness coating my thighs as I leaked for him.

"Fuck restraint," I moaned, arching up and shivering as my sensitive nipples rubbed against the thin material of my shirt.

He reached into his back pocket, pulled out a knife, and flicked it open. He carried the most random shit, but he always had a use for it. He was a damn boy scout.

My breath caught, and excitement pulsed through me. His eyes darkened as he watched me squirm, and the glint in them turned wicked.

"We'll explore that kink in a minute. But for now, it's purely a means to an end." He grasped the neckline of my tee and ran the knife over it, slashing the material from top to bottom effortlessly. I moaned and reached down to touch my clit, needing friction there before I combusted.

"Hands off my pussy, baby girl. When you're mine, I give you orgasms."

"What about when the others want to give them to me?" I challenged, sliding my fingers lower to my soaked cunt. Dipping three fingers inside, I moaned at the stretch. But it wasn't enough. I needed more. "Or when I want to do it myself?"

He slid the knife lower, pausing with a raised brow at my question. If he was surprised that I'd asked, he didn't even know me. "Then you'd better hope you've been a good girl so I let you come. Or I'll have your guys use you to get off and leave you aching for it." He parted the cut pieces of my top, exposing my body to him, and leaned down, running his tongue over my nipple as he pressed the blade to my other tit. The cold metal and the bite of the sharp edge pressing against my skin were like an electric shock lighting me up inside. My clit pulsed, and I widened my legs, begging him without words to fuck me.

With his lips against my nipple, he murmured, "And when you're my girl, you won't need to fuck yourself." He grasped my wrist, freeing my fingers from my cunt, and brought them to his mouth. He sucked on each one and growled when I cried out in desperation. The need to be filled to the bursting point was an ache throbbing inside me.

I wanted Ry over me and in me. I wanted him to fuck me until I couldn't walk, until I was delirious from the orgasms he'd given me.

Then I wanted the others to do the same.

I wanted to be his. Theirs.

Forever.

His voice was hypnotic when he leaned down and murmured in my ear, "Your pretty legs will shake so many times a day that you'll be walking like a newborn foal."

I slipped my eyes closed and floated on the sensation his words brought. My moan gave away just how needy I was, my hips rocking upward as I sought friction against my cunt, sought *him*.

"Fuck me, Ry. Just like that," I demanded, though it sounded more like a plea. I clawed at the hard muscle in his shoulders and tried to push him down to where my body needed him most.

But he didn't move, resisting my unsubtle direction.

The knife shifted, no longer pressing against my skin. I cried out, and Ry moved it, laying it so the point was sharp against the underside of my boob.

I was naked, my legs spread, and a man twice my size was hovering over me with a knife pressed to my tit. He could sink it into me, and I wouldn't be able to stop him, but I trusted him with my life. That feeling, the one that allowed me to jump without ever needing to second-guess whether he'd catch me, was empowering. I loved it. I loved him.

I loved the way he took charge and told me the way things would happen, our roles completely reversed from the every day. Which hole would he fill? Would he give me his fingers? His cock? His mouth? All of them? I had no idea, and yet that was just as exciting as it was freeing.

He trailed his fingers down my quivering belly and licked my nipple. "You want me inside you, baby girl?"

"Yes," I moaned, crying out when he circled my clit with his thumb.

"Good," he hummed as he slid what had to be a single finger into me. He was moving excruciatingly slowly, but he still knew exactly how to work me over, hitting my G-spot unfailingly. Except that it wasn't enough. The climb was too slow. It wasn't intense enough. I needed more.

But the bastard was a tease and was going to make me play his mind-fuck games.

Thing was, I loved them.

When I got off.

"Ry," I demanded, glaring at him and that stupid smirk he wore. "Stop fucking around and fuck me." I widened my legs, pulling them back and opening myself up to him, subtlety be damned.

He huffed out a laugh, humour making his eyes sparkle, then added a second finger. The third followed quickly after that, and the buzz in my veins started to build. God, the stretch was divine. The fullness, perfection. His lips left a burning trail on my sweat-slicked skin as he kissed his way to my clit.

His stubble brushed my cunt lips, and I cried out, desperate to ride his face, but he pressed my leg into place, stopping me from rolling my hips.

He had me at his mercy. I would do anything to get his mouth on me, to keep his fingers in me and get that dick in me again. Ry knew it too.

I watched as he swiped his tongue over my clit and licked up my essence. I was so wet, but Ry added lube to his fingers before dipping his face to my clit again.

He bit and sucked me, playing my body like a finely tuned instrument. I raced to the edge, teetering there as a monster orgasm built inside me. The *schlick, schlick, schlick* from his fingers driving into me pushed me closer. The stretch was a delicious torment, my body wanting more but loving it at the same time. "Fuck, yes," I breathed. "Harder."

"No, not harder," he growled. "Want to see your pussy suck my whole hand in."

He added another finger, and I cried out. "Jesus. Fuck. Oh, fuck. I'm there," I panted as heat washed over me in waves, every nerve ending sizzling and exploding with sensation. Noise rang out in my ears—shouts in a hoarse voice I didn't recognize but knew were my own. I gripped his shoulders, squeezing hard as I shattered in his arms.

Every part of my being was obliterated until I was only a mass of cells free floating in an ocean of ecstasy. The epicentre was my cunt. The sweet ache that had started in my clit radiated outward, and my walls contracted, clenching and releasing rhythmically as my body fought to keep Ry's fingers deep inside me while struggling with their combined girth at the same time.

But he was patient, and his thrusts turned to twists, his fingers curling and pressing down on my G-spot as he turned his hand side to side. The movements, although small, reignited my body, setting my already scorched nerve endings alight once more.

"Yes," I hissed, fighting to thrust my hips and get more of him inside me.

"Baby girl, you were made for this," he crooned, and my body lit up, his praise like a drug singing in my veins.

But then the thumb he'd been holding against my clit was gone. I sobbed out in frustration until he lashed it with his tongue once more. I gasped, then groaned, arching into his touch. He was a maestro.

Then it was there—his thumb at my entrance. He was going to try it, to get his fist inside me. "Yes," I cried, my voice more of a sob.

My chest rose and fell, my breathing choppy as my pulse hammered in my veins and anticipation stole through me. Could I take his fist? How deep could he sink inside me?

His mouth on me and his fingers inside me were overwhelming, but when he shifted his hand, pressing it down on my sternum and pushing the blade harder against my tit, I shattered again, splintering into a million pieces.

I shouted as he thrust his thumb in alongside his other fingers and curled them, stretching me from the inside as he worked his entire hand into my cunt. Orgasm after orgasm crashed into me, barely ebbing before renewing again. I didn't know which way was up. Everything was overwhelming, swirling around me like a vortex while my body was on fire and coming apart at the seams at the same time.

The way he played me, the way he knew exactly what I needed and wanted without me having to tell him, was so very Ry. He was my caretaker, the one who delivered on my heart's desire before I even knew what it was. Whether it was feeding me or taking care of the Noble Steed or my Mustang, mooring me where I needed to be to find peace, charging my yacht to kill an intruder, or making me come, he was there, orchestrating every move to make sure I was happy.

He'd told me he had feelings for me, that he'd wanted me, but he hadn't admitted the true depth of those feelings. I knew, without a shadow of a doubt, that he loved me, that I was it for him. I was his soulmate, his forever love.

He was mine too.

How could I—the girl who had a fucked-up childhood, who wasn't exactly a shining beacon of citizenship—be lucky enough to have found all of them? How had fate blessed me with not one, but four, great loves?

Ry shifted, and I needed to do more than just touch his back. I needed to make him feel as good as I did. Energy levels shot, I couldn't even open my eyes, but warmth radiated off him. He was holding himself up, hovering over me. He opened his zipper and hissed. I wanted that cock. I needed it. I needed to touch him, to make him come.

Reaching out with a shaking hand, he grasped my wrist and guided me to his length. He was long, thick, slick with pre-cum, and hard as granite. "I'm there," he groaned, his voice shaking as much as my hand.

"Come on me," I panted. I must have made a sight. My legs were spread, hiked up like chicken wings. His hand was still lodged deep inside me, and I was scrambling to touch him. Gripping his dick, I stroked him in long, languid pulls before twisting my wrist and coating his length in pre-cum. He took the hint and thrust his hips forward, fucking my hand as hard and fast as he needed. I was desperate for his cum, for him to mark me, to possess me.

"Show me, Ry. Show me how you own me."

He shouted out, his body bowing as he thrust his hips forward and let loose. Streams of cum painted my body from my cunt to my chin, settling in the valley between my boobs and my navel. It pooled in the dip between my collarbones and ran down my throat as I fought to steady my choppy breaths. One pulse after another, he let loose, choking out a cry as he fell forward, catching his weight on the armrest.

He shifted, pressing his face against my tit, resting his bare chest against my stomach. Cum coated my body, but Ry didn't seem to mind getting it on him. If anything, he was rubbing into me with the way he was lying on me.

Slowly, he removed one finger at a time from my core until I was empty, and I squirmed, hating the feeling. "I might need to do that again," I murmured with a huff of laughter as I wrapped my legs around his waist and held him to me.

SEVEN

Zali

"**I** volunteer," Ryder mumbled against my skin.

"Are you? Volunteering?" I asked quietly. I wiped my cum-soaked hand on my stomach and carded my semi-clean fingers through his hair, the soft-as-silk strands slipping through them. "As in, that wasn't a one-off?"

He absently ran his thumb over my nipple, the peak hardening under his touch before he shifted, lifting his face and meeting my gaze head-on. Almost defiantly, he tilted his chin and admitted, "I don't want it to be a one-off. I've wanted you for as long as I can remember."

I tugged a piece of his hair hard enough to sting. "Ow." He slapped my hand away and pinched my nipple in response. But the joke was on him—I fucking loved when my guys did that. My hips lifted of their own volition, and I bit back a groan.

His eyes darkened, but I wasn't ready to go again. Not yet, not when I had a chance to talk to him like Tristan had. My voice was breathy when I teased, "Hush, you big baby."

Running my fingers through his hair again, I gentled my touch. "Why did it take you so long? Christ, I've been parading around naked for years. You could have done something about it anytime."

His brows practically hit his hairline, and his mouth hung open in astonishment. "Are you serious?" When I responded with my own brow lift and half shrug, he huffed out a laugh filled with disbelief. "I'm… speechless. You have some awfully traditional beliefs around gender roles for someone who basically says, 'Fuck you' to every one of society's rules. Why didn't you say anything?"

"Because I'm clearly an idiot," I mumbled, shaking my head. "I don't know. You have this 'I make the decisions around here' energy, and I didn't want to fuck with that or risk you saying no. Besides, you're off limits—you're my brother's best friend, my employee, and my friend."

"You were friends with Flynn, and you work for Ezra. How are they different?" he asked, confusion and a sliver of vulnerability clouding his eyes. He kept it hidden well, barely a shaft of light under a door that Ry kept firmly locked, but I could see it. "Is that the difference—that you love them?"

His words broke my heart, and his uncertainty crushed me. I needed to fix this—Ry deserved to know that he wasn't just a convenient addition. I wanted him the same way I wanted my other men.

Permanently.

"I do love them. I love Tristan as well," I admitted. "But, Ry, I also love you."

He opened his mouth to respond, but I pressed my finger against his lips. He knew my story with Ezra. He'd seen our relationship change from one where we bickered and I taunted Ezra to one which admittedly wasn't all that different except that we admitted we cared for each other and now regularly fucked like bunnies. He'd watched it morph with his own eyes. He'd been there for all the key events.

But he didn't know about Flynn and me, how our relationship had developed. I needed to explain it so he understood.

"Flynn has always been my safe harbour, just like you are." I touched his cheek with my thumb and smiled, heat rising in my own at the same time. How was I shy in front of him? He'd literally just had his fist in my cunt. He'd fucked my arse only a few days earlier, or maybe a week—I was still all over the place since Monaco. He'd seen me at my best and worst, known me forever, and yet, admitting that he was special was enough to have me blushing like a schoolgirl. I huffed out a self-conscious laugh, and he smirked, tracing the colour travelling down my neck to my chest, smearing the drying cum on me.

"It was Tristan who made us face up to what was in front of us. That first time I met him, I wanted to kill him—drive the heel of my Louboutin straight into his eye."

Ry snorted out a laugh and gave a half nod in agreement.

"Then he went all caveman on me but said, 'Angel, kiss our kitten.' Flynn stepped up in front of me, and it was as if everything that had been right there the whole time snapped into focus." I snapped my fingers and shook my head in disbelief. I still couldn't fathom how much had changed.

"I had no idea. I was so clueless. I hadn't let myself think about you or Flynn that way other than in passing because I'd been too scared to lose either one of you. But I'd been hurting Flynn the whole time. And now you're telling me that I was doing the same to you?"

"So I have Tristan to thank?" he asked before he pressed his lips together in a ghost of a smile.

"You never answered my question," I reminded Ry. "Why didn't you say anything earlier?"

He hummed. "Noticed that, did you?" He nibbled on his cut lip again and winced before swiping his tongue over the raw patch of skin. "I wanted all of you, and you didn't see me the same way."

"Ry—"

"It's okay. It wasn't our time. But maybe now... maybe we can try for something."

"You know you have all of me, right?" I asked as I itched at the dried cum on my chest. I needed a shower, but I wasn't going anywhere. It'd be a miracle if we hadn't glued ourselves together by now anyway. "But I can't be exclusively yours. I can't—I won't—give them up."

"I'm still working shit out, Zali. I...." He shifted, pulling away from me until he was seated at one end of the couch with me at the other. He tucked himself in, zipping up his cargo shorts with short, sharp movements and then stood up, his back to me as he stomped over to the windows. "I don't know how I'm gonna go with the others, okay? I need it to be just us."

I tensed, my muscles going on high alert. Sitting up slowly, I shrugged off my torn dress and wiped myself down with it. "I need you to elaborate."

He shrugged, but I saw straight through his attempt at brushing off his concerns. The tense lines in his back and the way he held his head rigid told me just how stressed he was about it. "The guys are together too."

"And?" I asked, stretching out the word as I tossed the scraps of material aside and walked over to him. I held out my hands in supplication even though he couldn't see me. "You're not giving me much to work with, Ry."

Ry tangled his hands in his hair, and he let out a frustrated growl. He slammed his fist against the window, the toughened glass rippling under the force of his hit.

The picture before me was a study in contrasts. Ry's mood had turned dark and stormy, while outside, it was a picture-perfect night. Stars sparkled overhead, the moon low and full in the night sky, reflecting off the water and lighting up the surrounding bay.

"Fuck," he muttered under his breath before repeating it louder.

I moved over to him and wrapped my arms around his waist, resting my forehead against his spine. Every muscle was rigid, his body practically vibrating with tension. Smoothing my hands over his abs, I tried to soothe him, but he didn't relax. "It's important that we're all comfortable, Ry. If you're worried about them touching you—"

"No!" he barked before groaning. "Yes…. No. Fuck."

He's not worried, but he is? He was so damn worked up, but he had been ever since my close encounter of the shark kind. Except maybe it wasn't the shark that'd been the problem, but Ezra's suggestion that I enrol in Tristan's course. Things had changed pretty quickly after that. Was that what the issue was? Was he jealous?

But that didn't make sense. If he was jealous, he wouldn't be focussing on the guys being together. He'd have more of a problem with them touching me, not them touching him.

Oh. Oh. Was he saying what I thought he was? "This conversation goes no further than these walls. It's between you and me, and it'll stay that way. I'll never share what you say with anyone, okay?"

His grunt of acknowledgment sent a shiver through me, and I tightened my grip around his waist.

"Do you want one of them to touch you?"

He shook his head, his forehead rocking against the glass it was pressed against. But his movements were too quick and too jerky. It was as if Ry was overcompensating. He was intense, yes, but he was normally a lot more laid back than this.

"Okay. But I want you to know that it'd be okay if you did."

"I don't, okay?" he roared, pulling out of my grip and pacing to the other side of the couch, his hands back in his hair and his face turning red. Woah, as much as I wanted to slap his outburst back into submission, Ry was really bloody worked up about this. He was stressed the fuck out. If he was reacting like this, there was no way he and Tristan would have talked about it.

"Ry, that's okay too. Whatever your sexuality is, it's you. I love you for exactly who you are. I just wanted to reassure you that regardless of whether you wanted anything with anyone else, it wouldn't change my opinion of you. You're one of the most incredible people I know."

His shoulders slumped, and the tension ran out of his body like a balloon deflating. Suddenly it was as if all the walls around him had collapsed. I saw into his very soul, the tiny corner he'd reserved for himself. He was lonely and so tired of fighting, and my heart broke seeing him struggling so much.

"You ever think that life would be so much easier if we could change something about ourselves? Some detail that always stops us in our tracks?" I pointed at the wall and my computers.

He probably didn't understand what I was getting at, but it was one of the things we had in common. Once I got a thought in my head, I obsessed about it. It consumed me. It was why I worked hard to make sure I had some sort of balance between my work and life. If I held down a proper job, I'd never stop. At least the one I did have allowed me to turn work away when I needed a break. Ry was similar in that he focussed on a challenge until he perfected it—navigating my yacht, flying my plane, working on my cars, you name it.

Actions were easy for him. They were fine. But he didn't show his emotions. He buried them instead. He shut down and kept working, masking whatever the feeling was until he was a powder keg ready to blow.

Just like now.

His nod was small, but it was there. "But I can't."

"I know. We probably shouldn't want to either. But sometimes it's nice to imagine we could purge it from ourselves. We can shove down the feeling, but the peace never lasts."

"Yeah, if only it did."

"You know, if it's just a matter of doing something, you can do it," I hedged.

"I know what you're doing, Zali, and yeah, no. Not this. I can't *just do it*," he snapped back, the tension in him running hot again.

I walked over to him and rested my hands on his hips, rubbing my thumbs along his waistline. "Why not, Ry? As long as you aren't hurting anyone, why can't you?"

"Because I'd disappoint them. It's not what a *man* does." His eyes widened just a fraction and he continued quickly, as if trying to take back the words that had slipped out. "It's not what they'd want me to do."

He walked away from me, crossing his arms over his chest like a shield as he went back to the window. He rested his forehead against it once more. He was determined to run away from me, but I wasn't going to let him. The only way this conversation was going to be over was if he walked out of the room, but while he was here, while he was still engaging with me, it was still open for discussion.

"I'm just gonna come right out and say it instead of dancing around this." He went rigid again, and my heart twisted. "You were right about me hating society's rules. They're bullshit. The idea that a woman can't be with more than one man because it makes her a slut? Fuck that." I pointed my thumbs at myself and added, "It's my body, and I won't have some middle-aged white fuck-face bloke with a pot belly, sitting behind his middle-class desk, driving his beige sedan to church on Sunday with his Stepford wife and two point five kids, tell me otherwise just so the patriarchy can control a woman's body."

I sucked in a breath and clenched my jaw while fisting my hands at my sides. Anger sang through my veins, my racing pulse helping it along the way. I pointed out the door to my other guys.

"They think that Flynn's not manly enough because he doesn't have big muscles. They think any queer man is a pussy because they like dick, yet they wield theirs over women, thinking they're the fucking second coming. But they're running scared. They're all terrified of what they look like to others. All their hatred, all their vitriol are their insecurities mirrored onto everyone else. Instead of encouraging people to be themselves, they try to put us in boxes and trick us into believing the grass was greener back when society looked like it did in the good old days. It's all completely fucked up."

I threw my hands up in the air with a huff.

"Those fucking rules are there to keep people who aren't like them down. They're there to make people so desperate to be included that exclusion becomes bad. You become an 'other.' Well, fuck that," I hissed, my voice verging on a shout.

"You know why I do what I do? To show those bastards that they don't have everything right. That there is actual scum in this world, and we should be focussing on destroying them, not shooting down people who just want to live their lives. Why can't you do what makes you feel good? The truth is, you can, but society has us all fucking brainwashed. Everyone's too scared to step out of the lines. I call fucking bullshit. I choose to live outside the lines. You can too.

"And if they're disappointed in you because of it, fuck them sideways. Out of everyone on this fucking yacht, you are the one they should be most proud of. You are the best man I know. You would do anything for someone you love. You take care of us all. You protect us. You have this quiet confidence and this calmness that makes me feel safe. I trust you like no one else. If anyone is disappointed in you for any reason, they aren't worthy of you."

The silence that followed my outburst was deafening.

The others hadn't come into the office to see why I was practically shouting, and I had a feeling that was very intentional on their part. They knew Ry and I hadn't talked, and they were giving us the space to do it. But had I completely destroyed any chance of him opening up?

I looked at Ry, and he was thunderstruck, pale and standing stock still with his mouth open. Sometime when I'd been ranting, he'd turned to face me, but he was barely standing now. He was using the window as support, leaning back against it, his hands pressed to the glass to stop himself from sliding down them. It was as if I'd sucked the rage out of him, channelling it like a conductor, letting it surge through me, and there was nothing left to hold him up.

"I want to," he whispered, his voice hitching at the end. "I want to be free." His chest rose and fell, his breathing choppy. Colour slowly returned to his cheeks, and the hunch in his shoulders lessened. It was as if a weight had been lifted from him and he was no longer drowning.

"You can be yourself with us. I promise you that."

"I keep telling myself that I don't want it. But I do." He went back to gazing out the window, and it took so long for him to speak again that I thought that was all he had to say. "I'm scared I'll lose them. I'm scared they'll think I let them down, that I'm not the man they taught me to be, and they'll walk away."

I went to him and wrapped my arms around him. "Your uncle?"

"Yeah, and Tom and Chris. Mum too."

"It's scary," I agreed, pressing a kiss to his chest. "Thank you for telling me."

He wrapped his arms around me, clutching me as I held onto him. His grip was tight, as if he was trying to stop me from pulling away. "I shouldn't want anything like that." He huffed out a laugh, but it held no humour, only pain and disappointment.

"Why shouldn't you?" I pressed. "Why do you think it's wrong?" I could understand his uncle, Tom, and Chris saying something to him. They were chauvinistic pigs sometimes. But his mum was beautiful, so gentle and kind. She never had a bad word to say about anyone. She would never have drilled anything homophobic into him. Same with his dad. He was much more traditional—more of a man's man with ideals that reflected that—but I remembered him being a good guy. Had I been wrong?

"I don't want to disappoint them," he whispered, shaking his head. The tension was returning to his shoulders. "I don't want them to leave me."

"Let it go, Ry. Let all the stress go." I squeezed his waist and pressed my body against his from head to toe. "Let all the 'should-dos' and 'should-bes' go. You're safe with me." I nuzzled his chest, trying to communicate through that small touch what he meant to me. "It's okay if you're not ready, but you don't have to hide anymore. Not if you don't want to."

He sucked in a breath and let it out slowly. "When my dad died, so many people told me that I was the man of the house now and it was my job to be there for Mum."

"You've taken such good care of her. And of me too. You've been there for me in ways no one else has."

"When Ash died, I was drowning. Something inside me died with him. It was like all the happiness and light got sucked out of my life. I was so alone. I couldn't stop crying."

Tears sprang to my eyes, and my throat burned. I nodded, knowing exactly what he meant. Asher was the best of us all. He was like the sun—warm and happy. Everyone gravitated to him. With him gone, our worlds had turned dark and cold.

"They were trying to help. My uncle, especially. But...."

The silence stretched out again, and I waited.

"They kept telling me that I was a man now and that real men were strong. They weren't weak. 'Don't cry,' they said. 'Be brave and strong.'" His voice cracked on his last word, and he sucked in a shuddery breath. "Men don't cry like girls. They're not cowards like my dad." Ry let go of me long enough to wipe his face, but when I tried to pull back to kiss him, he kept me anchored in place. I hugged him tighter.

"My uncle used to say to me that being a man was important. He and Chris and Tom used to tell me secrets. It made me feel like I was one of them. I wanted to make Dad proud, you know? I wanted to slot in where he should have been. When they told me to look after Mum, I took it to heart."

His mum hadn't needed a man, she'd needed her family. Her child. They'd forced him to grow up too soon. They hadn't let him grieve, instead placing so much pressure on him to be there for everyone else. But who was there for him?

"I just wanted Ash back. I just wanted my best friend back." His breath caught, and this time he let me reach up and pull his face down to mine. I ran my fingers through his hair, rocking him while he cried.

"It's okay, let it out. Cry." I was doing the same, grieving for the little boy whose world had been shattered. He'd lost his dad and his best friend, the person who'd been his guiding light. Ash was his strength during his darkest times, and to lose that within months of another devastating loss had wrenched his world apart.

Slowly his tears dried, but he didn't move. I stood between his spread legs, one hand in his hair, the other wrapped around his shoulder as he clutched me like I was his lifeline. I was grateful I could give him some of the comfort he'd given me over the years.

"I dreamed about kissing Ash," he admitted.

Shock paralysed me. Had Ry been crushing on Ash? Was he grieving his first love as well as his best friend? My heart shattered, the need to comfort Ry overwhelming. But I dared not move, I dared not breathe in case I broke the spell that had Ry talking.

"It was the night before Mr Vella dropped off all the food he and his mum cooked. He sat me down, asked me how I was doing, and I don't know why, but I told him. He talked about how our minds can try to protect our hearts from the pain. Sometimes that happens in dreams where the person we've lost is alive again. He talked about how some people believe it's the other person's spirit. Other times it's a memory or a lost chance, sometimes for something we didn't even know we wanted. I never wanted Ash like that, but... I don't know." He paused, then shook his head as if clearing his thoughts before he continued. "Mr Vella told me his door was always open. He gave me his mobile number so that if I needed to talk to someone, I could call him. He said it didn't matter whether it was midnight, on a weekend, or over the holidays—I could call anytime."

"He helped me too," I whispered, remembering my own chat with him. He'd done exactly the same thing for me.

"But then our neighbour walked in just as Mr Vella was leaving. I hadn't even noticed the shirt he was wearing—I thought it was just black, but there must have been a rainbow somewhere on it. He started going on about how these queer fuckers parade around in rainbows, suck us in, and put shit in our heads. He said that it was unnatural and wrong. He started talking about how we needed to get back to real family values again, and then we wouldn't have so many problems. It hit me how much I was going to let everyone down if that was who I really was. I went over and over it, getting more and more lost, but the only thing that made any sense was hiding it. I buried it deep. If I convinced myself I wasn't one of them, I wouldn't let anyone down. I wouldn't let Mum down. I could be the man she needed."

"I'm sorry they put all that on you on top of everything else you were going through. It wasn't fair." I pressed a kiss to his hair, and he straightened.

He sighed. "I'm so tired of lying to myself. I'm tired of fighting with everything inside me."

"You must be exhausted," I murmured, running my thumbs over his cheekbones and the backs of my knuckles along his jawline.

"He makes me feel safe," he admitted. When I tilted my head in question, his lips tilted up in the ghost of a smile. "Tristan. Ezra made sure I was safe. He took my cuffs off in that interview room and checked my wrists." He huffed out a wry laugh. "Jesus, getting out of that ballroom in Monte

Carlo nearly turned to shit, but Ezra took over, all smooth and professional, and made sure we walked out without a scene. And Flynn doesn't hesitate. He shows me every day that he trusts me. He lets me lead."

"You know, if you ever… they'd be down." It was a conversation he needed to have with them, but I could at least pave the way for him to approach them.

EIGHT

Ryder

I couldn't believe that I'd admitted all those things to Zali. My deepest, darkest shame as a kid was realizing that I could never be the man I'd been expected to be for everyone else. So I'd faked it. I'd cast that part of myself aside, buried it and only let myself acknowledge that part of my sexuality which fit the mould of the type of man I wanted to be.

Now everything was unravelling. My sexuality was like a zombie clawing its way out of a grave that I thought had been dug much deeper and contained in a reinforced steel vault.

But my secret was free, and it was chasing me. Waiting to infect me.

Except that it wasn't really infecting me with anything except the antidote.

It was stripping away the decade of lies and deceit I'd perpetrated on myself. It was tearing away the disguise I'd wrapped myself in.

I didn't know how to live with this naked, exposed version of me. I knew Zali wouldn't tell the others. She'd leave it to me to come out, if I ever decided to do that. I shouldn't have needed her promises to keep our conversation confidential, but in a way, I'd needed the reassurance.

I'd told her the truth—I was tired. I wanted to be free too. I wanted to step into the sunshine and drop all pretences. I didn't want to lie anymore. I didn't want to be afraid.

But I didn't know how.

The easiest route would be to stay hidden. Smooth sailing and all that, but was it really easy? Was there a storm building on the horizon that would drown me when it hit? Some days I was barely able to hold on by the skin of my teeth. Other days I worked out my frustration on the yacht, scrubbing every surface until it was sparkling clean and I was too exhausted to dream of anything, much less the secret desires I'd hidden away.

I'd spent the plane trip home from Monaco going over how we'd come together, me underneath Zali while the others touched her. It was incredible. Something out of a dream. Since then, my dreams had been a series of vignettes. What could it have been like if things were a little different between us? What if I didn't have this chain around my neck strangling me every time I took a step closer to what I craved?

The possibilities had been endless, but my dream last night was simple. There were no triple-X-rated dreams. Flynn had kissed me, a chaste brush of his lips. Tristan had held me, and Ezra had told me how proud he was of me. That level of neediness was fucked up. But I'd been so scared of letting that part of myself out that it was almost a dream to think anyone could actually love me for it.

I'd slipped out of Zali's bed and spent the rest of the night pacing.

An early morning swim hadn't helped. Neither had a shower.

I was pacing again, stuck on how to deal with this. I wanted to shove it back down into the box I'd crammed it in when I was younger, but it'd outgrown the tiny space. It was too big for me to ignore.

Tristan came around the corner, stopping me in my tracks. He slipped his hands into the pockets of his pressed slacks. The collar of his button-down shirt was open, and he had the sleeves rolled up his forearms, exposing the tattoos there. He looked like the bad boy CEO, confident and re-laxed, which was ridiculous, considering it was a Saturday.

But the tension lines around his eyes gave him away. He knew my shit was about to hit the fan and dirty up their perfect world. Not that Tristan was arrogant like that. He was worried.

"You okay?" he asked with an air of casualness that was as fake as his relaxed pose.

I wanted to know. I *needed* to know. But I was terrified of what it meant.

I wanted to touch him, to touch all of them. But I didn't know how. I didn't want to be a disappointment. I didn't want to let them down.

Exhaling harshly, the irony of my worry hit me. I didn't want to let Tristan, Ezra, and Flynn down if I was a disappointing fuck. But twenty-four hours ago, I'd been worried about anyone finding out in case I disappointed my family— Mum, Uncle Kev, Tom, and Chris.

Holy shit, would I have anyone if I screwed this up? Or would they all shun me?

Fuck that. I was going to take this secret to my grave.

"I need to go. I need to get off the yacht," I responded, pushing past him so I could move aft. I didn't give him a chance to object or to stop me as I jogged to the ladder. My heart was hammering in my chest, my hands shaking as I raced there. A sheen of sweat coated my body, and my breathing was ragged as my legs nearly gave out, my knees buckling as I reached the couches.

He was there, catching me before I hit the deck. He wrapped his arms around me and hauled me up.

I shook him off and pushed him away. I couldn't let him touch me. Not now, when the foundation of the walls I'd built had been rocked to their core. Cracks were appearing everywhere, and I needed to shore everything up before I could face any of them—especially Tristan. He was enough like Zali that if he pressed me, I'd start fucking running my mouth.

"Ry, what's going on? You look like you're having a nervous breakdown."

"I probably fucking am." I huffed, wanting to kick myself. I had no filter around him, absolutely no ability to hold myself back. "I need to go," I deflected, looking for a way off the yacht.

Where was I planning on going? We were in a bay bordered on three sides by a sand island that was covered in scrubby bushland and very little else except the local wildlife. On the fourth side, there was an outgoing tide moving so fast, I could see the ripples on the surface where it was churning.

Fuck me, I was stuck.

I tried to pull away from him, to head into my stateroom or the wheelhouse, but he grasped my biceps, holding me firmly in place. I struggled against his hold, but it was no use. I had nothing left in the tank. I was a hollowed-out shell, and he was as strong as an ox.

Panic stole over me, my vision spotting and my chest tightening.

He shook me, snapping me back to attention. "You're not going anywhere until you tell me what's going on."

"Nothing. Nothing's going on."

"Bullshit."

His eyes nearly popped out of his head when I flicked open the button on my shorts and unzipped them, kicking them away. I was beyond the point of reason. I needed off this rollercoaster, and I didn't care how. "I'm going for a swim," I explained.

"Fine. I'll come too. Ez, we're going for a swim," he yelled as he undid the top couple of buttons on his shirt and pulled it over his head. With every inch of skin revealed, my gut twisted and want and need fought for dominance in me.

I bit back a groan, salivating over him. Try as I might, I couldn't pull my gaze away from his abs. The groove down the centre of his stomach and the V on either side of his hips formed the perfect arrow straight down to a cock that I knew was as ridiculously well-proportioned as he was and one that I'd been dying to touch for almost as long as I'd known him.

"Get undressed," he ordered Ezra as his man stepped into the sunlight, wearing nothing but a pair of ripped jeans that were more holes than material. Flynn was close on his heels, but he skidded to a stop and shook his head.

My brain short-circuited when Ezra unzipped them and instead of a waistband appearing, I saw his pubes. "Fuck me," I groaned, my resolve at breaking point and my sanity having long since sailed past it while holding up a cocktail glass and waving a white flag.

Zali was there in front of me, her soft hands on my cheeks. "Breathe, babe," she instructed, and I sucked in a breath. The vice on my chest loosened, and I closed my eyes, slumping into her touch. Tristan's hands landed on my shoulders, steadying me as Zali stood on tiptoes and tugged my face down to hers, whispering, "You're safe with us. Don't run. Please stay."

I absorbed her energy, her strength, clinging to her waist as I buried my face in the crook of her neck.

"They're worried about you," she continued. "But they'll give you space if that's what you need."

I didn't know what I needed. My hands were shaking, and my knees were about to give out on me. Fear the likes of which I'd only ever experienced once—when Flynn and Zali were getting shot at while we were escaping from the Reserve Bank—overwhelmed me. I was frozen in place, but every instinct in me told me to run. To find somewhere I could hide out until I had the strength to rebuild the walls that had kept me safe for so long.

"Ry, I'm here if you need me," Flynn murmured from next to me, and I couldn't help but reach blindly for him. I clutched him tight, needing his sunshine, his warmth at that moment. He wrapped his arms around my waist, and Zali shifted, letting him step in front of me.

Flynn didn't speak. He just held me tight.

A moment later, another set of arms surrounded me. Fingers tangled in my hair, and Ezra murmured, "Whatever you need, I'm here. So is Tris. You're part of us, Ry. You're not alone. We've got you."

My breath caught, and I trembled. I needed to get out of there, but it was impossible to move. Their arms around me were the only thing holding me up.

Tristan pulled away, his hands slipping off my shoulders, but I caught his wrists, keeping him close. I needed him there as much as I needed the others.

"Are you okay?" Flynn asked cautiously. "Do you need to sit down?"

"I don't think so." I hesitated, not knowing how to tell him what I needed. I didn't even know if I could go ahead with it.

Looking around for her, I spotted Zali a few feet away, giving us space without going too far away. I opened my mouth, ready to ask for help, but she was already moving closer. I swallowed, entranced by her graceful movements and in awe of the way she carried herself. She was confident, almost cocky, and often aloof, but when it was just us, she let down the façade. She was warm and loving, demanding and vocal, but fiercely loyal and protective.

And her body was rocking. Her breasts and that arse were curvy in all the right places.

Reaching for my hand, she threaded our fingers together and slid her arm around Flynn's waist. If I hadn't fallen in love with her a long time ago, I would have right in that moment. Without having to say a word, she gave me an out, a way to turn to her for comfort so I could distance myself from the men who had all my well-laid defences toppling.

She looked at Flynn before turning to Ezra, then Tristan. "Thank you for being here for Ry." It was a dismissal, but her voice was filled with a genuineness and warmth that couldn't be faked. Zali had promised I was safe with her, and she damn well meant it.

Flynn smiled, and it was like the sun coming out from behind a cloud. He was… beautiful. God, acknowledging that in itself was so freeing. Absolutely liberating. It was as if I'd turned the light on, shining a torch under the bed to scare off the monsters that were hiding there. But when he turned to me, his smile slipped. I wanted to capture it again, to give it back to him.

"Ry, what's wrong?" he asked, his bright blue eyes clouded with worry.

I let myself look at him, taking in the differences between us. He was slimmer than the rest of us guys, his muscles lithe and compact instead of bulky like Tris's or mine, and he was shorter than even Ezra's six-foot frame.

"Did something happen?" Flynn asked again, his voice wobbly. My gaze shot to his, and I reached for him without thinking, pulling him against my body and slipping my hand up the back of his shirt. I groaned when my fingers made contact with his heated skin. He sucked in a breath, and panic seized me. Dropping my arm, I stepped back in a flash, separating myself from both Zali and Flynn. I choked out an apology, hating that I'd already ruined things.

"Fuck, sorry. I didn't ask. I just…. Sorry."

"Ry, tell him," Zali whispered. "I guarantee he wants to hear it."

"Hear what?" Flynn asked. "Ry, you're scaring me."

I reached for his waist again, holding my hand a fraction away from his hip. "Can I?"

"Yes, of course." I placed my hand on his hip, and he tugged on my wrist, stepping closer as he slipped my hand back under his shirt. "If that's what you need, Ry, take it."

My eyes closed of their own accord, and my body trembled as I slid my hand higher, touching the long planes of his back.

A rough hand cupped my face gently, and I blinked open my eyes, seeing Tristan before me, his eyes warm. "We've got you."

He grasped Flynn's shirt and inched it up, his gaze never leaving mine. He didn't say the words, but I knew he was watching my reactions, waiting to see whether it was what I wanted or not. He was helping me, taking the pressure off me to express what I needed, and for that I would always be grateful.

Flynn raised his arms, and Tristan peeled the pale pink material up and over his head before dropping it on the deck, just out of reach.

Ezra ran his fingers through my hair again, and I groaned, his touch like a balm to my ragged heart. "You feel so good. Can't believe you're letting me touch you like this," he murmured, his voice holding the same incredulity as his words.

"I'm sorry for the way I behaved to you after Sydney," I mumbled, leaning into his touch.

"Hey." He touched my chin and waited until I opened my eyes. "My behaviour left a lot to be desired too. Let's call it even in terms of fuck-ups, yeah?"

I nodded, swallowing past the lump in my throat. The naked desire in his eyes, the tender way he was touching me, and the rasp in his voice drew me in. I needed to get closer. I needed to feel them.

Looking around for Zali, I spied her a few steps away. She was extracting herself from this, stepping away and letting them focus on me. "I love you," I mouthed to her, needing her to know.

A slow smile spread across her lips, lighting her up until she was incandescent. Knowing I did that, knowing I could make her happy, was like a shot of adrenaline. She made me brave. She gave me courage.

Flynn asked hesitantly, "Can I touch you?"

I nodded and rasped, "Please."

He shuffled closer until our thighs were brushing and shifted his hands from my belt loops to my abs. My stomach quivered, butterflies alighting at his soft touch. He bit down on his lip and slid his fingers up, dancing them over my skin, then up and over my pecs. His lips turned up in a smile as gooseflesh broke out over my body, and when his eyes met mine, the heat there nearly knocked me off my feet.

I sucked in a slow breath, inhaling his scent. He was like a spring day. Ocean breezes and warm skies. He licked his lips and trailed his fingertips over my collarbone, his gaze dropping to where he was touching me.

"Can I kiss you?" he breathed before looking up at me through long lashes.

"Fuck, yes," I said on a rush and leaned in as he raised his hands, tangling his fingers in my hair and rising on his toes to bring our mouths together.

He pressed his lips to mine gently, once then twice, before he asked, "Is this okay?" His lips brushed against mine as he spoke, and I moaned, pulling him closer. I needed to eliminate the distance between us, to feel every inch of his lithe body against mine. Gripping his hips to pull them against mine, I nuzzled our noses together before Flynn swiped his tongue over my bottom lip, and I opened for his exploration.

With my first dip into his mouth, his flavour burst on my tongue, rich like the dark chocolate he'd been eating. The tartness lingered on his tongue, and I couldn't get enough. I sucked on it before running my own against his.

Kisses landed on my shoulders and throat, and my cock pulsed in my shorts. I was as hard as an iron rod, and the sensation of their bodies against mine and their hands on me was enough to drive me wild. I was going from zero to one hundred in a matter of minutes—I knew that—but it had been so long coming that I couldn't stop myself. I wanted it all, everything they could give.

Breaking our kiss, I sucked in a breath and nibbled a path along his smooth jaw. He tightened his hands in my hair, holding me in place as I kissed his throat.

"I wish I could have been your first," I confessed, shocking myself with my words. It was true, but I never imagined actually admitting that out loud.

"You were," he replied without hesitation, and that confused the fuck out of me. How could I have possibly been his first? I'd seen him with both Tristan and Ezra before. I pulled back and tilted my head in question, my brows furrowed. Flynn blinked his eyes open slowly and licked his lips as he looked down at the way our hips were pressed together, my hard cock poking up and out of my underwear, Flynn's alongside it in his white cut-off jean shorts.

"Zali was my first kiss. Tristan let me top him, and I bottomed for Ezra that first time."

"How was I your first?" I groaned as he licked my throat and sucked on my Adam's apple, my fingers tightening on his lat muscles.

"You were the first boy I fell in love with."

I froze, and Flynn pulled back, his eyes widening at my expression. His mouth popped open as if he was about to retract what he'd just said. But I couldn't hear it, not when everything had gone fuzzy and static was electrifying my brain at the thought that he'd wanted me too. Grasping his nape, I hauled him closer, eliminating the space between us, and crashed our lips together. He gave as good as he got, gripping my hair hard as he rutted against me, and I kissed him like I'd waited a lifetime to do.

His breaths were pants, and his chest heaved as I palmed his arse. The meaty globe was a perfect fit for my hand, and I loved how there wasn't a single soft part to him.

I loved Zali's curves, her femininity too, but holding Flynn was something else entirely. Maybe it was because I'd resisted it for so long, maybe it was because I was admitting to myself that I wasn't straight—but this moment, right here, was perfection.

The others pressed closer to me, one at each of my sides. Two walls of muscle curled their hands around my hips.

"Let Ez taste you, Ry," Tristan pleaded. I moaned, loving that he pressed in closer to me, kissing a line up my shoulder. "Tell us if you feel overwhelmed. We don't want to do that to you."

I gasped when Ezra ran his hands up and down my sides, his breath ghosting over my nape as he nuzzled me.

"Please, Ry," Ezra begged. "Can I kiss you?"

I peeled my torso away from Flynn's, turning as far as I could without letting go of him. I reached for Ezra, holding on to him with one arm as if he was a life preserver. He brushed his lips over the corner of mine, his touch gentle, before he moaned and pressed in closer. With his hard cock lined up with my hip, he slanted his mouth over mine and kissed me. It was slow and deep, our tongues melding and exploring each other's mouths as Ezra slid his hand up my chest, flicking his thumb over my nipple.

My cock bucked in my underwear, a bead of pre-cum leaking from my slit and smearing between Flynn and me. Flynn moaned and dipped his head, kissing my chest and kneading my arse.

Ezra slid his hand down my chest to my belly, stopping when his pinkie brushed the elastic waistline of my boxer briefs. I choked out a cry and broke our kiss, my head spinning and my lungs burning.

Then Tristan was there, turning my face to his. Flynn let go of me, and I whimpered, but when Tristan took his place, standing front and centre before me, I sucked in a breath and held it. I waited for him to touch me.

But he didn't move.

It was probably only a split second, but it may as well have been eons. I needed him, the man who'd thrown my ordered world completely off its axis and forced all of us to face up to what had been staring us in the face for too long. We were all meant to be together, and while Zali was the glue that held us together, Tristan was the match that sparked the blaze burning between us.

His eyes darkened when I grasped his hips and hauled him closer. Our hard cocks nestled against each other, and his nostrils flared as he sucked in a breath.

"Fuck, I want to lick you all over," he growled before crashing his mouth to mine, our tongues fighting for dominance as we mauled each other. I took what I wanted from him—passion, aggression, and a rough ride—knowing that I didn't need to hold back with him. The knowledge that he could handle me caused the weight to lift off my shoulders. I didn't have to be gentle with him. I didn't have to temper how hard I held onto him or how rough I was.

Tristan ran his hands down my back before sliding them around to brush my hipbones. He pushed my underwear down, following the V leading to my pubes.

I moaned, and he smiled against my lips when my stomach quivered. "I like this," he murmured, collecting the pre-cum leaking from my slit with his thumb and bringing it to his mouth. I sucked in a breath and watched as he licked it clean, his pupils blown and turning his green eyes almost black.

Shivering with need, I whimpered, clawing at his back. The floodgates had opened. Now that I'd given myself permission to want this, I wanted everything. My hands shook as I reached for the button on his pants.

But Tristan stopped me, his hand closing over mine. "We have as much time as you need, Ry," he reassured me.

"Please, I need it," I rasped, shamelessly begging him to touch me. Tristan didn't hold back, jerking my underwear down and freeing my cock properly. The breeze against my heated skin was like a balm soothing my need while ramping it up again.

Tristan wrapped his hand around me, his rough hand firm and tight. He stroked my length in strong pulls, short-circuiting my brain and sending my nerve endings haywire. My balls drew up, my cock throbbing as I shot to the edge. Moaning, I thrust my hips forward, driving myself into his grip. Desperation washed over me, my body in a sprint to the finish line. But I didn't want it to end so quickly. Not yet. Not when I'd only just gotten their hands on me.

I tried saying the alphabet backward, focussing on the sounds around me, the barnacles growing on the hull of the yacht. I tried to remember mathematical formulas I'd been taught and started reciting the safety procedures I'd put in place with so many of us on board.

But it was no use.

Flynn kissed down my back while falling to his knees and gripping my arse, kneading my cheeks, and Ezra bit my shoulder, his cock nudging my leg as I chased more of Tristan's touch on my cock.

It was decadent and salacious, Ezra as naked as the day he was born, me with my underwear around my thighs, and Tristan and Flynn still half-dressed, all of us kissing and touching here on the main deck high up enough that anyone traversing the waterways would see. Flicking my gaze to Zali, I smiled at her watching us from the sidelines. I loved her for giving me this—for letting me finally own my sexuality.

I sucked in a breath and savoured the freedom coursing through my veins. There was a healthy dose of fear too, but I was beyond reason. I'd shaken off the binds that had kept me trapped in my own head. Instead, I reached for Ezra's cock.

But he was already sinking to his knees. "Want to taste you," Ezra breathed, nipping my hipbone as he eased my underwear the rest of the way down my legs.

"Want you inside me too," he added.

The final strings I hadn't even known were tethered fell away, freeing me from their binds. It was time that I voiced my own desires. It was time I got to touch them too.

"Me too. Both of you," I admitted, palming Flynn's head as he licked along my hamstring where it intersected with my arse. He was so close to the most intimate part of me, the place I hadn't ever been able to imagine being touched.

Tristan let go of me and raised his fingers to his mouth, licking my pre-cum from them before cupping my face with his free hand and reaching down to his pants with his newly cleaned one. He drew me in for another decadent kiss, our tongues tangling as I moaned, the backs of his hands brushing against me as he shoved his pants down.

I cried out when heated breath washed over my sensitive shaft. My gaze snapped down to the beautiful man on his knees. Ezra, who was gorgeous enough to be offered a modelling job, had his fingers curled around my dick. My cockhead was pointed at his open mouth as he watched a bead of pre-cum leak from my slit and roll down my length.

It was worthy of billboard signage. It was fucking sexy. He was fucking sexy.

"Please," I begged. I didn't have to ask twice. He licked my sensitive glans and hummed at the pre-cum smeared there before engulfing my cock with his hot mouth. He laved me with his tongue, sending shivers of sensation through my entire body. Tingles erupted from the top of my head and the tips of my fingers and toes.

Ezra sucked me to the back of his throat, the tight heat closing around me and nearly setting me off like a bottle rocket. He worked me, sucking in long pulls before he released my cock, then swallowed me back down. I saw stars.

But then his mouth was gone. I cried out, never wanting the sensation to end, but he closed his fist around me and jacked me with the perfect amount of twist in his wrist as he reached my crown. I watched him take Tristan's cock to the back of his throat the same way he'd swallowed me down.

Jesus Christ, watching them together was like my own private porn show. I fucking loved it.

Flynn ran his finger down my cleft, almost tickling me with his gentle strokes, getting nearer to my hole with every pass. I grunted when he spread my cheeks, then shouted out as he circled my rim with his tongue. I gripped Tristan so I could hold myself up, my knees threatening to give way from the sensation overload.

When Ezra turned his attention back to me, I was a goner. My orgasm rushed at me like a freight train, collecting me and obliterating every cell in my body. I shouted out, the waves of ecstasy crashing through me as I pulsed, unloading jets of cum into Ezra's mouth.

Flynn pulled back as I came down, and I watched through hooded eyes as my cum dripped down Ezra's chin, landing on his chest. He pulled his mouth off my softening cock and stood up, crashing his lips to Tristan's. Their tongues parried, but Tristan licked Ezra's chin, tasting me on his lips. I reached for both of them, closing my hand around both their shafts and marvelling at the feel of silk-coated steel against my palms. Their shafts were hot, damp from the pre-cum leaking from their slits, and I used it to lube my way.

Flynn stood up too and came around to share in Ezra's kiss. They were drinking me up, each of them tasting the evidence of my orgasm. I was inside each of them, and I wanted them all over me.

Dropping to my knees, I kept going, jacking them and wishing I had another hand. Tristan growled as he opened his eyes, pointing his cock at my face. He shuddered as I jacked him, licking my lips. That was all it took, his cock thickening in my grip and pulsing as his balls unleashed. He moaned, his voice sounding like he'd swallowed gravel as he shot pulse after pulse onto my chin, throat, and chest.

Using his cum as lube, I spread it over Flynn and Ezra before jacking them hard and fast.

Flynn's pierced monster was so different to my own. He was thick and long, bigger than me on both counts, and the metal adorning his shaft was a complete contrast to the preppy outfits he wore and his sweet, innocent personality.

Never in a million years would I have imagined him having any kinds of piercings, never mind a Jacob's ladder. I ran my thumb over the metal embedded under his skin, and he cried out, stiffening as I twisted my wrist.

I couldn't tear my eyes away, but I needed to get a look at Ezra too. My mouth watered as I flicked my gaze to his cock. He was longer than me, but not as girthy, the perfect handful. He was fucking beautiful. Everything about him was sublime.

His skin colour was more golden than my tan, and Flynn's was pale against my hand. They may have been different to me, but our similarities—our masculinity, no matter the form it came in—was the hottest part for me. We fit together, all four of us having fallen for each other as well as for our woman.

"Give it to me. Paint me," I ordered them, and Flynn cried out, his cock twitching in my hand. I watched as Ezra's balls drew up and his cock thickened, getting impossibly harder as both of them let loose on me, hitting my face and chest with pulse after pulse of cum. It was dripping down my body, making a beeline straight for my own semi-hard dick.

I understood how Zali felt. She was our cum slut, but I wanted to rub it into my skin, walk around with their marks on me. I wanted them to own me just as much as I wanted them.

"My pretty sir," Flynn murmured, running his fingers through my hair before touching my cheek and spreading the cum he collected there onto my lip. I licked my lips, tasting their spunk for the first time, and my eyes rolled back into my head. I reached for my straining dick again.

"You ready to kiss me yet?" Zali asked, straddling my knees and pressing her naked body against mine as she wrapped her arms around my neck.

"Yeah, I think I am," I murmured as I slanted my mouth over hers and kissed her. It was slow and deep, our tongues melding and exploring each other's mouths as she ground against me. She tasted sweet, like the mango I'd cut up for her for breakfast, and she smelled of sunshine and salt. I moaned, a thrill of wonder coursing through me that I was finally kissing her and here with them all.

NINE

Flynn

I leaned against Zee's desk and watched her as she closed the window in her office. The wind had picked up, and despite being calm only a few hours ago when we were on the deck, it was now blowing a gale. The papers ordered in neat stacks were curling in the breeze, the weights holding them down the only thing stopping them from flying about the room.

We'd all gone our separate ways after Ry had come out to us, giving him some space and time without abandoning him. But Zee had asked me to sit and go through the information with her before she spoke to the others. I wasn't sure that I was much help though. It was like my brain couldn't wrap itself around what had happened that morning. I kept replaying what happened over and over. I still couldn't believe it was real, that Ry let us touch him, that he admitted it was more than just needing to get off. His kisses…. Damn, they were hotter than Hades.

His kisses were drugging. All-consuming.

I sighed happily. I got to kiss him. I got to call him ours. I bit down on my lip, my smile escaping anyway. I was giddy, my insides dancing like I was doing the can-can.

This whole morning had, quite frankly, been life changing. It sounded ridiculous, but it wasn't an exaggeration. I hadn't lied to Ryder. He was the first boy I'd fallen in love with. He may not have had my physical firsts, but he'd had my heart long before Tristan and even Ezra had come along. And that meant something.

I'd kept my crush on him on the down-low—my sexuality would have been a reason for my family to take notice of me rather than forgetting I even existed—but more than that, I was terrified of Ry's reaction. If he'd been repulsed by me being bi or my schoolboy fantasy of kissing the bad boy and my best friend, my teenaged heart couldn't have handled it. I would, quite literally, have been a walking, talking Olivia Rodrigo song.

Zee was looking at me with a soft smile. "You're happy," she said. It wasn't a question. There was no need. I knew it was written all over my face.

"I am. I'm walking on air."

"Me too." She hugged herself and grinned happily, her eyes sparkling like she was incandescent. "When he spanked me in the plane, I was spun out. But I totally thought it was a one-off. Then when he joined us in Monaco and went further, I had my fingers crossed that he'd come around. But I didn't think it was actually possible. I figured I'd be pining for him forever when he walked away that second time."

"Imagine how I felt." I laughed, shaking my head. "I didn't think I had a snowball's chance." I wrapped my arms around Zee's waist and smile-kissed her. "And now I can call you both mine."

The smile slipped from her lips as she became serious. Cupping my face in her soft hands, she brushed her lips against the corner of my mouth and whispered, "Even when we weren't together, I was still yours, Flynn. You mean everything to me."

"I love you too." Sliding my hand into her hair, I tilted her face up to mine and kissed her slowly, stroking my tongue languidly against hers, taking us both higher.

I tugged her with me into her executive chair, pulling her onto my lap. She'd called me into her office for a reason, and I didn't want to keep distracting her—she needed a break, and the sooner we finished up in here, the sooner she could take it. "Go on, fill me in," I suggested.

"Okay." She nuzzled my face and pressed a kiss to my cheek before clearing her throat and shifting so she could reach the keyboard and mouse.

When she was comfortable, she jiggled her mouse, waking up her screens, and pointed at the spreadsheets there. "Whoever is using these accounts is smart. See these withdrawals?" Zee highlighted the lines I'd ordered by amount. "They're cash withdrawals. But they're not being made from ATMs or anything like that. They're withdrawing cash from the same location—Monaco—and given how regular the withdrawals are, my guess is that they're living off it."

"So they're in Monaco?" I asked, confused. I thought that all the evidence was pointing us to Mauritius.

"I don't think they are. Look at this transaction. It's one of the first ones from the accounts, but it wasn't a withdrawal like the others. It was a transfer. The card expired years ago. It was issued, it received one transfer, one withdrawal for the full amount, then the account was closed down shortly after. From Mauritius."

"How did you find that out?"

"It was an Australian card. The bank kept note of the ISP that processed the request for verification purposes." She didn't add anything further. Unless she'd managed to hack into the issuing bank, the only way she could have gotten that information was out of the historical records from Reserve Bank. She'd never admitted downloading anything—she'd denied it outright, in fact—but we all knew she had the records.

My chest warmed and my belly flip-flopped. I loved this woman. She was incredible. No matter how cold-hearted she portrayed herself as, she had the biggest heart of anyone I knew. She was still protecting us, determined to make sure we had plausible deniability.

Leaning in, I kissed Zee, tightening my arms around her waist. She sighed happily and snuggled into me, playing with the top button of my shirt. "You've been working a lot," I murmured.

"What do you have in mind?" she asked, her voice turning seductive.

"A naked swim. You and the guys. You need to destress."

She hummed, her voice wistful. "I love that idea. But not yet. I think I may have cracked who it was."

"What?" I exclaimed, incredulity and shock lifting my voice to a squeak. "What more do you have?"

"This first transaction. It's the beginning of a pattern."

Scanning my eyes down the spreadsheet, it was impossible not to notice that every transaction was for the same amount, bar the first one. That was a whole lot more than the others. "It doesn't match though, and it was a transfer to a card, not a withdrawal. Why do you think they're related?"

"Look at the timing. Once a month, every month on the same day. There are a few random interim transactions, but this one is the first of the regular amounts."

Holy hot dog, she was right. She continued, "When you think about it, if you're moving to a new country with just luggage you can carry, even if you are going home, you're going to need a lot of stuff. Our guy could have spent most of that on groceries getting their pantry and cold foods stocked up. Then there's linen, extra clothes...."

"Who do you think it was? Why do you think they were going home?"

She sighed, leaning back against me and snuggling into my embrace. I ran my hand up her back, her bare skin soft under my hand. The only thing she had on was a loose camisole and a pair of ruffled panties that showed enough skin to make me salivate. But that wasn't what I was focussing on. It was her warmth and her vibrancy that had been dulled by the weight she was carrying. Maybe she needed strength, and if that was the case, I was privileged to be the one she called on.

"Remember when Tristan said that he'd been trying to find the staff members who were at ReimagINC when it went under and how there were a lot who'd dropped off the radar?"

"Yeah. Did you find a connection to one of them?"

She opened a staff profile that included a photograph of a man who was probably in his mid-forties if the greying in his closely cropped beard was anything to go by. He was handsome, with dark skin and eyes. He filled out the light blue shirt he wore nicely, and he had a killer smile.

"This guy was the assistant to the CFO. The credit card that received the transfer was in his name. He was born in Mauritius but immigrated here a year before he got the job with Mum. Before that, he worked for the same liquidators that handled ReimagINC's winding up."

"That's a lot of coincidences."

"Yeah." She groaned and scrubbed her hands over her face. She was mentally and physically exhausted, but Zee wouldn't let up on this until she'd solved it. "There are too many."

She gritted her teeth, her eyes turning cold and hard. "He's also one of the people who went completely radio silent when the company went under. I think it's him, Flynn. I think he did it."

"Far out." I exhaled on a shudder and squeezed her tight again. "What can I do, Zee? What do you need?"

"I need to nail this bastard to the wall and make him beg for death."

My gut twisted painfully. I'd told Tristan and Ezra that they needed to be okay with Zee or Ry ending this… person. But I also needed to be okay with it. Knowing that it might actually happen, that they could be about to take a life, shook me to my core. Fear coursed through me.

What if they got caught? What if they ended up in some scummy overseas jail that destroyed them? I'd seen pictures of Kerobokan Prison in Bali. I couldn't imagine that Mauritius jails were any better. Did the death penalty exist in Mauritius? Holy hell, if they were caught, they could be sentenced to death. Killed themselves.

My breathing quickened and my pulse skyrocketed. No, I was doomsaying. There were protections we could take, preparations we could make to ensure that this didn't go wrong.

And we would. I'd wrap it up until it was airtight. There was no way I would let anything happen to them. Just like Zee would do anything to protect us, I would do anything to protect her. Ry too.

What we couldn't protect against was either of them struggling to live with having pulled the proverbial trigger. I would never forgive myself if they were haunted by the moment this guy's eyes turned dull as the life seeped out of him. I ached at the thought of regret eating them alive.

That fear flared in me again, but it wasn't the act of killing someone that terrified me. It was what it would do to the people I loved. It was my job to stand beside them no matter what so I could support Zee and Ry until my dying breath.

We needed to do whatever it took to get them through this as unscathed as possible.

A calmness settled over me. I had my mission—care for them, be there for them. Now I needed to give them the closure Zee and Ry both needed.

How did we do that? How did we find this person? We suspected he was in Mauritius, living in a luxury compound. "We have to narrow down the properties. We can't just doorknock fifty estates all over the country, randomly looking for one person. We'll be arrested long before we ever find him."

"We've got the addresses of the houses we think could be our targets, but we need to narrow them down. Some of them might not have even been built at that time. I have to get into the Mauritius land registry. If I can narrow those fifty back down to the few in that article, it'll be manageable. We might be able to get the number down more if I can find out anything about the owners. Hopefully he's stupid enough to have used an entity that I can tie back to him."

I nodded, skimming my fingers down her back again. Her muscles were bunched up, tense and knotted. That swim was looking further away than ever, but I knew Zee wanted this finished. She needed closure.

"Should I look at whether we need visas and how best to get there and back?"

"Get Ry in here. We're taking my plane. Tris and Ez too. We have a bit more research and a shit ton of planning to do."

TEN

Ezra

The interior of the plane was all lacquered oak and cream leather. It was plush and uber luxurious without being pretentious. It suited Zali to a tee. But riding in it was also unlike anything I imagined an international flight on a private jet would be. Instead of the champagne flowing and joining the mile high club, we were quiet, each doing our own thing. Ry was in the cockpit, flying the plane, and Flynn hadn't left his side. He'd nominated himself Ry's unofficial co-pilot, and Ry was teaching him what all the gadgets and gauges were for. I'd taken them drinks and snacks a few hours earlier, then walked away overwhelmed by the array of screens in front of them.

Tris had his head buried in his laptop. The plan was for him to run formal scheduled classes for the first half of the research project, then meet individually with groups to continue to guide their research and gather it into a useable format. So far, he'd met the groups via video chat, and now he was compiling the information he'd been presented, starting to put together the outline for each episode in the podcast.

He'd wanted to pull the pin, but after speaking with the funding board and Ethics about pulling it, they'd been insistent that *Tarnished Crown* be published. Even then, he was resistant. It wasn't until Zali had sat him down and begged him to keep going, to get to the bottom of what fate had befallen her mother and brother that he agreed and started to compile the episodes.

Zali was determined to get justice for her mum and brother. I didn't blame her, but Jesus, it was taking its toll on all of them. I was proud of Zali too. She'd been stressed, barely sleeping and constantly working, but a couple of nights ago, it was as if she'd reached her limit. Instead of burying herself in research like she'd done every night since making her discovery or demanding sex, she rang Cara. An hour later she was out the door. They went out to dinner, caught a movie, gorged themselves on popcorn and slushies, and came home smiling a few hours later. I'd never known her to have a girlfriend—I hadn't even known her to have friends other than Ry and Flynn—but she gravitated toward Cara, and Zali couldn't have picked a better friend for herself. Cara was sweet and seemed pretty sheltered, but she was genuine and fiercely protective of Zali.

When Zali had returned to the yacht, she was in a much better place mentally. She wasn't as weighed down. She got a good night's sleep and hit the research again the next day.

The transfer to the Australian card had been like finding the switch for the spotlight. And that spotlight shone straight onto one person.

Auberon Benedict.

His background was much of a mystery except for what we'd been able to find in the company records. Somehow, Tristan had managed to get a hold of them. I still wasn't sure how, but I knew him. I knew it was legit.

I'd been working behind the scenes too. I'd meant what I said to Tristan. I needed to protect Zali and Ryder. I'd gathered what evidence we'd obtained legally and sought to have a warrant for Benedict's arrest issued. But it hadn't come through. My inspector had refused to sign off on the application to the court. She'd been unimpressed, not even convinced that a crime had occurred.

Looking at the case from her perspective, I agreed. What Tristan and his students had legally obtained barely scratched the surface. It was all circumstantial at best with giant gaping holes in their theories. Zali's evidence filled the gaps and actually established the link to Benedict. But it was all inadmissible. I couldn't use anything she'd obtained from the Reserve Bank's records or it would risk the charges against her reappearing. If she hadn't retrieved those records, she wouldn't have been able to verify that the transfers were made to different accounts than the ones in ReimagINC's accounting records. Without them, I had no evidence of a crime.

But if I could get past that, I couldn't tell Puglisi anything about who received the transfers or what they did with the money. That data all came from the Grande Banque Unie.

As far as Puglisi knew, I'd been sick for the week. I couldn't very well tell her that we'd breached more international laws than I could count to hack into the bank and download the critical records. That ruled out the possible purchase of the house and credit card transaction that would establish the connection to Benedict. Without those essential pieces, standalone property transactions in Mauritius were irrelevant.

It didn't matter that the owner of one of the properties we'd identified was a corporation named Blessed Royal. I hadn't picked up on the connection immediately, but Flynn had. He'd searched for what Auberon meant, wanting to know more about the heritage of the name. Of German origin, it meant noble or royal bear, while Benedict's meaning was blessed. It was yet another coincidence that we couldn't ignore but was irrelevant without all the data.

The arrest warrant didn't matter anyway though. Turns out that Mauritius was a non-extradition country. Even if I got one, I wouldn't be able to get assistance from the local police to take him into custody and begin the extradition process.

I needed a confession from him.

Harder yet would be persuading Zali and Ry not to execute this fucker.

If I did that, I could bring him back.

It didn't much matter how I got him onto Australian soil—hogtied and gagged was a perfectly good option—but once I did, I had jurisdiction.

Once I had him in custody, I'd get the evidence I needed to get him locked up.

I'd make sure he went away for life.

Then, it'd be my pleasure to conveniently let slip to his fellow inmates that he was a child killer. His stay at His Majesty's pleasure would be less than pleasant—exactly what the bastard deserved.

I looked across at our girl. She was preoccupied, staring out the window at the cloudless blue sky, her knee bouncing. She was dressed casually in one of Tristan's button-down shirts, the sleeves rolled up to her elbows. Her stilettos had long since been kicked off and her legs were now covered with a blanket, but she was still cold. Her nipples were peaked, hard buds under the material of the shirt.

I closed my laptop, not in the mood to finish the report I'd been writing. Shifting over to sit opposite her on the armchairs, I asked, "Want to talk about it?"

She blinked, her gaze slowly coming into focus as she turned to me. "Sorry?"

"Want to talk about what's going to happen?"

"No. It's better if I just go there alone and kill the fucker myself."

I couldn't help the bark of incredulous laughter that bubbled up. I softened the blow by reaching for her dainty hands and threading our fingers together. Hers were cold. I rubbed them, trying to warm her up, but she needed another blanket. First, though, I needed to clear up the misconception she was living under.

"You have four men who love you like the earth loves the sun and the moon."

My gaze flicked to Tristan, who stood up and gestured at the extra blanket perched on the end of his seat. I nodded, and he brought it over, then wrapped it around her shoulders before tucking a loose lock of hair behind her ear.

"There is no way on earth that you're seeing that man alone," I continued, leaving no room for argument in my tone. She may be our queen, but I was prepared to risk her accusation of treason if it meant keeping her safe.

Tristan added, "If he was dangerous enough to kill your mum and brother, he could do the same to you. Between the five of us, we can stop him, but only if we're there too. We can't keep you safe if you go alone."

"He killed my mum and my brother—"

"Sure, okay. Let me just go tell Ry that you're doing this alone, then," I threatened.

She huffed and rolled her eyes. It was a low blow, but if he had any inkling that she'd even thought of doing it alone, he'd turn the damn plane around.

Tristan added, "We know how important it is to you to get justice. But if he hurts you, then what? If we're together, we can take the bastard down."

"Fine," she grumbled, but I suspected it wouldn't be the last we'd heard of her cockamamie suggestion.

Flynn chose that moment to walk down the corridor from the cockpit. "We're about half an hour out from starting our descent. The resort knows we're on the way. They'll have transportation waiting to take us to the hotel."

The resort he was talking about was a private getaway for the uber rich on an island off Langkawi. It was serviced by its own private airport. Even though the reason for our trip was hanging over us like a storm cloud, I couldn't wait to see it. I was more excited for Zali. Tristan had wanted to treat her to a night of luxury. He'd looked in Kuala Lumpur, but Ry had asked for a smaller airport. It wasn't until Zali had handed Tristan her platinum card and cancelled the price ceiling on his search that he found the resort.

And it was perfect.

There were four traditional chalets on the island, each one resembling a log cabin constructed on a platform over the water. But while they looked simple from the outside, inside they were opulent. The beds—covered in silk sheets and mounds of pillows—were strategically placed under retractable ceilings, allowing for stargazing at night. The lounge featured a sunken glass viewing floor to the reef below, and the deck immediately outside allowed easy access to the water and the perfect spot to watch the sunset over the Malaca Strait. The staff, including the Michelin-star chefs who prepared every meal and delivered them anywhere on the island, were on call 24-7. They catered to guests' every whim.

We would be sticking to the chalet, but the island itself looked magical too. Walking tracks that meandered through the jungle led to twin waterfalls with deep clear pools perfect for swimming in. Others led up the steep slope to the lookout—the perfect place for a proposal if the photos online were anything to go by.

Despite the staff and the other chalets, the resort was entirely private. The chalets were secluded, separated from one another by both the natural landscape and swipe card access to the private beach they were perched over. Apart from the private airport and obvious luxury, the main draw-card was the resort's seclusion. The only guests we wanted to see were the ones we were travelling with.

Clothes would be optional from the moment we stepped into the chalet until the moment we left.

It was exactly what Zali needed.

It was exactly what we *all* needed—a chance to connect with one another before this next step. It was naïve to think that we'd be the same people on the way home. Tris had admitted to needing a moment for all of us to be together before everything went down, and I'd wanted something special that we could remind ourselves of when we were facing dark days. I only hoped it worked.

* * * * *

The sun was starting to dip low in the sky as I looked out at the ocean beyond the cove our chalet was situated in. Icy mocktails were waiting for us on a tray, and there were more in the frozen slushie machines on the deck behind us. A fruit platter was delivered to our door as the porters were carrying our luggage into the chalet.

Dinner was three hours away—the staff would deliver our seafood spread so that we didn't even have to go to the restaurant. It was enough time for us to have a swim and possibly even snorkel at least part of the reef surrounding us.

Tristan's heat blanketed my back, the sun warming my front. It was humid, not even a faint breeze coming off the Strait of Malacca to our west. The glasslike surface of the water, marred only by the occasional ripple from a fish's tail breaking the surface, was calling to me, but I didn't want to get in without the others.

My shorts were riding low on my hips, but when I went to pull them up, Tristan stopped me, pressing a line of open-mouthed kisses to my shoulder and up my throat. I shivered, and he growled, "These need to come off," as he grasped my hips and ground his erection into my arse.

I arched into his touch, canting my butt so it left him in no doubt that I wanted to be filled by him.

"Want you naked in that water," he rumbled, tugging on the laces holding my shorts up. They slid lower on my hips, and he pushed them down, my semi thickening as he trailed his lips down my back and bit the meaty part of my butt. Licking the sting away, he slid his hands back up my thighs and brushed them over my cock. I moaned and bent at the waist, spreading my legs so he could play.

I gasped when the hard slap landed on my arse, a rushing sensation travelling straight through me and filling my cock until it was hard enough to hammer nails. "None of that yet," Ry ordered, his voice playful but seductive too.

"We have our lady to get wet first and our boy to take care of."

Straightening up, I cast my gaze sideways at Ry, biting back my groan at the sight. He was naked, his shorts and shirt lying in a pile on the sunbed next to him. His cock was heavy between his legs, the dark thatch of trimmed hair at its base like a neon sign for my senses. I wanted to bury my face there and inhale his musk.

Now that he'd grown more comfortable with directing things between us, being on my knees for him was revelatory. I loved the way he took charge, choreographing movements and driving us all to wild climaxes. I'd always thought of Tristan as the one in charge, but even he'd demurred to Ry a few times, swapping the role between them effortlessly.

Right now, the desire to bend over and offer my hole to whoever could get in me first was almost overwhelming.

"I think our lady is already wet," Flynn said playfully, brushing his fingers over her mound, her inner thighs glistening with her juices as she rubbed her legs together.

Out of all of us, Flynn was the only one still fully dressed. I raised my eyebrow, and he shook his head, knowing exactly what I was about to ask. "I'll sit this one out," he explained.

"Please, Flynn," Ry begged, his voice a soft purr. "Swim with us."

Flynn didn't like water. He wasn't a confident swimmer, but we weren't getting in the water to do an ocean swim. It was purely to relax together after a long few weeks.

Wrapping his arms around Flynn's waist, Tristan cuddled him close and murmured, "You don't have to get in, but we'd love it if you did."

He sighed and grumbled his acquiescence under his breath. Tristan's smile was like the sun coming out from behind a storm cloud, his whole face lighting up with delight. Ry's matched it, and my belly flipped when I saw how happy they both were.

Zali rested her hand on my shoulder, leaning her head against my arm as she hummed softly. "They make one another happy, don't they," she murmured loud enough that only I could hear.

"They do. Seeing all of you happy is wonderful. I don't want it to stop." I wrapped my arm around her waist, pulling her close.

"It won't," she replied confidently. "It took meeting Tristan to kick us into action, and now that I have you all, you're stuck with me."

"You'll find me if I run away, will you?" I asked playfully.

"Oh, I'll stalk you better than anyone has ever stalked you before," she warned with a laugh.

I couldn't help my bark of laughter as I nuzzled her hair and dropped a kiss there. "Have to say, if I'd realized what would happen, I would have introduced you to Tristan years ago. I never expected to be standing here like this with you."

"Are you okay with making this trip? With work, I mean. Was the inspector okay with giving you time off again?"

"I think she's relieved I'm out of the office, and I'm back on HR's good side. They've been telling me for months to get my unused holidays down, so when I said I'd be away for a few weeks, they were ecstatic."

I was still worried about work. I wanted things to be okay there, but I'd reached this weird kind of tipping point. I needed to either be all in or out. If I kept going down the path I was, I'd get myself into trouble. Puglisi had been right—I was off the rails—but I wouldn't change a thing if faced with the same decision. There was no way I'd choose my job over my partners. They all deserved the best that I could give them.

Being a copper was in my blood. I loved my job. I loved the responsibility and the chance to make a real difference to people's lives. I didn't get off on the power, though. I wasn't some loose cannon who was physically dangerous to people.

But I was a little too lax on following the rules.

For someone who was supposed to enforce them, I had no trouble crossing the line when I felt it was necessary.

And that was a problem.

A fundamental clash of morals with my profession.

I had some thinking to do, and I needed to make the decision quickly because if Puglisi thought I'd stepped out of line even one more time—exactly like I was doing now—I had no doubt she'd sic Ethics onto me.

Flynn's movements caught my attention again as he slowly flicked open the buttons of his pale blue shirt, biting down on his lip and revealing each piece of skin torturously slowly. Tristan didn't know where to look—his gaze was ping-ponging up and down Flynn's body, and he was openly salivating at what he was seeing while Ry watched him like a lion ready to pounce on his prey.

Ry's transformation over the last couple of weeks had been like night and day. He was still hesitant sometimes, but Tristan encouraging him to pull his head out had been good for him. He'd talked with Zali, and then after that first time together, he and Tristan had left the yacht, swimming over to the island and walking the beach until they'd slipped out of our line of sight. They were gone for hours. I don't know what they'd spoken about, but Ry was somehow lighter after it. I know that Tristan had encouraged him to speak with his old teacher too. A few days later, he'd docked the yacht at the city marina and had been gone for the day, then arrived home at the same time as me.

Huh, home.

I smiled, warmth ballooning in my chest. I was home. The people surrounding me were my home. No matter where we were or what we were doing—including what happened in the next couple of weeks with this trip or with work when we were back in Aus—I was home. I'd found my place, my people.

I kissed Zali's temple again and tightened my arm around her before nudging her closer to Flynn. It was time to let loose for a while, relax, and have some fun.

With the four of us surrounding Flynn, walking around him, and eying him like he was our next meal, Flynn moved quicker. His face flushed a pretty pink, and his hands shook as he rushed to strip his shirt off, dropping it unceremoniously on the deck at his feet. His knee-length denim shorts were next, but he paused when he reached the tiny pair of navy-blue briefs. His chest rose and fell, his breathing choppy and his body trembling with need.

Ry stroked his cock, licking his lips as he eyed off all the naked skin before him. Tristan's jaw ticked, and even though he wasn't as tall as Ry, his bulk and that bossy alpha side of his personality made him seem larger than life. Zali ran her fingernail down Flynn's back, and he arched, tensing every muscle in his torso and making his erection flex.

"Take them off, beautiful boy," I ordered, a distinct rasp in my voice. I stepped closer, the heat of his body in front of mine drawing me into him. We swayed closer, my hands brushing his abs as I reached up to hook my fingers into the elastic at his waist. Flynn sucked in a breath, his back pressing against my chest, and I dropped to my knees, skimming my lips down his back before I nuzzled his arse cheek.

He turned in my arms, and I tugged his underwear down, humming as I freed Flynn's hard cock. Running my lips over the barbells in it, I inhaled deeply, getting high on his musk and tasting the drop of pre-cum that had beaded at his slit. Flynn sucked in a shaky breath and threaded his fingers through my hair, holding me in place as I laved him.

"Let's take this into the water," Zali said from beside Flynn as she jacked him slowly. Flynn's eyes rolled back into his head, and she positioned his cock at my mouth, letting me get another taste of his pre-cum. I fucking loved it when he leaked for us. Closing my lips around his crown, I sucked and was rewarded with more of his flavour on my tongue. I wanted all of it. But Zali had other ideas.

She grasped his cock, using my spit to lube the way for her strokes before letting go and walking backward to the ladder. She crooked her finger in a come-hither motion and made shimmying down it look sexy. She picked up a set of goggles and a snorkel, and a moment later, she was treading water as she fitted the mask into place.

Ry was next, diving off the bottom step of the ladder into the water below, mask already in place. "Flynn, you next," he called. I stood up and fitted Flynn with his mask before I grasped his hand and led him to the ladder. I didn't give him a chance to debate Ry's order, but he didn't resist. Flynn didn't like the water or the creatures that lived in it, so snorkelling was pushing him outside his comfort zone.

Ry pulled Flynn into his arms as he sank into the water, and Flynn wrapped himself around Ry, riding on his back like a baby koala does to its mother. They lingered at the ladder, letting Flynn get used to the water.

"Go," I said to Tristan, planting a kiss on his luscious lips before handing him another mask and snorkel. "I'm right behind you."

I grabbed my underwater camera and hooked it around my wrist before swimming out after them.

Ducking my face down, I breathed through the snorkel and looked around, watching as Tris pulled his snorkel out and Zali mirrored his move, kissing him as they floated underwater above the coral. I snapped a photo of them, the kaleidoscope of colours a beautiful contrast to their bodies and the shafts of sunlight penetrating the surface casting a shimmery glow that haloed them.

Ry and Flynn swam over to them along the surface, Flynn still holding tight to Ry but no longer on his back. He was pointing at the schools of fish darting in and out of the protection of the coral. It was in constant movement but also at peace.

I wanted to remember this moment forever. Utter tranquillity settled in my soul. I wasn't sure we'd ever manage to recapture the relaxation that we'd stolen in this moment during an otherwise chaotic summer. That was the part of all this that I worried about the most. I had to keep Benedict alive despite Zali and Ry's intentions.

Would they hate me for it? Probably.

But if it meant saving them from suffering the guilt of taking his life, I'd take their being pissed at me every day for the rest of mine.

Nerves from contemplating the future betrayal churned in my gut. Even though I had a good reason, I hated acting like a double agent trying to push my agenda on the people I loved the most.

I had to cling to the knowledge that it was necessary. I may be a shitty cop who flouted a hell of a lot of rules, but there was one I wouldn't let the loves of my life cross. I didn't give a shit about the law's stance on murder, but I knew once they crossed that line, there was no coming back. It would eat them alive.

I swam closer to our centre—Zali—and duck dived under. The water was warm and crystal clear. The tide was about to turn, the incoming current from deeper in the Strait would make diving deeper necessary. But for now, I looked at the marvels of the natural world, letting the lingering worries wash away in the late afternoon sun and the tepid sea.

The water flowing around my naked body was unlike anything I'd ever experienced. It was sensual and freeing, as if it was kissing my skin, touching all the places that only I or my lovers touched. I basked in the sensation, floating underwater and just feeling the push and pull. I got it now. I knew exactly why Zali loved it. After experiencing it, I wasn't sure whether I'd ever be able to put on a pair of togs again. Swimming in board shorts or even Speedos could never live up to this.

We swam like that for what felt like hours, Ry and I taking it in turns to swim along the surface with Flynn and taking photos of everything. It didn't matter whether we were at the surface or below it—it was magical. But I didn't argue when Ry swam up and said breathlessly, "Go and check out the coral down there. There are so many fish."

I ducked underwater and was again surrounded by the incredible beauty. Tiny brightly coloured fish darted in and out of the seagrass and soft corals. Larger silver fish—the size of a baseball but flat—schooled, turning on a dime in perfect synchronicity. Others, larger still, swam along the reefs at a more leisurely pace, their life moving in slow motion until prey caught their eye. It was like being in a city, movement everywhere, but no city I'd ever seen compared to the one I was looking at. The bright corals in all shapes and sizes were incredible. Even the soft corals were amazing. But the fish absolutely stole the show—yellow, hot pink, blues, greens, and orange with stripes and spots—as far as the eye could see.

I stayed under as still as I could for as long as I could. I didn't want to surface, but my lungs were screaming, my body's instinct to breathe overriding the wonder I was seeing.

Breaking the surface, I could already see Tristan and Zali in the shallows. Reclined on her back in the water, Zali floated leisurely in the lagoon. Her lightly tanned body was a beautiful contrast to the aqua water and deep blue of the late afternoon sky.

Zali held her hand out to me, and I swam into the shallows toward them. It was only chest deep and closer to the shore, and the lapping of the water increased the rushing against my body. I moaned, my dick thickening as the push and pull stroked against my skin.

"You should feel it when you're floating," Zali said knowingly with a wicked smirk.

The moment we linked hands, rightness washed over me like a comforting blanket. It wrapped around me, warming my chest and sending butterflies fluttering around in my belly.

"Lie back with me," Zali encouraged. With my arms out to my sides and my legs spread, I let my head relax back in the water, its lapping kissing my sides and between my legs. My nerve endings lit up, and my cock stood tall, like a flower reaching up toward the sun. I gave myself a pump and choked as I sank below the surface, my body locking up tight as sensation shot through me.

Zali maneuvered me so my head was at her waist. I looked up at the chalet, and the stress from an hour ago seemed like ancient history. But it still niggled at the back of my mind, my thoughts snagging on that anticipatory sense of betrayal that I couldn't help but feel.

She ran her fingers through my hair, and I fell back into the moment. My plans and everything else swirling around inside me settled. I was protecting them—it was the right thing to do. I hummed and brought Zali's hand to my lips, kissing her softly.

Zali sighed happily. "Promise me that when we get back, we'll find a way we can be together. I want us to move into one place."

Hooking my pinkie through hers, I silently promised her it'd happen. I had no idea how to do it, but the thought lit a spark in me, and once ignited, it gathered speed like a wildfire burning out of control. I could imagine it. Waking up next to them every morning, then coming home after work and spending time together sounded like a dream.

"I want that too," I said on a rush.

Tristan hummed and added thoughtfully, "We'll need a bigger bed. Four in Zali's king was a tight fit. There's no way we'll fit all five of us."

Ry, with Flynn back on his back, glided to a stop in front of me. Ry parted my legs and pressed between them, pinning my thighs in place with his elbows. I wanted him to be there just as much. Wrapping my legs around them both, I pulled them closer and rubbed my foot over Flynn's arse, loving the way he squirmed when I brushed my toes down his crack.

Flynn moaned quietly and said, "We need one of those Alaskan king beds. They're twice the size of a normal king. And I want to be on the bottom."

"The bottom, hey?" Ry teased. "Who's on top?"

"All of you. Zee can ride my cock, and the rest of you can divide and conquer us."

Zali arched up, her nipples hardening as Flynn's words turned her on.

"I like the sound of that," Ry growled, running his fingers up and down my belly. My cock flexed, standing tall and begging for attention. Flynn was the one to reach for me first, though, closing his fist around my shaft and teasing my slit with his thumb.

Sensation ricocheted through me once more, the same high I'd had when getting naked on Zali's yacht making an appearance now. I moaned, shifting so I could get closer to Zali. I needed to feel her core tightening around my fingers as I brought her to the edge and helped her fly. But Ry beat me to it, teasing her folds with deft strokes of his hand. He held me in place with his other one, his big palm covering nearly all my arse cheek, his fingers brushing closer to my hole.

Ry was close enough to suck on me, my cock right in his face, and if Flynn didn't slow down, he was going to get painted in cum. Ry moved his fingers, trailing them down between my cheeks but stalling just shy of my hole, the tease. "Please," I begged.

Ry's breath caught and he squeezed his eyes closed, his Adam's apple bobbing in his throat. He shifted his hand and looked away from me. But it wasn't quickly enough. I saw the dimming of the desire in his gaze. "Hey," I said, pulling free from Flynn's grip and standing up. Water sloshed around us, and Zali choked out a cough as it washed back over her.

I knew Tris had her, so I concentrated on Ry, cupping his face and laying a soft kiss on the corner of his mouth. "If you don't want that, it's totally fine. We haven't gone there yet, and if we don't, that's okay. I'll never push you for more than you're ready for or want."

His shoulders dropped and he held his head low. "I do want it," he mumbled and looked away before slowly inhaling, his chest expanding with his breath. On a rush, he added, "But I don't know if I want to receive. I mean, Flynn eating me out was fucking hot, and a finger might be okay, but I don't know if I want to take a dick, you know? You probably think it's shitty—"

"No, I don't," I said, cutting off his nervous rambling. Zali and Flynn both wrapped their arms around Ry, and I was so very grateful for the way we championed one another, but especially that they'd given him their tacit support when he looked like he needed it.

Shaking my head, I added, "Not at all, Ry." When he looked up at me, his expression sheepish, my heart flipped and my belly swooped. This man. This beautiful, strong, sensitive man was both adorable and so brave. He was finally comfortable enough to voice his insecurities rather than needing to escape them. I fell in love with him more every time he did it.

"I don't expect you to bottom for me just because you topped me. This isn't a tit-for-tat arrangement. We all do what makes us feel good." I held out my hand to Tristan, and he came closer, joining me as we faced Ry. "Tris only ever tops me. That's our dynamic. If you want the same with me, I'm more than fine with it."

"What about Tris topping me?" he asked.

Tristan ran his hand down Ry's side, looking through the clear water at the spot where it rested on his hip. Their equally tanned skin was a stark contrast to the white sand below us. His hold was possessive but not controlling. "Only if you want me to. As for you topping me...." He gave a small chuckle before colour rose in his cheeks, and he flicked his gaze to Flynn. "That's kind of Flynn's and my dynamic. If it feels right in the heat of the moment, then maybe, but Flynn's the only person who's topped me, so..."

"Okay," Ry murmured, nodding and leaning into Tristan's side. "So neither of us tops the other."

"For the record," Flynn interjected, "anyone who wants to top me can."

I snorted out a laugh and pinched his cute bubble butt playfully. "Don't worry, baby boy, one of us will get all up in there soon enough." I gestured between Ry and Tris. "I'm extending Flynn's offer to me too."

"There's a whole lot of talk of dicking each other and no action," Zali complained playfully, moving us past the sex talk and back to the sexy times. "Let's move this party somewhere you can actually get all up in me, given I don't have a dick to share around," she demanded with a huskiness in her voice that had my dick perking back up to rock solid again.

"And yet, you have the biggest dick of all of us," I teased, planting a hard kiss on her lips.

"I prefer yours when it comes to getting me off though."

"Once again, for the record, I'm totally up for pegging." I wiggled my eyebrows and took my time running my gaze down her body. The thought of her wearing a strap-on had my cock achingly hard and leaking.

"Race you to our room," Flynn challenged, hopping on Ry's back again. "Whoever wins gets Zee's pretty pussy and my butt." Ry launched himself forward, laughing as Flynn pretended to ride him like a jockey on a horse, and Tristan grasped Zali's ankle, tugging her back toward him.

"You're forgetting her mouth," I called, shooting a wink at our girl before swimming toward the chalet.

I watched as Ry stopped swimming at the ladder to let Flynn scramble up it. Our beautiful boy stood at the top, his dick swinging freely, the metal adorning him glinting in the late afternoon sunlight. He raised his arms above his head while doing a silly dance, celebrating.

"Zee, get up here," he called out, waving her over.

Ry was up the ladder in a few steps, and my swim strokes stuttered as I watched the flex of his arms, back, and arse as he moved. He dragged the wicker coffee table away from the couch and tossed the long cushion from the couch onto it, softening the surface for Flynn as I climbed the ladder.

"On your back, beautiful boy," I instructed, parting his knees once he'd laid down. I licked a stripe up his cock. The bump of his piercings on my tongue made me jealous of Tristan's arse. He got to feel those inside him, rubbing his prostate and lighting up every nerve ending. "You know, one of these days, I'm gonna pin you to a table just like this and ride this monster. I want to feel these piercings inside me."

Flynn's breath stuttered, and pre-cum bloomed at his slit. I lapped it up and hummed as I sucked his thick cock down as far as I could, my gaze never leaving his.

ELEVEN

Zali

I climbed up the last rung of the ladder, completely re-freshed. It was as if the weight of the world had been washed away in the ocean and my well refilled. I needed the water to feed my soul. Maybe it was the connection to Mum and Ash that did it—like getting a shot of adrenaline from being close to them again. Maybe it was as simple as being able to disconnect from what was weighing on me— the pressure, the driving need to give them some kind of justice. Whatever it was, I needed it. My body craved it in the same way an addict craves their drug of choice.

Now, though, it was craving other things. That sweet prelude of what was to come was nothing but a tease. And I wanted more. I wanted it all.

Stepping onto the deck, I saw Ry flick open the lube and Flynn prop his heels up on the coffee table, spreading him-self open as Ezra licked at him like he was a lollipop. My clit throbbed at the sight of them making each other feel good.

I wanted in too.

"Zee, come here. I need you," Flynn rasped, holding out his hands for me. I went to him, and he tugged me closer. "Straddle my face. I want to taste you."

I didn't hesitate to follow his orders, and he rewarded me with a lick of my cunt before he sucked my clit into his mouth, biting down on it gently. I cried out, sensation licking over my body and pooling in my belly. I covered him with my juices, and he hummed, lapping them up as I ground on his tongue.

Tristan's hands were at my arse, his thick fingers rimming my hole. "You want to do this, Ry?" he asked as Ryder tipped the lube, coating his fingers in slick before handing it to Tristan. The cold of the viscous liquid hitting between my cheeks was a shock to my system, and my cunt tightened, anticipation thrumming through me. I couldn't wait to have them inside me.

He hummed. "Think I might prep Ez, actually. Want my cock in him."

"Me too," Flynn gasped as he repositioned me and slid his fingers deep inside my cunt. I cried out and pinched my nipples, arousal singing through my veins and my clit already tingling. Fuck me, I needed this. I needed to get out of my head and let them take over my body, using me to get off. I wanted them to fill me, to fuck me and use me like I was their sex toy. I wanted to be brimming with cum and have it spill out of me every time I moved. I wanted to be stretched open and fucked.

When we got on the plane again tomorrow, I wanted to still feel every pump of their hips against me, the ghost of their fucking a dull ache every time I moved.

Then I wanted them to do it all again.

"Get inside me, Tristan," I begged. He obliged, sliding without hesitation what had to be two fingers inside my hole. The burn was like kindling to a match, setting me alight. I moaned long and low, my cunt clenching as it begged to be stretched like Tristan was doing to my arse.

"She's already close," Flynn growled against my clit, the vibrations sending me spiralling. "Add a finger, Tris."

They were worshipping my body, Tristan following Flynn's suggestion and stretching me more, finger fucking me harder.

The rushing started at my core, tingles exploding from my clit.

My cunt tightened, and Flynn added another finger. I twisted my nipples hard, my fingernails biting into the skin there.

A wave of heat blasted over me, and I cried out, my orgasm slamming into me after only a minute of them touching me.

My legs nearly gave out, but they were there to catch me. Ezra hooked his arms under my shoulders, and Flynn lifted my arse, both of them shifting me like I was weightless. Tristan was there too, holding Flynn's cock up so they could impale me on his dick while my cunt was still convulsing. The stretch and the caress from the warm metal of Flynn's piercings as he entered me was an electrical shock to my system, making my muscles lock up, then release as he hit my G-spot and kept lowering me until he bottomed out. He was so hard and thick that I paused for a moment, savouring the stretch.

"Zee, I need you to move," Flynn groaned, and I rocked my hips tentatively, wanting more than his cock inside me.

"Lie on him, kitten. I need inside your arse," Tristan ordered, and the resistance in my body gave way. I laid on his chest, pushing my hips up, and Tristan climbed onto the table, straddling my hips and nudging my hole with his thick cock.

"Do it," I begged. "Fuck me so I'm fucking Flynn too."

He didn't hesitate, surging forward in one deep thrust, not stopping until his hips were pressed against my arse. The burn rocketed through me, the sharp stab of pain/pleasure stealing my breath. I gasped, and Tristan pulled all the way out before jamming his hips forward, breaching my ring and slamming his cock into me.

I shouted out, the sizzle of pain igniting my insides. He was relentless, fucking me hard and fast and not giving my body a moment to adjust to his intrusion. I fucking loved the way he refused to treat me with kid gloves, knowing how much I craved that bite of agony with my orgasms.

His breathing turned ragged, and a drop of sweat landed between my shoulder blades. I arched up, my muscles locking tight, the movement changing the angle of my hips. Flynn's cock hit my G-spot, and it was enough to send me over again. I screamed, my cunt clenching Flynn like a vice as Tristan kept up his frantic pace.

Ecstasy washed over me in waves, my insides shattering, and with every thrust, the pieces melted and morphed back together, only to repeat the process again barely a second later.

Tristan pulled out, and I sobbed, the emptiness like a void inside me that needed to be filled.

Hands on my face distracted me as they brushed my hair away and turned me. A cock—Ezra's—prodded my lips, and I opened to him. He sank in to the back of my throat and bent at his waist, bracing himself on the table. With one foot propped next to my side and the other planted firmly on the floor, he fucked my face at the same frantic pace that Tristan had my arse. Gagging, spit dripped down my chin, and I heaved in a breath, crying out in relief when a cock nudged at my arsehole again.

Canting my hips, I silently begged whoever it was to fuck me again, and they didn't disappoint. At the snap of his hips, I knew it was Ry, his movements hard and fast but different to Tristan's. I couldn't explain how I knew it, but I did.

Flynn cried out from underneath me, and I knew that Tristan was working him, his fingers deep inside him as he rubbed his prostate until Flynn was seeing stars. His cock thickened even more, and I moaned, loving the stretch and burn of being taken in such a primal way.

My body was keyed up, my clit tingling and my stretched arse burning as I laid there taking it like their fuck toy. My moans were incoherent, and the grunts above and below me were music to my ears, like a symphony lifting me to another epic orgasm.

One of my guys gasped, and I let my mind wander, imagining the resort staff watching them take me. Fuck me.

Ezra hit the back of my throat again, and I choked, my cunt tightening as my stomach clenched.

"Fuuuuck," Ry groaned.

"Don't you dare come," Tristan ordered. "We're not done yet."

But he was gone. Ry pulled out, his breathing ragged, the whoosh of cool air he left behind hitting me like a bucket of ice. But then he was there again, using his fingers this time. The burn was back as he stretched me. "We're gonna try my fist in your arse soon aren't we, baby girl?" he crooned, breathless. "Just like your pretty pussy swallowing my fist, your arse will love it too. Want to sink in to my wrist."

Oh, fuck yes. I wanted them all to see it, to watch as Ry curled his hand inside my arse and punched his hand forward, stretching me to breaking point. I wanted their cocks inside me too, as many of them as could fit inside my cunt and my mouth. I wanted them fucking my tits and covering me in cum.

I wanted our onlookers to gasp and take out their cocks, fucking their fists until they came. I wanted them to get off on how I was being used. I wanted to be the one responsible for all our orgasms, to ride the wave of power at the knowledge that they fell apart looking at me.

I wanted my guys out of their minds with lust. I wanted them to come all over me, paint their releases deep inside me so I could carry it around.

My scream was silent as another orgasm crashed into me like a tsunami. My cunt tightened and my arse clenched like a vice around Ry's fingers, needing to keep him and Flynn inside of me. Ezra pushed deep inside my throat, cutting off my air supply, and I saw stars, the need to gasp in a breath rendering me powerless and heightening the sensation running through my body simultaneously.

I sobbed as he pulled back to let me suck in a breath.

"We're gonna take turns fucking you, kitten," Tristan whispered by my ear, his voice a harsh rasp. "Hitch up your pretty arse and mount you. We'll fuck you into the mattress until you're filled with our cum, and then we'll plug you up." He hummed, and I gasped, my orgasm renewing itself.

"Fuck, she's coming again," Flynn cried. "I'm there too."

He shouted out, his voice a mixture of pain and pleasure, and Tristan continued. "You'll carry it with you like our pretty little cum slut. Then when we want to fuck you again, we'll uncork you and bend you over. We'll fuck you anytime we want."

"Yes," I cried around a mouthful of cock as my cunt tightened again, my renewed orgasm stronger than the one that had hit me a moment ago.

My vision turned dim, my body going lax against Flynn's, and the sensation of being full disappeared. I sobbed when Ezra pulled out of my mouth, but I had nothing left. My body was a shell so overwhelmed with the sensation bombarding me that I was static.

Hardness slid inside my arse again, and I sighed, my whole body shifting as someone maneuvered my legs so I was bent in half while still being impaled by Flynn's dick. Heat at my back and a soft kiss to my nape told me that Tris was inside my arse, his thick cock spearing me open.

Another cock prodded my arse, pressing against my hole. I moaned long and low as the tip breached my ring, my arse stretched just as tightly as it had been with Ry's fingers in me. My cunt spasmed again, and I cried out. A cacophony of moans followed as my guys pushed in deeper, their cocks splitting my arse open. The pain was overwhelming, sharp like a knife wound.

My cunt tightened, and the tingling began. But they stayed still. I needed them to move.

Weight shifted on top of us, and my breath gushed out of me as Tristan leaned more heavily on me. Three cocks— two in my arse and one in my cunt—were more than I'd ever taken before, and yet I still needed more. But blessed relief hit me as someone snapped their hips forward, lurching into me and shoving that second cock in my arse as deep as it would go. I shattered again, my scream barely a whisper as my body exploded around me, my nerve endings firing and my vision going dark.

Gentle hands petted me, fingers brushing through my hair and another set each on my waist and down my legs. I was empty, my body achy as I blinked open my eyes. I was floating in a cocoon of warmth and softness. "There you are," Tristan cooed. "Drink of water?"

I opened my mouth, unable to speak, and let Tristan bring the straw to my lips. I sucked down the water and snuggled against Flynn's thigh, his warm hands massaging my scalp.

"Do you need anything, Zee?" he whispered from above. When I shook my head, he added, "Our guys are still strung out."

I flicked my gaze to the table. Ezra was kneeling on all fours, his cock red and angry between his legs. His arse was up in the air, and Ry had his fingers lodged deep inside him. Tristan was behind Ry, arms wrapped around his hips as he leisurely jacked Ry off. Ry's groan was filled with agony as Tristan twisted his wrist over his cockhead and, as slow as molasses, ran his hand back down Ry's length.

"Please," Ezra gasped, a line of pre-cum dripping from his slit and hitting the cushion he was kneeling on. "I need you both."

Ry hissed, "Fuck, I'm gonna come if you don't stop, Tris."

I watched them move into place, and my clit pulsed, my core tightening as my body replayed the ecstasy of having them buried inside me only minutes earlier. Slickness between my legs warmed my belly. I had Flynn's cum inside me. I wanted the others' too, but I didn't think I could move—or even talk—to ask for it.

Tris let Ry go and slapped Ezra's arse, leaving a perfect red handprint on the paler skin below his tan line. Ry closed his eyes and positioned his dick at Ezra's entrance. Ezra mewled, but Tris was moving again, walking back to Ry. "Hey, if you're not ready—"

Ry opened his eyes, and his smile was dazzling. He leaned forward and pressed a kiss to Tristan's lips. "I'm ready. I'm pinching myself that this is actually happening."

"Guys," Ezra barked. "Fuck me, please."

Ry grasped Ezra's hip with one hand and with his other rubbed his cock against Ezra's hole, teasing him. The move elicited a pained groan from our guy as Ezra dropped his head and canted his hips in a blatant invitation. Ry eased himself in, moving slowly without pause, not giving Ezra the chance to adjust to his intrusion until he was stuffed full. Fuck. They were beautiful together. Dark and rough-edged against our golden pretty boy. Ry's hips were pressed against Ezra's, both their faces etched with restraint.

Tristan hooked his finger under Ezra's chin and lifted his face up before running his thumb along Ezra's bottom lip. He waited for Ezra to open, and Tristan replaced his thumb with his cock, rubbing it on Ezra's lips just like Ry had done to his arse.

Flynn hummed, and I felt every bit of yearning in his voice to the soles of my feet. Being between them was a dream come true for both Flynn and me, but given how rocky Ry's relationship with Ezra had been of late, I was so glad that they were taking this step together, cementing their connection and taking it to another level.

Like a finely tuned machine, Ry withdrew as Tristan pushed forward, not stopping until he was buried in Ezra's throat. They kept going, not hard or fast, but steady and un-relenting until Ezra was shaking and his dick leaked a steady stream of pre-cum. The noises were illicit—deep grunts and groans and whispered praise that lit Ezra up. I could see him flying, reaching that pinnacle of ecstasy until he was so blissed out, he was having an out-of-body experience.

I knew the feeling well. These men had a knack for taking me there.

Repeatedly.

Ezra's moan was long but muffled as he came undone completely untouched. Ry followed him over the edge, choking out a cry as he snapped his hips forward one last time and shuddered through his orgasm. Every muscle in Ezra's body locked up as his chest heaved and Ry pumped him full. Pulse after pulse erupted from Ezra, painting the cushion under him with each flex of his cock.

"That's it, Ez. Show us how much you love being pumped full of Ry's cum," Tristan ground out through clenched teeth.

"Fill him up, Tris," Ry ordered breathlessly in that deep gravelly voice that commanded attention.

As if he'd been waiting for Ry's instructions, Tris shouted out a curse, and with his hands on Ezra's cheeks, shuddered through his orgasm.

TWELVE

Zali

My gut twisted as we drove past Benedict's compound in our Tesla rental, slowing down so we could scope it out. I was in the middle, pressed between Tristan and Flynn, and I normally loved it there, but right now I had a hand pressed low on my belly, trying to stop the cramp.

I couldn't see much except that the white iron gates were closed. The privacy granted by the gardens surrounding the fence would hide anyone trying to scale it, but it was high enough that it wouldn't be an easy task.

"Can we get the gate open?" I asked, not particularly wanting to have to Spiderman it in.

"Ry or I will be able to get over it. It's likely got cameras connected to it, though, so we won't have the element of surprise if we do," Ezra answered, his voice contemplative.

The house was hidden behind a lush tropical garden that was junglelike in its density. A smooth concrete drive wound through the property, disappearing around a bend in the dappled sunlight cast by the towering trees. That element of surprise would come in handy if Benedict took off and we had to go searching for him in the jungle. There were too many places he could disappear into and not enough of us to find him easily.

It wasn't only the land that we had to be concerned about either. The compound took prime position on a picturesque beach. The water was too shallow for a boat of any size to be kept there, but there were plenty of marinas nearby where larger yachts were moored, making for an easy ocean escape should Benedict need it.

We were staying close—two doors up from Benedict's house to be exact. Our holiday rental was owned by Benedict's next-door neighbour, but she rented it for short-term accommodation for the rich and famous. The pictures I'd seen so far didn't do the landscape or the houses justice. I couldn't wait to see whether ours was the same.

This stretch of coastline wasn't famous for its tourists if the surprised looks on the locals' faces at the markets were anything to go by. The quiet fishing village was quaint, and the socio-economic differences between the residents and the billionaires who'd slowly been encroaching on the local beaches obvious. There were more privatized beaches now than public ones from what we could see, longer stretches of sand and hectares of land in lush forest gardens locked behind high fences, like the one Benedict owned.

Ez kept driving, picking up a little bit of speed as he passed Benedict's neighbour's house and the one we were staying in before he slowed again, pulling into the slate stone driveway of our temporary home. Like the other houses, lush gardens were planted along the road, creating a privacy barrier and almost entirely blocking out the minimal amount of noise that would be heard along the quiet street.

But once we passed the barrier gardens, the grounds opened up to a breathtaking scene. Palm trees dotted the wide lawns, and sand drifts danced along the drive. Birds chirped and waves lapped gently at the turquoise waters along the shoreline only a stone's throw away.

The house was a picture of elegance and style. White walls and a high-pitched thatched roof were a beautiful contrast to the rich blue sky, the ocean, and the greenery surrounding it.

I understood now why Benedict was drawn here, unable to leave his homeland forever.

It was heaven.

I couldn't help but take in the wonder of it.

Ezra pulled to a stop, and we piled out, Ry moving slower than the rest of us. An older woman stood at the foot of the stairs, waiting to greet us with a warm smile. Smiling at her, I gazed up at the wide verandas stretching out invitingly, picturing myself lying down under them, reading a book and relaxing. We weren't here for that, though, which only intensified the yearning for it.

White, gauzy curtains billowing in the breeze from the open doors and windows drew my attention next. I itched to see the view from the opposite side of the house, the peek I'd had during the drive coming in a tease to whet my appetite.

"Welcome," the woman greeted, her American accent pronounced. "I'm Martha Holt, your host."

"Pleased to meet you, Martha," I responded with a smile. "I'm Zali, and this is Ryder," I explained, slipping my arm around his waist. With my free hand, I gestured to Tristan and added, "This is Tristan, and Flynn and Ezra are getting our bags. You have quite the place here. It's stunning."

"I hope you enjoy your stay tremendously."

"Thank you." We'd booked the home for a week, but we had the option to extend it for another two if needed. The idea of extending our stay hadn't been appealing before, but I could easily be swayed after seeing it now. Who knew what the next few days would bring, though.

"The keys are on the kitchen counter. Treat the home as your own. If you change your mind on the chef or any other staff, just call preset one on the telephone, and my staff will arrange for whatever you need. I'm right next door—" She gestured in the same direction as Benedict's compound. "—so it's no trouble. My chef took the liberty of preparing a meal for you for lunch, and the refrigerator is fully stocked."

"Thank you, Ms Holt," Tristan added, the wonder in his voice obvious as he looked around.

"It's always a pleasure having special guests," she demurred graciously. "Now if you'll excuse me, I'll let you enjoy your stay. Reach out if you need us. One of my staff will drop off some fresh bread for you tomorrow morning."

We shook hands, and I watched her retreat as she made her way over to the golf buggy. Her driver held out his hand, helping her onto the seat, but his gaze never left mine, his stare boring into me. After a lingering moment, he walked around the buggy and took off along the grass toward the beach.

"We're going to take today off and relax," Tristan ordered. "Ry, you must be exhausted from that flight."

The first leg of our flight had seen us travel from the Gold Coast to Darwin, then Darwin to Langkawi in one day. Today's leg had been another double-header, with our first stop in Sri Lanka to refuel, then another flight from Sri Lanka to Mauritius.

As a passenger, it had been luxurious, but as pilot, Ry had to be constantly on the ball, concentrating the whole flight. So it didn't surprise me that Ry was exhausted. When he'd handed Ezra the car keys, I'd been shocked. But his silence on the drive from the airport here had spoken loudest. He was drowsy and dragging his feet. Even his leaving the bags to the others was unlike him.

"Want a shower or bed?" I asked Ry.

"Let's check out the house first." Arm in arm, we went inside, and my jaw dropped. Ezra and Flynn had picked this house purely for its proximity to Benedict, but I was incredibly glad they had.

Towering cathedral ceilings soared above us, and wainscoting along the walls gave the home a luxurious feel. Timber floors of the most beautiful warm red brown drew us inside the open-plan living area. White leather couches were gathered around a fireplace on a thick rug that sat opposite a grand white kitchen with Shaker cabinets, farmhouse-style sink, and pendant lighting above the island bench covered in white marble swirled with a blue grey. Outside the French doors was a covered patio complete with plush furniture and an outdoor kitchen.

But all of that paled in comparison to the view.

The rolling waves of the ocean sparkled like diamonds, and the sand was almost white. Coconut palms swayed in the breeze, almost at the high tide line. A firepit sat on the deserted beach with loungers surrounding it. A volleyball net was set up further along, just waiting for playtime.

I wanted to slide on out those doors and enjoy the beach. I wanted the sun to warm me and to see smiles on my guys' faces. And I would, no matter what happened with Benedict in the coming days.

* * * * *

I rubbed my eyes and wandered naked into the kitchen. I'd slept late—later than I wanted—but Ry was still asleep, so I wasn't the only one who was wiped out.

I set the kettle to boil on the stovetop and took in my surroundings, still amazed that we were here. We'd only used three rooms inside the house—the bedroom, bathroom, and kitchen—since we'd flown in the day before. The outdoor patio was by far my favourite spot.

Tristan and Ezra were out there now, lying on the sun loungers, their interlaced hands spanning the gap.

Flynn dodged around me, carrying a carton of eggs, bacon, an onion, and a block of cheese. My stomach rumbled right on cue, and he grinned, gesturing with his chin to the cupboard nearby. "Green tea is in there with the mugs."

"Thank you." I yawned and rubbed my eyes again, exhaustion sitting heavy on me. "I feel like a zombie," I muttered.

"Go for a swim. It's beautiful out there, and there's no one around. I've already got a towel for you on Tristan's chair."

"You know I love you, right?" I slipped my arms around his waist and kissed his cheek, nuzzling into his throat as I held him. Flynn—all my guys, in fact—always managed to anticipate exactly what I needed and most days delivered it without me even having to ask.

There was a knock at the door, and I waved Flynn off, slipping on the robe I'd worn the night before as I padded over to the front door. The smell of fresh baked bread permeated the air as I swung the door open, and I inhaled deeply, my eyes slipping closed and the smile spreading across my face. "Oh my God, that smells divine. Thank you."

There was a beat of silence, and my smile slipped, wariness crawling over my skin at his stare. But he snapped out of it quickly when he saw my discomfort. The man cleared his throat and pasted on a charming smile, but it didn't reach his eyes.

Truthfully, he looked like he'd seen a ghost. His eyes were wide and his smile strained. But with steady hands, he handed over the basket of food he was carrying and spoke in a melodic accent that sounded like French with a twist.

"Bonjour, madam. It is my pleasure. I have freshly baked bread, milk, and fruit picked this morning."

I lifted the lid on the basket, and my stomach rumbled again. Laughing, I added, "I am going to go and eat all of this right now."

He nodded and stepped back with a smile, and I began to close the door, stopping only when he opened his mouth to speak again. "Madam, what is your name?"

It was my turn to hesitate, neon warning lights flashing in my brain. My stomach knotted, and I stuttered out, "Queen."

A warm hand on my waist startled me, and I would have dropped the basket if not for Tristan reaching for it.

"You're very beautiful." He flicked his gaze to Tristan and smiled politely.

"Can you go and take this into the kitchen, kitten?" Tristan asked, handing me the basket once more. I nodded, shooting him a small smile. I hated that I'd been uncertain for even a moment, my normal bravado escaping me. But every woman experienced that fear—the momentary uncertainty at how dangerous a man was—at least once in her lifetime. I was no exception.

Tristan had asked me to take the basket into the kitchen, but I didn't want to abandon him either. If he needed me, I'd be there. I watched Tris through the glass as he stepped toward the man, the murmur of conversation too low to make out the words spoken between them.

Barely a moment later, Tristan returned inside, closing and locking the door before he came to me.

"What was that about?" I asked, curiosity getting the better of me.

"Nothing." He shook his head, waving off my concern. "I was asking where the closest petrol station was so I could get some gum."

I blinked, not knowing whether to believe him. Had he just lied to me? I opened my mouth, then snapped it closed again, unsure of what to do.

"It's all good, kitten." He held out his hand for the basket, and I passed it to him, then he continued smoothly, asking, "Why don't you go and wake Ry, and I'll make your tea for you while Flynn whips up breakfast?"

I nodded, trying to shake off the imbalance from my conversation with Tristan and the wariness our visitor had caused. Climbing into bed with Ry to wake him up sounded like the perfect distraction.

"Go," he encouraged with a warm smile that crinkled his eyes and made me want to lick him. "Call out if you need any help waking him up," he added, his grin turning wicked.

"Why don't you pop that milk into the fridge and get Flynn to hold off starting the eggs," I suggested, slipping off the robe and adding a swish to my hips as I walked away from him. "Ry's always a handful."

Ry was on his back, the white sheet low on his hips, a distinct tenting happening at his groin. His dark hair was tussled, his stubble thicker after not having shaved for a week or two. I loved him like this, at peace and completely relaxed. I tugged the sheet down gently, exposing him, and crawled up the bed between his legs. I rubbed my face against his thigh, nuzzling his sac as I breathed him in. His scent, that natural musk, had my mouth watering. I did it again, inhaling deeply and keeping whatever part of him I could inside me.

I licked the seam that ran up the centre of his sac to the base of his cock, and Ry's breath caught. He moaned.

Looking up, I met his hooded gaze, his eyes barely open slits. The heat in them singed me in the best possible way, making my cunt tighten and my nipples peak. He reached down, tangling his fingers in my hair, and widened his legs. I licked his crown, closing my lips around his bulbous head, and sucked before popping off him to lick him like a lollipop.

"Don't stop," he rasped, the combination of sleep and desire making his voice gravelly. I returned to his cockhead, sucking it back down and taking him to the back of my throat. I wrapped my index finger and thumb around the base of his cock, jacking him as I sucked him deeper. He squirmed, gripping the sheets with his free hand.

His muscles strained as footsteps sounded behind us.

"Now that is a beautiful sight," Tristan hummed.

"On the bed, Tris. I need to taste you," Flynn ordered in his no-nonsense tone. Their eyes lingered, their stares warming me from the inside, ramping my desire up. Fuck, I loved being watched. I loved knowing how much they wanted me, how they wanted to take me apart, owning every part of me and giving me themselves in turn.

A shiver passed through me, want and need coiling in my belly as my cunt tightened. I rubbed my legs together, needing to ease the ache. Ezra's hands on my arse held me in place, stopping my movement, his touch both gentle and firm at the same time. I huffed in frustration, my mouth still filled with Ry's length. I wanted him, needed him to touch me.

Thank fuck Ezra wasn't in the mood for teasing. He pressed a kiss to the back of my thigh, laving his tongue over my leg toward my core. I inhaled sharply when he spread me open and his mouth met my cunt lips, licking and kissing me. I moaned, the vibration setting off a chain reaction of deep grunts and groans.

I looked up at Ry, and my heart melted at the sight before me. He and Tristan were kissing slowly, their tongues tangling as Ry searched for Tristan's hand, interlacing their fingers when he found it.

Flynn reached over and brushed a piece of my hair off my face and pushing it behind my ear. "Want to be able to watch you too," he murmured before taking Tristan deep into his mouth.

The tightening started slowly, that throb low in my belly building with every swipe of Ezra's tongue and teeth. I closed my eyes, my lids fluttering as he delved deeper, fucking me with his tongue. My breath caught and my thighs quaked as I soared higher. Ezra read my body like an open book, stepping up his movements. He gave sharper bites, twists of his fingers, and faster flicks of his tongue on my clit as I cried out.

I sucked Ry deeper, rolling his balls and brushing my fingers over his taint. He stiffened for a moment, and I instantly moved my hand, taking the hint. But he lifted his knees, opening himself to me and issuing an invitation I couldn't refuse. He was letting me play with a part of himself he'd been so nervous about sharing only a couple of days earlier.

I wouldn't push him too far out of his comfort zone, but I wouldn't deny his gift either. Gathering my spit from the base of his cock, I swirled my thumb over the tense muscle, rubbing until he'd relaxed a fraction. I didn't dare breach his hole—my nails were too long, and I wouldn't risk hurting him, especially not the first time—but his dick thickened, and a rush of pre-cum landed on my tongue. Pride welled in me at the knowledge that I was giving him something.

I cried out when Ezra added a finger, and then I shot straight to the edge when Tristan choked out a grunt and his body locked up tight. He twitched, his hips thrusting forward. His cock choked Flynn as he came. I was on the edge too, the ripple in my inner walls starting as the focus of my entire being centred on my clit. Ezra hummed, and it was my undoing, sensation shooting through me at the vibration, my orgasm sideswiping me and sending me flying.

Ry gasped, and his fingers tightened in my hair as he flattened his feet and fucked my face. It ramped me up higher. The way he used my mouth to get off sent another bolt of electricity through my body.

I shouted out in frustration as Ezra pulled away from my cunt, a draft of cold air replacing his mouth. He slapped my cunt, and tingles raced through me. I moaned, and he grasped my hips hard, driving his cock deep in one thrust.

I shattered apart, the rhythmic clenching of my cunt gripping him tight as I came. Ry filled my mouth, his salty essence my prize. My eyes rolled back into my head, and I swallowed. Ezra snapped his hips forward in fast movements, and he shouted out. His cock thickened, going impossibly harder inside me before the pulses of his cum painted my inner walls. It renewed my orgasm, the heat like a live wire directly inside me.

My arms shook, no longer able to hold my weight up. My body was jelly. Collapsing forward, I rested my head on Ry's belly, still nursing his softening cock in my mouth. I ran my thumb down his abs, following the V to his pubes as I breathed him in, trying to steady the tremble inside me, yet wanting the moment to last forever.

Ezra was breathing hard when he pulled out, and I mewled my protest, the emptiness inside me a void that needed to be filled. He petted my back along my spine, raising gooseflesh all over my sweat-soaked skin, and murmured, "Come over here, beautiful boy. Zali needs you to finish inside her."

They shifted around, Ezra letting go of my hips only for Flynn to manoeuvre me into position. He rubbed his cockhead against my still-throbbing cunt but didn't give me a chance to beg him. He ploughed forward with a deep thrust, his piercings lighting me up. Sensation overload. Moving with slow, hard pumps of his hips, he hit my G-spot with every pass, driving me toward a climax that would rearrange my atoms.

My cunt spasmed, and I cried out again, my body climbing hard and fast. He pinched my clit with his deft fingers, and I shattered once more, my body splintering into a million pieces and taking Flynn with me. He moaned long and low as his cock twitched inside me, unloading his cum in deep pulses.

I groaned when he pulled out, a shiver travelling over me, heat sparking again as my nerves flickered with the remnants of desire.

THIRTEEN

Tristan

I fingered the piece of cardstock with a handwritten number that Ms Holt's staff member had handed to me. He was a different person to the man with her the day before, but he'd had the same flicker of recognition in his eyes that I'd seen in Ms Holt's driver.

Zali had been shaken up, his comment that she was beautiful throwing her for a loop. He'd surprised her, but he'd also creeped her out. As soon as I'd seen her by the door, every protective instinct roared to life. Something told me to get her away from him. I hadn't thought he was dangerous, but this was already hard for her. I didn't want to make it worse with some guy trying to come on to her.

I was glad I did. He hadn't been there to try to hook up.

It was something a whole lot more unsettling.

I closed my eyes and bounced my knee, the pent-up energy inside me needing an escape valve.

"Who are you?" I asked. "It's hardly appropriate to go around telling your guests that they're beautiful. Your boss wouldn't appreciate it."

"I apologize, but she is very familiar. We know who Zali is. But please, rest assured, she should feel very safe here." He reached into his pocket and took out the white card, then handed it to me with the number facing up. *"Call this number, please, professor."*

Without another word he turned on his heel and walked away. My mind raced as I tried to process exactly what he'd told me.

I'd been debating what to do with the information I'd been holding all day long. Dusk had settled over the island, and we'd lit the firepit down on the beach. The others were gathered around it, waiting for darkness to descend fully before we made our move.

But the questions I had were still unanswered. Should I call the number? Should I tell Zali? Should we all be there to call together? I swallowed hard, confusion and indecisiveness swirling around in my gut. I needed to decide on the course, but I was stuck.

Looking up, I spotted Ezra walking over to me. I'd been sitting alone on the patio for a while, and he was either coming to get me to join them or to tell me that our plan had just kicked into action.

I slipped the card into my shirt pocket and smiled at him, patting the seat next to me.

"It's just about time to go," he said as he sat down and rested his elbows on his knees, clasping his fingers together and looking at me with a worried frown.

The questions that had been circling through my mind were pushed into the background. I had other priorities that I needed to focus on.

We were about to head over to Benedict's house.

This was quite possibly it—the moment our lives changed. I needed to protect them. If I had any hope of doing it, I needed a weapon. The knowledge that at least one of us wouldn't be the same person we were right now after it was over sat heavy in my gut. But if it meant protecting Zali and Ryder, I would do it. Steeling myself, I sucked in a breath and held it, counting my heartbeats as I willed myself to find the strength to pull the trigger when the time came.

"Before we go, can I talk to you for a sec?" Ezra asked, and I nodded, grateful that I had a moment longer to gather myself.

There was no risk of the others overhearing from their spot down the beach, but he leaned in close, pitching his voice low anyway. "I need your help tonight. Benedict might not even be home, so it may all be for nothing, but if he's there...." He paused, his shoulders slumped like he was carrying the weight of the world on them.

I reached for him, pulling him closer, and pressed a kiss to his temple. "We'll do this together," I promised.

"I couldn't get a warrant. Mauritius is a non-extradition country too. If I can get him onto the plane alive, I can arrest him the moment we're in Australian airspace. I'll have forty-eight hours to interrogate him and get a confession." His frown was pronounced, the tension around his eyes pulling them tight. But I knew Ezra, and I knew that he wouldn't leave things to chance, especially not something like a confession.

"How will you get it?"

He huffed out a humourless laugh. "I can't torture it out of him, if that's what you're asking." I nearly shook my head, but he'd already continued on, knowing that's not what I was asking. "I've put together every piece of evidence that we've compiled. I have a folder stashed in the plane with it all in there. I can only guess what his motivation was—money, jealousy over Rosa's success—who knows? But I'll find out. He's fucked, and he'll know just how badly by the time I've finished with him. I'll tell him that I can get a plea deal if he cooperates. I'll promise immunity on a few charges if I have to."

"Zali and Ry will fight you—"

"Zali and Ry want to kill him, Tris. I need your help to make sure that doesn't happen."

"What do you want me to do?" I asked. My stomach clenched, yet hope soared in me. Was this the solution? Was this the means to protect them that I'd been looking for? If I had to kill the bastard, I wouldn't hesitate, but there was no way I'd let them do it.

"I need you to be a witness. Take everything in, write a contemporaneous statement. Help make whatever confession we can get out of him irrefutable. I want to put him away for life. I'll make sure justice is served. Proper justice, not vigilante justice. I can't watch them destroy themselves, Tris."

"I want to kill him myself," I confessed. My gut churned, nausea climbing up my throat. "If it means saving them, I'll do it."

Ezra spun and grabbed my hands, squeezing them tight. His eyes flashed with fear, and his face drained of colour as he shook his head and breathed, "No."

I lifted my lips in the ghost of a smile and squeezed his hands back. "From the moment I found out somebody had stolen Rosa's identity, I knew Zali would want to end them." I shook my head and took a steadying breath.

"Finding out what happened to Ry's dad—seeing his loss so raw—has made me want to wrap them in cotton wool."

Ez leaned in closer, pressing his forehead to mine, and I knew he felt the same. It was why he'd come to me with his plan. He cared as much as I did.

"I've been trying to figure out how I can get in there and do it first, finish him off before they even get a chance to raise the proverbial gun." I huffed out a laugh and shook my head. "But your insistence that we not bring weapons put that idea to bed. How am I supposed to steal yours if you don't have it?"

"I have my revolver. But you aren't touching it." His voice took on a hard edge, a no-nonsense tone that I knew there was no negotiating with.

I sighed, closing my eyes and letting my head hang low. "I can't let them take a life any more than you can, but my reasons aren't so noble—"

"I don't give a fuck about the law on this, Tristan," he hissed, standing up to pace. That edge in his voice was gone.

Now it was doused in panic, a frantic need for me to hear him.

"I don't care what the Criminal Code says or even what morality says about it." He gripped his hair and pulled it the way he always did when he got frustrated, and I reached out for him, clasping his hand and pulling him between my legs. He turned to me, agony in his eyes, the crease in his forehead deeper than usual. With his thumb pointed at his chest, he shook his head and said, "My reasons aren't noble, Tris. They're selfish."

He gestured to the three of them walking up the beach toward us. "I won't let Zali and Ryder live with the knowledge that they've taken a life. I won't watch them destroy themselves with the guilt. I can't. I've seen it before, and it changes a person. I won't let you do it either."

"I'm with you," I said. I wouldn't tell Ezra, but I'd overheard his conversation with Puglisi. I'd listened to every word of his impassioned plea and heard her cold response back to him. Nearly all the evidence we had was inadmissible, but Benedict didn't need to know that. If we could get a confession, we could nail the bastard.

Then once he was in jail, we'd let natural selection take its course. I'd seen what inmates did to people serving time for crimes against kids. Hardened criminals might have a moral code that differed distinctly from that of the rest of society, but they shared its abhorrence for child killers.

Benedict's confession would be his death warrant.

Karma might have been a bitch, but she was a patient one.

He'd get what he deserved.

I was determined to protect Zali and Flynn, and Ezra had the answer—make him talk. I believed in Ezra, in his experience and expertise. I had faith that he could pull this off. I knew in my gut that once we got Benedict on Australian soil, Ezra would take care of it.

"If we can get him, we can prove that Rosa was innocent. We can prove Benedict murdered them."

I nodded, my mind made up. "We finish this properly. We find out why and how he did it, and then we nail the fuck to the wall with his own confession."

The fight rushed out of Ezra, and he sagged against me in relief, dropping to his knees in front of me. His breath came out in shuddering pants. I held him close, my arms tight around his shoulders as he buried his face in my neck. "Thank you," he whispered, his voice choked up. "Fuck, it'd kill me if you had to live with having ended him."

"I know, Ez," I murmured. "I love you too."

I reached into my pocket, but Ry's words cut through me. "Let's get ready."

My gaze cut to Ezra's, and I nodded. He and I were going to finish this the proper way, the one in which Zali and Ryder wouldn't have to live with the consequences of their actions today.

FOURTEEN

Zali

I didn't know why, but Ezra insisted on driving to Benedict's house. Tristan and Flynn were coming in via the beach, and we were going straight through the front door. I watched as Ry scaled the fence and Ezra pulled onto the curb, waiting for him to do his magic.

A moment later, the gate began its slow roll open. Ezra pulled in, headlights off, and paused long enough for Ry to climb back in. The grounds were quiet, no movement in sight. The only lights on were those in the gardens, spotlights pointing up at the trees illuminating the branches with a soft glow.

We were all wearing the same mics and earpieces we'd had on in Monaco, and I heard Tristan's murmured, "We're in the grounds. Heading toward the house now."

"Copy," Ezra responded. "We're through the gate and coming up on the front door."

Apparently, most locks were easy to break—true of both digital and physical ones I supposed. But these houses made me pause. Surely they'd have more security than what we'd seen. Ry had spotted a couple of cameras at the entrances, but that was it so far.

Ezra parked the Tesla in a darkened corner where the brake lights wouldn't alert anyone home of our arrival. We got out, closing the doors with a quiet snick. He'd disabled the automatic lock of the doors, and the key—a nondescript black card—was in the cup holder. Any one of us could jump in and drive if we needed to make a fast escape.

We crept around to the front door, and I held my breath, waiting to see if sensors activated the lights. But when it stayed dark, my breath left me in a relieved rush.

Ezra pulled two thin tools out of his back pocket and dropped to his knees. Ry shone a light on the door as Ezra jiggled the tools in the lock. Barely thirty seconds later, just like schools of fish parting for shark on the hunt, the lock clicked. Ezra eased the door open a crack.

He hadn't been kidding around—locks really were for keeping the honest thieves out.

Ry fed a camera attached to a screen by a foot of posable wire through the gap in the door. It was used for checking whether a drain was blocked, but it was perfect for what we needed—small and intended for dark spaces. He panned the width of the room, making sure the coast was clear. There was nobody in the entrance, but we couldn't see into the room where light from a floor lamp blinded the night vision camera.

"We're in," I whispered, creeping after Ezra and Ry.

"All the doors around the back are locked. There's someone in the living room, so we couldn't check them.

Come and let us in. We're at the laundry, eastern side of the house," Flynn answered.

Ezra gestured to Ry with a tilt of his chin, and I could see the indecision in his gaze. He wanted to be with us when we stormed the room.

"We go together," Ezra whispered.

Ry nodded and went in search of Tristan and Flynn. But I didn't want to wait. That fucker was right there, so close that I could just feel my hands closing around his throat as I choked the life out of him. I wanted him to bleed. To suffer in pain the same way Mum and Asher had. I wanted to see the fear in his eyes when he realized he was breathing his last breath.

I was moving before I knew it. But I was yanked to a halt before I could even process what I was doing. Ezra had wrapped his hand around my wrist, holding me in place.

Struggling, I tried to yank my hand free, but he gripped me tighter. I gritted my teeth and glared at him, but his only response was to shake his head.

"Together," he whisper-hissed.

An eternity later, Ry reappeared, Tristan and Flynn on his tail. Tristan and Ezra gazed at each other and nodded, a silent conversation passing between them before Tris turned to Flynn and did the same. Some of the tension dropped out of Ezra's shoulders, and alarm bells rang in my head. Something was off. What did they know?

The television in the living room was on, but the volume was muted. Soft classical music played through the overhead speakers instead. The warm light from the lamp created an intimate space, leaving the room in shadows except for the bubble of peacefulness that the fucker who murdered my family was enjoying.

I took in the moment, letting my anger boil in my veins. The need to avenge my mum and brother built until I was shaking, the pressure mounting until I was set to explode. Was my brother scared in his last moments? Did he see the light of the surface get further away as the yacht disappeared into the depths of the Pacific? Or was he already unconscious? I'd never prayed before, but I did then. If I could wish for anything, it was that they died not knowing the horror befalling them.

The soles of our shoes were silent on the marble floors as we crept forward and scanned the area. We'd gone in as prepared as we could on short notice—but it wasn't anywhere near enough. But neither Ry nor I were willing to scout the property for days, waiting to find out who lived there. We couldn't risk Benedict becoming aware of our presence, and we didn't want Martha to send us packing for creeping out the neighbours either. So we were moving fast. Getting in and out as quickly as we could. This was supposed to be reconnaissance to try to find out if anyone was home, and if they were, who was there.

The first question had been answered in the affirmative.

Now I just needed the answer to the second.

Ezra had insisted on no weapons. It was fucking ridiculous if you asked me—if he'd bought his gun, we could have walked straight in there and executed the fucker without a moment's hesitation.

Ezra wouldn't be swayed.

Knowing my boy scout, he wanted to take Benedict into custody and bring him home. Hell, he'd probably gone and gotten a warrant for his arrest.

But Ry didn't take orders from Ez, and for that I was grateful. I'd seen the throwing knives ensconced in his wrist sheath as he pulled the sleeve of his black Henley down over them. Knowing they were there was small comfort— at least we weren't completely defenceless.

But maybe it was a good thing too. Watching the fuck bleed out from his cut throat would be a whole lot more satisfying than a bullet to the brain ending things quickly.

I wanted to send him off knowing exactly whose eyes he was looking into.

He would beg for death, and I would gladly oblige.

After I'd extracted my pound of flesh.

Testing the weight of a marble statue on a side table, I took it with me. Destroying his shit would be a bonus.

The sound of a glass being picked up drew my attention, my muscles coiling to attack. The others had heard it too, all moving soundlessly in that direction.

Adrenaline rushed through me, the desire to fuck him up overwhelming.

We were in position, spread out on either side of the high-backed armchair he was sitting on, Ezra and I on one side and Ry flanked by Tristan and Flynn coming in on the other.

Ezra drew a gun from the back of his pants, and my eyes boggled. Cheeky fucker had lied to me.

I saw a head rising above the couch.

A woman, not a man.

Oh, Jesus Christ, we'd caught his wife or daughter. Where the fuck was he?

My heart hammered in my chest. If he came in from behind us, he could hurt my guys. I twisted my foot, preparing to pivot and guard our rear.

She turned.

Time stopped.

My vision swam.

My knees went weak.

Ezra squeezed my hand until my knuckles cracked and I sucked in a breath.

Everything snapped back into sharp relief.

I looked at her.

Blinked.

Looked again.

This couldn't be real. It couldn't be happening.

"Mum?" I breathed, my chest constricting. I tried to breathe again but couldn't.

The statue fell from my grip, the quiet of the night shattered by the dull *thunk* the marble made.

Confusion reigned supreme.

I didn't understand.

I couldn't understand.

This couldn't be happening.

"Martini?" she asked, completely unfazed.

"You fucking bitch," Ry roared, lunging for her. I watched the scene unfolding in slow motion as if I was outside my own body. Tristan and Flynn launched forward and grabbed Ry around the waist, holding him back.

He struggled, elbowing Flynn and throwing his head back against Tristan's.

But they didn't let go.

Tristan dodged a moment too late. Ry's head glanced off his cheek, and a bloom of red bruising appeared immediately.

"What the fuck?" I asked, utterly bewildered.

Mum moved, but Ezra clicked off the safety on his gun. "Freeze."

"Oh please," she laughed, a cold sound that chilled my bones. It was so unlike the woman who'd raised me. I was still struggling to comprehend what I was seeing. She was so familiar, yet incredibly different too. I'd gotten used to seeing her face in the mirror—the only obvious differences between us were her brown eyes and light brown hair to my blue and blonde.

"When Kavi said he'd seen a woman who looked like me, I didn't believe him at first. But when I overheard the gossip that the Holt staff agreed, I realized I'd underestimated you. I'm impressed."

I tilted my head, my brows furrowing in disbelief. "Is that all you have to say? You underestimated me? You're impressed?" I asked, my confusion turning to betrayal. "What the fuck, Mum? You died? Asher died?" A sudden bloom of hope exploded in me. If she was alive, maybe he was too. "Where is Asher?" I asked, looking around the room, waiting for him.

Was he here with her?

Was he safe and sound too?

"Clearly, I survived. So did Asher, but not for as long as I did."

My heart shattered, hitting the ground like a skydiver whose parachute had failed to open.

Grief swamped me. We'd grieved him. We'd cried endless tears. But he'd lived, at least for a little while. What had his life been like? Had he missed us like we'd missed him?

She smirked then, as if she was proud of herself for outliving her only son, and it hit me. She'd seen him alive and well after that day, yet we'd thought he'd died. Why had she gotten to have him but we didn't?

Anger surged through me. Dad and I deserved his time too. We should have been here with them.

But no, that wasn't right either. If Benedict wasn't here and she was, that meant….

Fuck me, that meant she was the one who'd embezzled the money. Her identity hadn't been stolen. They were her accounts—accounts she'd set up in an unhackable bank that prioritized their clients' privacy above all else. The bank had been charged numerous times, paying larger and larger fines for refusing to hand over information ordered by the courts at various national and international levels.

She'd choreographed this whole thing, planning every detail. She'd taken the money and left the country, never to return. She'd faked her death and never looked back at the carnage she'd left behind.

Why did she take Asher when she ran?

Why did she leave us behind?

The unfairness of everything that had happened hit me head-on, the combined force of Dad's and my grief stealing my breath. My hands shook, and that cold smirk she wore grew more self-satisfied.

I saw through her disguise to the evil lurking below the beautiful veneer, and I knew.

I just knew.

Ash's death hadn't been an accident.

Blind fury washed over me. It drove me forward, my hands shaking as the desire to rip her apart limb from limb pumped through my veins.

A shout. Agonized and primal.

Curses and a scuffle next to me.

But I couldn't look away from her. I couldn't take my eyes off the only threat in the room.

This woman—this monster—wasn't my mother. I didn't know who she'd turned into, but she was a stranger.

The Rosa Weatherall I'd known was dead.

This woman wearing her skin like an outfit was a psychopath.

The money she'd stolen was only the tip of the iceberg, the least valuable of it all. She'd taken my brother. She had his last memories. She had his final days.

And now he was dead.

Dad and I had grieved for them while she'd been off living in paradise.

Oh, God. Dad.

The fight drained out of me, and Ezra pulled me into his arms, lending me the strength I didn't know I needed.

"I see you're still following my daughter around like her shadow," she sneered at them.

"Don't you dare talk to them," I hissed, disgust dripping from my voice. "How could you? You betrayed everyone. For what? Money? You bitch."

She raised a brow and gestured around the room with open arms. "You and your father could have been right here with me. I planned on the four of us disappearing, but no, he had to work." She spat the words like they left a vile taste in her mouth.

"Oh, that makes it all okay?" I asked, stunned. "What the fuck is wrong with you?"

She pointed at herself with her thumb and raised her chin in defiance. "I deserved that money. People gave it to *me*. It was mine."

I blinked in disbelief, sure my ears were playing tricks on me. Was she serious?

"Then they wanted it back," she huffed incredulously. "That wasn't going to happen."

"So, you took it. You made it look like you were investing the money and siphoned it into international accounts instead," Tristan accused.

She smiled at him, the kind of expression a snake might make. "Yes, professor." Her smile turned to a glare. "Yes, I know who you are. You're a stubborn fuck too. Normal people back off after receiving one death threat." She set her glass on the table and carelessly flicked her long hair over her shoulder before tapping her chin with long red nails. "Where were we? Oh yes, the accounts. I transferred the money, and then I covered my tracks." She sat on the other couch, stretching out until she was comfortable.

My gut twisted, bile rushing up my throat. I sat like that too, spread out and acting like queen of the fucking world.

"Hiring the liquidator with a connection to my assistant CFO, his credit card, the accident... I orchestrated all of it."

"Then you just hopped on a plane and left?"

She shrugged. Fucking shrugged like it was no big deal. Like she hadn't abandoned her husband and daughter, her parents, in a giant fuck you to them, fucked over countless families, and disappeared, leaving us thinking she and my brother were dead.

"We went to Moreton Island, hopped on a charter flight to Cairns, changed our looks, and used fake passports to get out of the country without the authorities"—she gestured with a sneer to Ezra—"knowing a thing."

"What happened to Asher?" I gritted out.

"It's better now that he's gone," she sighed happily.

Rage exploded in my chest, and I saw red. She didn't deserve him, not one single piece of his existence or memory from his time on this earth. I fought against Ezra's one-armed grip, trying to get closer so I could claw the bitch's eyes out.

"He complained so much," she continued unperturbed, gesturing to Ry, who'd gone as still as stone. "He missed him, and you, and your father."

"You killed him?" Ry whispered, my heart shattering into a million pieces at the anguish in his voice. Ezra tightened his arms around me, catching my weight and holding me up as my legs gave out, all the fury draining from me in a gush.

"How could you?" I asked. Tears sprang to my eyes, my chest tightening and my breathing shallowing out.

"I didn't kill him," she scoffed, like the concept was ridiculous. But I didn't put anything past her. She was fucking insane. She waved her hand, dismissing my concerns, and my gut twisted. "He fell." She rolled her eyes, and I didn't recognize the roar that came from me. "His balance wasn't what it had been before he had to lose his foot—"

"How?" Ry asked, his voice sounding like he'd swallowed broken glass.

I dared a look at him, and I couldn't bite back the sob that wrenched from my very soul. Tears streamed down his cheeks, his face pale under the salty tracks. Both Tristan and Flynn had their arms around his waist, but they were no longer holding him back. They were holding him up, much like Ezra was doing to me.

"How did he lose his foot?" he persisted.

"I had it amputated," she replied as if the answer was obvious.

"Before we left the Coast. I gave him a little something in his drink and he went to sleep. I had a... *friend* on board, and he took care of it for me together with sinking the yacht after we'd gotten off."

She did it.

She cut his foot off for no apparent fucking reason. "Why?" I whispered, my voice catching in my throat. I curled into myself, her words striking me like physical blows. "Why would you do that? What did he ever do to you?"

I blinked in disbelief, sure my ears were playing tricks on me. Was she serious?

"Then they wanted it back," she huffed incredulously. "That wasn't going to happen."

"So, you took it. You made it look like you were investing the money and siphoned it into international accounts instead," Tristan accused.

She smiled at him, the kind of expression a snake might make. "Yes, professor." Her smile turned to a glare. "Yes, I know who you are. You're a stubborn fuck too. Normal people back off after receiving one death threat." She set her glass on the table and carelessly flicked her long hair over her shoulder before tapping her chin with long red nails. "Where were we? Oh yes, the accounts. I transferred the money, and then I covered my tracks." She sat on the other couch, stretching out until she was comfortable.

My gut twisted, bile rushing up my throat. I sat like that too, spread out and acting like queen of the fucking world.

"Hiring the liquidator with a connection to my assistant CFO, his credit card, the accident... I orchestrated all of it."

"Then you just hopped on a plane and left?"

She shrugged. Fucking shrugged like it was no big deal. Like she hadn't abandoned her husband and daughter, her parents, in a giant fuck you to them, fucked over countless families, and disappeared, leaving us thinking she and my brother were dead.

"We went to Moreton Island, hopped on a charter flight to Cairns, changed our looks, and used fake passports to get out of the country without the authorities"—she gestured with a sneer to Ezra—"knowing a thing."

"What happened to Asher?" I gritted out.

"It's better now that he's gone," she sighed happily.

Rage exploded in my chest, and I saw red. She didn't deserve him, not one single piece of his existence or memory from his time on this earth. I fought against Ezra's one-armed grip, trying to get closer so I could claw the bitch's eyes out.

"He complained so much," she continued unperturbed, gesturing to Ry, who'd gone as still as stone. "He missed him, and you, and your father."

"You killed him?" Ry whispered, my heart shattering into a million pieces at the anguish in his voice. Ezra tightened his arms around me, catching my weight and holding me up as my legs gave out, all the fury draining from me in a gush.

"How could you?" I asked. Tears sprang to my eyes, my chest tightening and my breathing shallowing out.

"I didn't kill him," she scoffed, like the concept was ridiculous. But I didn't put anything past her. She was fucking insane. She waved her hand, dismissing my concerns, and my gut twisted. "He fell." She rolled her eyes, and I didn't recognize the roar that came from me. "His balance wasn't what it had been before he had to lose his foot—"

"How?" Ry asked, his voice sounding like he'd swallowed broken glass.

I dared a look at him, and I couldn't bite back the sob that wrenched from my very soul. Tears streamed down his cheeks, his face pale under the salty tracks. Both Tristan and Flynn had their arms around his waist, but they were no longer holding him back. They were holding him up, much like Ezra was doing to me.

"How did he lose his foot?" he persisted.

"I had it amputated," she replied as if the answer was obvious.

"Before we left the Coast. I gave him a little something in his drink and he went to sleep. I had a… friend on board, and he took care of it for me together with sinking the yacht after we'd gotten off."

She did it.

She cut his foot off for no apparent fucking reason. "Why?" I whispered, my voice catching in my throat. I curled into myself, her words striking me like physical blows. "Why would you do that? What did he ever do to you?"

She huffed as if my question was ridiculous. "To throw the scent off us, of course. People readily assume you're dead when you're missing a body part. I didn't want to lose any of mine—" She shrugged like it was no big deal. "—so I chose Asher's foot. He didn't miss it much."

My heart stopped. White noise buzzed in my ears, filling my head with static. Shock rendered me speechless. I opened my mouth, but nothing came out. I had no words. Nothing. I was numb all over.

Ry wailed, and from the corner of my eye, I saw him turn to our guys for comfort, burying his face in Flynn's hair and clutching Tristan tightly.

"People assume you're dead because no one can fathom the kind of evil it takes to chop up a defenceless child," Tristan gritted out through clenched teeth, his tone murderous.

"Who was the *friend* you had on board?" Ezra asked, his voice hard.

She smiled serenely as if she was thinking about a loved one. "He was the same man who delivered the death threats to your professor here." She gestured to Tristan and her lip curled in disgust before she sighed, the sound almost happy. "The Martinelli family really came through with him and the liquidator."

Fuck me. She was... I didn't even have the words to describe her. She hadn't been accidentally caught up in them and suffered the consequences. She'd been the one directing their moves.

"How did Ash fall? Where?" I demanded, anger and agony tightening my chest.

"Oh." She waved me off with a small laugh. "The roof. I have a deck up there. I wanted him to see the view standing on the top of the wall." Her smile fell, her eyes turning cold and that evil glint reappearing. "But he slipped."

FIFTEEN

Ezra

Fuck me, this woman was unhinged. Looks-wise, she was so familiar—the resemblance between Rosa and Zali was remarkable, and I'd heard so many stories about her that I should have felt like I'd known her for years—but she was a stranger.

I didn't see a single iota of the warm, loving woman Zali and Roe described.

She was monologuing like a nineties supervillain, and that suited me fine. She'd all but confessed to everything except Asher's murder. That was the one thing I wanted though. It was the most important charge to make stick. Without even realizing it, Zali was building the case against her mother with every question she asked.

"You're lying," Zali replied. "Asher didn't slip."

"He climbed on the wall with a prosthetic foot, and he lost his balance."

"You said yourself you wanted him to see the view. You put him up there, didn't you? He was scared of heights. You talked him into getting on that ledge where he didn't want to be, and you pushed him," she growled. Taunting her, Zali added, "Say it. Own it. Be proud of your achievements. Don't be a coward now."

Rosa sneered and lifted her chin defiantly. "Fine, you want the truth? I did exactly that. I got him onto the ledge, and then I shoved him off. I watched him fall—and I liked it. I liked being free of him and his whining."

Zali's pained cry was agonizing, but it changed something in Rosa. Like the flip of a switch, the laid-back woman reclining in the chair was no more. She was on her feet, gun in hand and pointed at Zali in an instant. I didn't even have time to blink. Chaos erupted around me. I heard shouts and frantic scrambling.

But my focus zeroed in on my target.

No one—no-fucking-one—pointed a gun at my girl.

I let go of Zali, then pushed her down and behind me, using my body as a shield. Whip fast, I brought my hand up, steadying my grip, and shouted, "Drop the gun."

The safety was off, a round already chambered.

Each beat of my heart was like a gong being struck, loud and reverberating through me. My pulse rushed through my veins. My lungs expanded with my breath, and I held it.

I didn't wait for her to comply.

Time slowed to a crawl.

I fired.

It was only a warning shot. I didn't want to kill her, just slow her down.

Everything moved in slow motion, the kickback from the gun taking an hour.

The bullet ejected the chamber, firing in a straight line to Rosa.

From the corner of my eye, I saw Ry break free of their grip, launching himself out of Tristan's arms.

My aim was off.

I was going to miss.

Tristan pushed Flynn, shoving him back and out of harm's way. He scrambled for Ry, trying to stop him from tackling Rosa.

The bullet impacted, grazing her arm.

Rosa screamed.

Blood poured out of the flesh wound.

She was distracted.

Now was my chance. I squared my aim again.

White marble soared through the air, catching my eye. *Fuck. Rookie mistake.*

It was the foot-high statue Zali had picked up.

A body crashed into me, blond hair flying.

Rosa screeched, "You motherfucker."

She fired.

Another blast of sound ricocheting through my head.

Tristan pivoted on a dime. He vaulted the table. Bent at the waist, he charged Rosa like a linebacker.

The breath whooshed out of my lungs as we hit the ground.

My body cushioned Zali's fall.

A heavy weight landed on us—Ry.

Rosa's gun clattered to the floor.

Zali's throw hit its mark.

A hiss of pain.

A deep groan.

Fuck. Tristan.

"Tristan," I screamed, scrambling out from underneath Zali and Ry.

Without thinking, I moved. Instinct drove me to him.

"Ry," Tristan cried. "Fuck. Flynn." Panic intoned his voice, fear making it high pitched and thready.

I spun, looking for what he'd seen, and a choked-out cry bubbled up my throat.

I dropped to my haunches, then ripped off my Henley and pressed it to the back of Flynn's head. I needed to stem the blood oozing from the gash.

Tristan went for Ry.

Flynn hissed. He reached up, pressing the balled-up shirt against the wound. He tried to sit up.

Waving me off, he said, "I'm okay. Just hit my head."

I eased him upright, and he grasped my bicep, leaning around me. "Fuck," he breathed, his voice a panicked whisper.

Ry was on his back, clutching at himself.

Oh God, no. Fuck. Had he been shot in the throat?

Tristan was shirtless, applying pressure to the wound. I still couldn't tell where he'd been hit.

Ry was struggling underneath him.

"Ry," I gasped, tears springing to my eyes.

Fuck.

A gunshot rang out. "You fucking cunt bitch. That's for Ry."

I stilled, my gaze snapping up to Zali.

She gripped my gun in both hands. It was aimed directly at Rosa.

Rosa touched her chest and lifted her blood-soaked hand to her face.

"You shot me?" she breathed as she stumbled back.

Zali adjusted her aim.

I jumped up, scrambling over to her.

Two shots were enough to disarm her.

I could still get Rosa onto the plane.

I could still get her home and into custody.

I could make her pay for what she did.

But before I could reach Zali, another shot rang out.

"That's for Dad."

A second direct hit to her chest.

A bloom of blood soaked the white satin slipdress Rosa was wearing.

No. No, no, no. No more. "Zali," I cried, begging her to stop. Begging her not to fire again. Her mother couldn't survive it.

Zali would be responsible. She would have to live with the knowledge that she'd killed her.

Rosa fell back, each breath a wet rasp. Blood oozed from her mouth with every exhale.

Zali stepped forward, squaring her aim at her mother's head.

"No," I screamed, scrambling over the couch to get to her. Need drove me to protect Zali. To stop her from making a mistake that would change the direction of her life.

"I watched him die. I watched the light fade from his eyes as he bled out," Rosa gurgled, a deathbed confession.

I froze. Shock held me immobile. She really was evil. Everything else—the theft, the hiding her tracks, even the death threats to a certain extent—could be excused as greed. But that? Murdering her own child?

"This, you fucking monster, is for my brother," Zali spat, her voice laced with venom.

She fired.

The shot landed true. Right between Rosa's eyes.

A circle appeared on her forehead, blood instantly painting her eyes red.

They bulged for a split second, her skull elongated as the bullet sped through her brain and hit the back of her skull.

Rosa's head exploded.

A gruesome mix of blood, bone, and brain matter splattered backward.

The white couch turned red.

Rosa's body slumped.

Dead.

"Good fucking riddance," Zali muttered.

She placed my gun on the table.

Then she turned on the balls of her feet and headed for our guys.

"Hold tight, Ry," Tris said, his voice tinged with desperation. "We'll get you help."

Sixteen

Zali

blinked, taking in the scene in front of me. Blood and gore were everywhere, sprayed like a head-sized paint-ball had exploded. I supposed it had. *Ew.*

Her eyes were glazed over, unseeing forever more. Her mouth was slack, open a fraction. She lay at an awkward angle with the top half of her body on the couch. Her leg was bent unnaturally, and her arms were splayed out by her sides, palms up.

But even in death she wasn't still.

She slid to the floor, a slow wet squelch leaving a trail of smeared blood down her white couch.

Disgust filled me.

"Good fucking riddance," I spat. I wanted to unload the entire clip into her. I wanted to make her as unrecognizable as she'd become to me. I wanted to wipe her face away so that I didn't see her in the mirror every time I looked in it.

Instead, I gathered every ounce of strength I possessed and placed Ezra's gun gently on the table.

Then I turned and walked away.

She was no longer my mother.

She was a stranger, and I wouldn't grieve another moment for her.

"Hold tight, Ry," Tristan begged. "We'll get you help."

"Zee," Flynn cried, standing up and racing over to me.

"I'm okay," I reassured him, turning him away before he could see what remained of her. I abso-fucking-lutely wouldn't let the vision of the person who birthed me lying there on the floor upset one of the sweetest, most beautiful souls in my world.

I couldn't even call her my mother anymore.

She'd ceased being my mum the moment she made the decision to leave without Dad and me. She became a smear I had to wipe off the face of the earth the second she decided to kill my brother.

I'd cried my tears for her.

Now I'd fulfilled my promise for vengeance. I'd served my brand of justice to Asher's killer.

I hadn't expected it to be her sitting in that seat. I was looking for a man who'd been framed. He was completely innocent.

But now I knew the truth.

She deserved her ending.

I didn't expect to be happy about it—I wasn't—but I thought there would be more than the nothingness I was currently experiencing.

No, that wasn't right.

I was relieved.

I was angry too. The sense of betrayal was overwhelming. We'd grieved for her, wasted a decade's worth of our tears on her. Our hearts had shattered, and we'd barely survived ourselves.

Dad and I had missed her every day. Yet she'd been alive.

We'd lost Ash.

She'd stolen him.

She'd hurt him and kept him away from us—her fucked-up reasons didn't even make sense.

Then she'd killed him.

Yeah, the overwhelming emotion was relief.

Relief that she was gone, that there was one less monster on this earth.

Now she had an eternity in hell before her.

She deserved every agonizing second of it.

"I'm fine," Ry groaned. "Get the fuck off me."

"No, hold still. You're bleeding," Tris grumbled.

"We need to get out of here," he snapped back. "Let me get up."

"Ry!" Flynn barked, kneeling beside him.

Ry shoved Tristan off him, dislodging his grip. Flynn lunged forward and held the makeshift bandage in place while Ry slowly sat up and took a few deep breaths. He was pale. Blood was smeared all over his throat and fingers. The sight of it had my heart rate climbing. Fear coursed through me. He needed to be okay.

He needed to survive.

"Listen to me, Tris," Ry implored, calmer but no less determined. "We can't stay here. There are staff quarters on site. There are neighbours. There's no way someone didn't hear those gunshots." He breathed again, his eyes closing as he looked like he was fighting off nausea. "We need to leave the country. Tonight. Our stuff stays at the house. It's gone."

Ry got one knee under himself, and Flynn steadied him, still holding the dark shirt in place. Tristan wavered, knowing the truth of Ry's words. It was why we'd packed the essentials into the Tesla—our passports, money, computers, and our phones. They were the only things we needed to get out of Mauritius.

Tris hooked the arm on Ry's uninjured side over his shoulders and helped him to his feet, making sure he was steady enough to stand.

"Help me get to the car. I'm not dead yet, so the bullet didn't nick an artery. I'll be fine. Flynn and Ezra can patch me up after I take off."

"I need to stay," I rushed out. "I have to scrub the security cameras and check—"

"Absolutely not," Ezra ordered, grasping my hand, ready to haul me out of there. "We can't be extradited back here—"

"But it's possible to get stopped on the way," I argued. "What if they corner us driving to the airport? Or we get to Sri Lanka or Malaysia and get boarded?" I held up my hand, my fingers extended. "I need five minutes, Ez."

Gesturing to Ry, I added, "Get Ry to the airport. I'll wipe the servers and be right behind you. The longer we stand here arguing about it—"

"Fuck no," Tristan declared. "I'm not leaving without you. Ez and Flynn, you take Ry. He needs you more than he needs me. Call ahead. Get them to prep the plane for an immediate take-off. I'll stay with Zali and make sure we get out of here."

Ez shook his head, and Tristan added, "She's right. We finish this properly."

Ezra's shoulders dropped, and he reluctantly swapped spots with Tristan, helping steady Ry's injured arm. My guys needed to help Ry more than he needed the assistance, but neither of us called them out.

Flynn's lips were turned down in a frown, and he shook his head. "So help me, Zee. If you aren't five minutes behind us, I'll unleash hell to get you back by my side. You hear me? Make sure you come home to us. You too, Tris. I'm not giving either of you up."

"What he said," Ry added with a wince.

"I love you. All of you," I whispered, my heart overflowing with love for these men. Even now—especially now— when we were on the run for our lives, they were fighting to protect me. "I'm five minutes behind. I promise."

Tristan went over to the crumpled body, not giving it a second glance, and picked up the gun she'd dropped. "Let's go. Clock's ticking."

With a nod to the others, he dragged me away from them. "Where do we look?"

"Find an office. The security system will be controlled via a laptop."

My steps stuttered to a stop, and Tris hugged me close to him. "We'll be out of here soon."

"I can't believe we've just sent them off. Jesus, what if Ry's not okay?" My heart thumped hard, adrenaline running through me, my breathing too fast.

Tris gripped my arms and waited until I looked up at him. "Ry is okay. Ez and Flynn both have first aid training. They're looking after him. We need to do our job and get the hell out of here."

We really did have to move—there was no way I was spending a lifetime in jail for doing the world a fucking favour.

Nodding, I tilted my chin toward the stairs off the large living area. "Let's go."

"That's my girl."

We dashed up the stairs to the third level, and I stumbled out onto the deck. But I didn't linger. My only regret of the night was that I didn't throw the bitch off the roof myself, but the realization on her face that she was a dead woman was good enough for me.

Going up to the second level, we ran through the house, turning lights on in every room we passed. It was enormous, bedrooms and sitting rooms, a library, a music room, and a main suite that would rival any one of the ones belonging to Kardashians. Room after room of designer furniture and pristinely kept spaces passed in a blur, and my disgust grew.

She'd stolen all that money for what? To live alone on the opposite side of the world to her family? This house was a museum. It had no life in it. There wasn't a single personal memento, not a single photograph. Had she ever had a visitor? Or had she been alone in her castle, bar her staff, for a decade? It would have made for a lonely life, one that was still far too good for her.

"Got it," Tris called out from a couple of doors away from me down the long hall.

Relief swamped me, and I dashed past him into the room. If you'd told me ten years ago that I'd be in this room and not giving a shit that it was my mother's, I wouldn't have believed it. Hell, even a week ago, I wouldn't have believed it. Un-fucking-believable what the truth does to a person.

I sat down, the latest model slimline laptop in front of me, and wiggled my finger on the touchpad. Precious seconds ticked by as the operating system loaded. I laughed, relief crashing into me.

Lady luck was on my side tonight. Karma must not be too pissed off.

Navigating to the security software, I deleted both the feed and the cloud backup without hesitation. I'd worked with these systems before. They were nothing more than a feel-good platitude, virtually useless for anything except recording the goings on at the property. But the recordings often weren't clear enough to view. Salt spray and rain played havoc with the cameras, and even the night vision was sub-par.

I should have finished up with that, but I wanted her photos. I did a quick scroll through, and the album looked complete. She'd obviously been bored enough to have put them all in order, including saving a folder marked "Asher." I didn't hesitate, yanking the charging cable out of the wall and racing out.

I wanted to know everything the bitch had done so I could systematically scrub the memory of her life off this earth.

"Tris," I called. "Where are you?"

"In the garage," he replied. He was on the opposite side of the house, and I got turned around, finding a different set of stairs to take me to the ground floor. I jogged down them, holding on to the railing as the laptop cable dragged behind me, bouncing off the marble tiles as I went.

With each room I passed, my revulsion grew. A library, a theatre room, an indoor plunge pool, a miniature roller-skating rink—she didn't need to go anywhere. She'd brought the world to her doorstep.

I rounded the corner into the kitchen and found the garage off it. "Have you got everything?" I asked. "We're not coming back in."

"Why would we?" he asked, poking his head into where I was rummaging through the cabinets. "What are you looking for?"

"A lighter. I'm going to burn this motherfucking house down. Not one memory will survive. Or any stray fingerprints."

He nodded and took the bottle of whiskey I was holding before striding over to the gas cooktop and turning a burner on. "Get in the car," he ordered.

I hit the button to open the garage door and grabbed the keys to the sleek Jaguar before running straight for the driver's door.

The moment the garage door started to open, I heard sirens.

"Tris," I called. "Let's go."

I thrust the laptop into his arms before he'd even managed to close the door, and I slammed the car into gear, floored the accelerator, and dropped the brake. Tyres squealed on the slick surface, and we launched forward.

"Stop!" Tris screamed.

Right there in front of the car was the man who'd visited us the day before. He was carrying a duffel bag.

He ran to Tristan's side and opened it, thrusting the bag onto Tristan's lap.

"We called the police once we thought you'd left, but I saw lights coming on. You must hurry. Call Ms Holt when it's safe. Take this bag. Do not leave it behind." He pointed to the left. "Go that way. I'll delay the police."

His words didn't make a lot of sense, but I wasn't waiting around to find out what he was talking about. He slammed the door closed, then banged on the roof, and I peeled away.

Before we rounded the corner in the drive, I flicked my gaze to the mirrors and saw flames flickering through the windows and smoke starting to billow out the open garage.

Tristan was trying to pull his seatbelt on when I swerved to the left through the open gate and bounced over the bumpy verge to the left of the drive. I was following on blind faith the loose directions our new friend had given us. I had no idea where I was going or what was ahead of us, but the gate being open was a bloody good start.

I screamed out onto the deserted road, fishtailing all the way past Ms Holt's house.

The car was responsive, the steering light, and it was fast as fuck. She had decent taste—at least she didn't rely on a push bike for transport, or Tristan and I would have been shit out of luck.

My hands were shaking and my heart beating at an erratic pace as I drove like a maniac through the quiet streets. I had no idea where I was going, operating on a wing and a prayer that I was at least headed in the right direction. I couldn't hear sirens anymore, but that didn't mean they weren't close—the Jag muffled every noise. Even the engine's roar was barely a purr.

Finally, Tristan got the navigation system to work, directing us to the airport. I was white-knuckling the steering wheel, constantly flicking between looking at the road and rearview mirror. My breathing was ragged too, and I was on the verge of laughing like a hyena.

"We're fifteen minutes away," he breathed. "Slow down. You've got this, kitten. I'm right here with you."

"Fuck, I'm freaking out." I wasn't proud of the wobble in my voice, but I sucked in a breath as Tris spoke again.

"They won't catch us. We have a headst—"

Two police cars rounded the corner close behind us.

Lights flashed. Sirens blazed.

I slowed down. Pulled to the side so they could overtake.

But they weren't easily fooled.

They slowed too, pulling up beside us.

Fuck, they were readying to box us in.

Screw that. This queen wasn't going down without a fight.

I dropped down a gear and floored it. The Jag surged forward, immediately pulling away from the Toyota four-by-fours the officers were driving.

There was traffic dotted ahead of us.

Tristan held the grab bar.

My concentration narrowed to the road before us.

My mind mapped out a route, instinct guiding my movements.

It was a game of tag, but the stakes were so much higher.

I zipped left, swerving around a car turning right into a parking spot.

Swerved to the right, passing a slow-moving truck.

Over and over like a game of Need for Speed, I dodged the traffic, trying to put as much distance between us and the police cruisers as possible.

A light turned red up ahead.

"Punch it," Tristan gritted out.

I sucked in a breath and hit the accelerator.

Crossed to the wrong side.

Ran the red light.

Swerved back to the left.

Exhaled.

"Fuck," I whispered, my voice shaking.

The police cars followed us through one intersection after another.

"We're nearly there."

I saw the officer deploy the road spikes a moment before we hit them.

I swerved. Hard.

We hit the curb.

Mounted the footpath.

I fought to keep control, the rear end fishtailing and smashing against the stone wall of a building.

Every instinct in me told me to look away, to close my eyes.

I held tight, speeding up.

The mirror clipped a streetlight. It ripped it clean off.

Glass shattered into a spiderweb of cracks.

We were through the intersection in the blink of an eye.

Swerving right, I wrangled the car back onto the road.

Tristan's head whipped to the side, the dull *thunk* against the glass making me wince.

"You okay?" I asked, not taking my eyes off the road as I dodged a man on a moped veering onto the wrong side of the road.

A car flashed its lights.

Honked its horn.

I played chicken, daring them not to move as I passed a truck.

They pulled over.

"Fuck me, Zali. For the love of God, get on the right side of the road," Tristan gasped, a hint of panic in his voice.

"Hold on," I muttered as I threw the car to the left.

It hit a pothole and bounced.

Hard.

My head slammed against the window, a sting above my eye.

I blinked, clearing my vision.

The suspension was fucked, the tyres probably on their way to exploding, but all I needed was a few more kilometres. We'd survived the town centre. If the tyres held out, we might actually make it.

I accelerated again, pushing the car to its limits. The streets passed in a blur, one long line of lights as the navigation struggled to keep up.

"Take the exit on the left," Tristan groaned.

I slowed, taking the turn and punching it again. Up ahead was the entrance to the private terminals. But the airport was closed, the boom gates locked down. It didn't matter. There was no way I could come to a complete stop in time anyway.

So I didn't even try.

I floored it again. The car rocketed over the speed humps and blew straight through the gate.

An alarm wailed, but there was no obvious movement otherwise.

I tore through the second gate, the boom cracking the windscreen as it was shorn straight off.

I couldn't see my Falcon 2000 on the tarmac. Where the fuck was it?

"There," Tristan said, pointing toward the hangars. One bay door was opening.

We were almost there.

Five hundred metres.

Four hundred.

Three hundred.

Two hundred.

Holding my breath, I hit the anchors.

The car slid sideways.

Closer and closer to the door.

Fuck, were we going to stop?

"Shiiiit," I cried, wrestling control of the beast.

The Jag screeched to a halt just in time.

Only a few metres leeway before Ry wouldn't be able to get the plane out of the hangar.

But we didn't pause. We couldn't.

There hadn't been movement a moment earlier, but now security guards were arriving in droves.

The siren still blared in the distance.

A Toyota pulled up, police piling out.

"Fuck, run," I screamed, throwing open the door and sprinting for the plane.

Tristan was right behind me.

Ezra dashed back to the plane, waiting for us to get there too. We shot up the stairs, our shoes squeaking on the smooth concrete below our feet. Ezra tumbled into the cabin. He closed the flight stairs behind us, and Ry accelerated out of the hangar.

"About bloody time," Ry said, his disembodied voice coming through the speakers. "We're doing this blind, so it might get bumpy."

Code for strap the fuck in.

He wasn't joking.

Ryder

The sirens were deafening.

Police and airport security were converging on us.

It was like a car chase scene from a Hollywood movie.

Trust Zali not to do things by halves.

If she'd come with us, we could have had a few minutes more to break into the hangar, steal our plane, and get in the air.

But our girl was stubborn, and even though I wouldn't admit it, she'd probably saved our arses by insisting that the security footage be scrubbed.

"They're here," Ez yelled, and within a moment, the sensor confirmed that the cabin door was locked.

I taxied the plane out through the half-open door to the cavernous building.

"About bloody time," I muttered through the PA system. "We're doing this blind, so it might get bumpy."

The guys didn't have time to patch me up when we'd sped into the airport. By the time we got past the lame attempt at security and into the building, the alarms were already going off. I'd only done the crucial pre-flight checks, so we would at least get into the air.

Then I could stop and take some painkillers—anything to dull the razor-sharp shocks of pain through my shoulder every time I moved.

The bullet had hit my collarbone. It was definitely broken—I could feel where it was separated—but I wasn't sure whether the bullet was still embedded in me or had exited somewhere out the back of my shoulder.

An officer stood in front of me, using a loudspeaker. "EWB269, you are not cleared for take-off. Power down."

I ignored him and pushed forward, heading straight for the runway.

But fuck, we weren't moving fast enough.

We needed to get on the runway. We needed to pick up speed.

If I didn't get moving, we'd be surrounded and utterly fucked.

I gave her some speed, letting the jets deter anyone getting too close from behind. It didn't stop our problem of being cut off, but at least it was a good start.

Heading straight across the deserted tarmac, I aimed for the closest runway, lit only by emergency lights.

There was no tower to check in with, no one there to authorize our take-off.

So I punched it.

The moment I had a straight shot, I pushed up on the thrust lever, urging Zali's baby to take-off speed.

Pain rocketed through my shoulder as I gripped the yoke and guided her into the air.

We climbed and climbed, levelling out at forty-one thousand feet.

I was in agony.

My breathing was shallow.

Sweat poured off me.

I gritted my teeth and fought back the nausea.

"Get the autopilot on, Ry. We need to get you checked out," Flynn murmured from beside me. "I'll stay in here and call you if anything happens."

"Yeah," I groaned. "Yeah, okay."

I scooted back my seat, and Ezra was there to help me up. "Let's get you taken care of," he said gently. With an arm around my waist, he led me over to the armchair and eased me down into it.

I was woozy, unsteady on my feet. It could have been shock or blood loss. Whatever it was, I hated it. I hated not having my wits about me. But if I was going to choose any-one for it to happen with, it'd be these four people. I knew I was safe even though I was the one who had responsibility for everyone in the plane.

Ezra peeled back Tristan's balled up shirt and cut away my own. "Jesus, you're torn up." He cleaned my shoulder, the saline solution freezing against my clammy skin. I shiv-ered and clutched my arm, trying to stop the agony-causing movements.

The liquid shot straight into the Grand Canyon that had been carved through me, and I hissed, then ground out, "Motherfucker."

"Sorry, hon. I'm trying to be gentle."

"Not you," I panted, squeezing my eyes closed. "That fucking bitch for shooting me."

I don't know how long he worked to clean me up, but each agonizing second was like a lifetime.

"Your collarbone is broken. It's going to need to be set. Without knowing a whole lot, I think it needs surgery. It's a mess." He was poking and prodding, strapping gauze or some other sticky stuff over my shoulder, but I couldn't look at him. Blood was never my strong suit, but if I saw it now, I'd puke.

"The bullet exited your shoulder through your trapezius." He eased a sling over my good shoulder before helping me slide my arm into it. "This should help take the weight off your collarbone, but you're going to be sore for a while."

He pressed a kiss to my forehead, and I leaned into his touch. "Five centimetres," he whispered, his voice hitching. "That's it. We would have lost you."

I wrapped my good arm around his waist and tugged him to me. He wasn't a small guy, but he managed to gingerly straddle my hips. He threaded his fingers through my hair and eased my face against his shoulder.

"I'm not going anywhere," I mumbled against his chest, needing him to just hold me for a moment. My world had been rocked on its axis. Turned upside-fucking-down.

The things I'd been struggling with—my sexuality, my identity—seemed so inconsequential now. Insignificant in the face of what we'd seen in the last few hours.

Tris had initially thought she was guilty, but he'd changed his mind when he'd read her diaries. Those bloody things were red herrings. They were decoys to try to convince anyone looking that she was innocent. We'd all fallen for it so completely that we'd been blindsided. Even in those early days before Zali changed his mind, I don't think Tris imagined for a second that she'd faked her own death and disappeared overseas.

We never believed her capable of killing Ash.

The truth was horrifying.

An absolute nightmare.

My throat closed up, and I bit back a sob. How could she? He was sunshine and laughter. He was happiness and love contained within a lanky kid.

How could she have killed him?

Why didn't she just send him home? To us. To all the people who loved him and would have kept him safe from her.

If only she'd called. Hell, Roe would have dropped everything and gotten on a plane in an instant if he'd heard her voice. He would have swum that fucking ocean if it meant getting Asher back.

I would have too.

We fucking loved him.

Why couldn't she have given him back to us?

He was my brother in all but blood. He'd saved me. He'd been there for me through what I'd thought were my darkest days after losing Dad. They were nothing when his death was added onto my already broken heart.

Hot tears flowed, and I clutched Ez harder, crying into his shoulder. He rocked me gently and held me tight, never letting go. He kissed me wherever he could reach and ran his fingers through my hair, calming me even as he let me cry.

I didn't know how long we sat there, but it was long enough that Zali came over and sat on the armrest. I wanted to reach for her, to gather her into my arms and clutch her tight. But the sling held my arm fast to my body.

Tenderly rubbing my back, she waited until I'd composed myself enough to pull away from Ez. She wiped my cheeks with her thumb and the backs of her fingers, the tears in her own eyes cascading down her cheeks. Her smile reflected my heartbreak, her lip quivering as she sucked in a breath and tried to compose herself. When she had, she offered me a glass of water and some tablets.

"They're just paracetamol. Probably won't even take the edge off, but I've got stronger meds—"

"I can't have them. I need to be alert enough to fly. Flynn's nowhere near ready to take over."

Zali nodded and cupped my face, pressing a kiss to my cheek as she stood. "Let's focus on getting you patched up. We'll go straight to the hospital once we land in Sri Lanka," she promised.

I shook my head. "I'll get us home. I can wait."

Zali slipped the tablets onto my tongue, and I swallowed them, downing the glass of water she pressed to my lips.

Ez tilted my chin up and pressed a soft kiss to my lips. I sighed, a confusing mix of joy and devastation fighting for dominance over me. Everything was upside down except for these four people. They were my rocks. They wanted me safe and well. They wanted me happy. I was home when I was with them.

Ez pressed his lips to mine again, lingering longer before he repeated the action and swiped his tongue along my bottom lip. I let him in, touching my tongue to his in a slow dance.

Without words, he showed me he loved me.

I poured myself into the kiss, losing myself to the horrors of the knowledge we'd discovered that evening. The kiss wasn't leading anywhere, but it did more than getting off could ever do. We were reconnecting, showing each other what we had in our hearts. I sank into his arms, and when he finally pulled back, I was at peace.

"Thank you for looking after me," I whispered.

"You never have to ask."

I smiled, knowing the truth of those words. "You're a good man, Ez. One I'm proud to say I love."

He laughed, his eyes lighting up with happiness as he cupped my face in his big palms and kissed me again with a hard press of his lips. He didn't call me out for still being in the closet—I hadn't known how to broach the subject with Mum or the rest of my family. I'd been so fucking worried about losing them, but now... now I knew. I was done hiding. I was done being scared and living the way I thought other people wanted me to. The people here with me now made me happy, and I wanted to be able to shout from the rooftops that Zali and her men were mine too.

Ezra's eyes softened as if he knew what I wanted to do. He nuzzled my nose with his in a ridiculously adorable move and smile-kissed me before adding, "I think our girl wants my spot."

"Should we make her jealous?" I teased.

"You're already feeling better," she grumbled, but there was no heat in her tone. If anything, it was relief. Ez slipped off me and pressed a kiss to my forehead before going to sit with Tris.

Zali curled up on my lap, needing me as much as I needed her in that moment. I wrapped her in my one good arm, and we sat quietly, my eyes closed as I breathed her in.

After a time, she sighed. "I'm just like her." Her voice was quiet, filled with vulnerability. I opened my mouth to disagree, but she kept speaking, adding, "I hate her, but I'm just like her."

"You're nothing like her," I challenged.

"She stole all that money. How the hell do you think I made all of mine? I took it. She's disregarded every law, every moral code there is. How is that different to me?"

Tris was on his knees before us in a heartbeat. "You're nothing like her. I promise you."

"How, Tris?" Her plea was impassioned, the fear in her voice very real.

"The Zali I know may very well be the world's best hacker. She says, 'Fuck what society thinks' a lot, but you know right and wrong." With one hand on my leg and the other on Zali's, he held her gaze, a promise in his eyes. "You don't hack people to cause them damage or to hurt them unless they truly deserve it. Every person you've taken from has done horrible things."

"So shouldn't I have turned them in?"

Ezra laughed, but the sound wasn't happy. He took Zali's place on the armrest of the recliner we were sitting on. "The legal system is fucked up, Zali. Sometimes I think we need karmic justice more than court systems and jails. Today was the perfect example."

"How much money have you paid out to your mum's investors?" Tris asked. I could tell her the exact amount Mum had received in her bank account—the amount she invested plus the returns Rosa had promised Mum and Dad for the full ten years. Instead, I tightened my arm around her and kissed her hair.

"A couple of hundred million," she mumbled.

"Right, so you've seen a wrong, and you've fixed it," he confirmed. "You do that with everything, Zali. Flynn told me what you did for him, sticking with him through all the bullying, then buying him an apartment and a car just to get him out of his parents' place. You protected him. You did the same for Ry too, giving him what he needed to survive losing Asher. Even your old teacher told me what you did for his friends, no questions asked. He asked for help, and you were there. The one who runs Spectrum—"

"That was for the LGBTIQA youth service he volunteers at," she explained.

"How terrible of you to help them," Ez teased, his voice full of sarcasm. He smoothed his hand down her hair, caressing her cheek as he did, his touch gentle.

"And the other one who got screwed over by his football team?" Tris challenged, raising his brow.

Ez continued, "You made things right for them. It's what you do, Zali. It's what you've done tonight too."

"I killed her. I'm a murderer. How can you love me?"

"We will never stop loving you," I promised, my voice fierce. "If I'd done it, would you hate me?" I didn't wait for her to answer before I shook my head. I knew her answer. "You gave my best friend justice. You made sure his murderer couldn't hurt anyone else. You fulfilled *our* promise, and for that, I'll always love you."

Tears spilled over her lashes, running down her cheeks. She nodded and pressed her lips together. "I just wish we'd been there when he really needed us."

"You were only a kid," Tristan countered. "It wasn't your job to protect him even though he did that for you."

Ez brushed the tears from her cheek with his thumb. "None of you knew what she was capable of. I know without a shadow of a doubt that if your dad had any inkling, the outcome would have been different."

"I'm going to jail, aren't I?" she asked.

Instinctively I tightened my arm around her, trying to protect her. "No," I gritted out, daring Ezra to even try to arrest her. There was no way I'd let her take the fall for defending us against that monster and getting justice for Ash.

He shook his head with a soft smile. "I'm way out of my jurisdiction. But that wouldn't matter anyway. I'd never let you be charged," Ez murmured, pressing a kiss to her forehead. "It'll never be a problem again either. I'm handing in my badge when we get back—"

"Ez," Tristan started, but he held up his hand to halt Tristan's words.

"I'm done, Tris. It's the right time. But this isn't about me."

Tris reached for Ezra's hand, squeezing it after he threaded their fingers together. He turned his gaze to Zali and nodded. "Ry's right, you know. You're nothing like her. She murdered a defenceless child—her own son—after she'd already hurt him. And for what? Her lifestyle? For a bit of peace and quiet?" He closed his eyes and shook his head, sorrow radiating from him in the downward tilt of his lips and the frown between his brows. "I'm sorry. I'm so sorry." He sucked in a shuddery breath and exhaled slowly before blinking his eyes open again. They were glassy, like he was on the edge of tears himself. "Zali, she would have killed you too if she had the chance. She very nearly killed Ry. You could never be like her."

"It was self-defence, and I never want you to think otherwise," Ezra supplied simply.

* * * * *

Landing in Langkawi, after a pit stop in Sri Lanka to re-fuel, was like returning home. It was a tiny slice of familiarity that we had good memories of, even if our stay was only brief. We were greeted as old friends and fussed over by the resort staff. They weren't even worried by my grumpy arse. They took one look at our bloodied and bandaged state and took over, bringing each of us a change of clothes and insisting on a visit from a doctor for me.

The doc checked me over and agreed with Ez, declaring an operation necessary to set and pin my collarbone before it would heal properly. He cleaned me again and reband-aged me. He ordered ice and gave me instructions to keep it cold to minimize the swelling. Zali had listened raptly and had been checking me ever since, insisting that I put my feet up and relax.

All I wanted now was a whiskey or five, Zali in my arms, and sleep.

I yawned, my body heavy but my mind spinning like a ride on sideshow alley. I don't think I'd ever be able to fully comprehend Rosa's thoughts; she was so completely fucked up. I'd wanted vengeance. I'd wanted revenge. I never thought for a minute that it would be against Rosa herself.

But I was relieved.

We hadn't been able to save Ash, and I would never for-give myself for that.

But I know he'd be proud of us, Zali in particular. We were all proud of her. The way she'd relentlessly tracked down every lead to find his killer was awe-inspiring. She was scary good.

I just hoped she didn't linger on the thoughts she'd had in the plane. Sure, there were similarities between her and Rosa, but she was nothing like that fucking bitch.

"What's this?" Flynn asked, picking up the straps of the black duffel bag sitting on the table.

I'd watched Tristan keep it close to him on the plane. Then when we'd arrived at the resort, he'd made sure he had it in his sights, setting it down with our overnight bag stuffed with our electronics.

"One of Martha Holt's staff gave it to us," Tristan explained. "She owned the house we stayed in. When he dropped off bread and milk this morning... no, yesterday morning, he told me that they knew who Zali was. Then he said she should feel safe there—"

"I couldn't figure out why they were staring. They recognized me," Zali murmured as if the pieces had just fallen into place. She looked so much like her mum that it was impossible to miss the resemblance.

Tristan nodded. "Yeah, I'd say he did. He told me to call Martha. He gave it to us when we were leaving. He asked me again to call her too."

"What's in it?" Ezra asked as he ran his fingers along Zali's shoulders, gently massaging her before leaning down to kiss her hair.

"We haven't looked," Zali said and rubbed her eyes. She was exhausted too, her usually bright blues dull with dark circles under them. "After what went down tonight, I honestly don't know if I want to look. I'm done with surprises."

Flynn moved over to us and sat next to me, squeezing my knee affectionately before gathering Zali's hands in his. "You're completely justified in feeling that way. You tell us if or when you're ready. One of us can check it and let you know whether you need to see what's in it, or we can leave it be. Same with calling Martha—"

"She asked me to call her," Tris interrupted. "You don't have to be there, but you can be if you'd prefer."

Zali sighed, and her shoulders slumped. "As much as I don't want to know, I think I need to find out."

My hands shook, and I swallowed past the lump in my throat. Bile churned in my belly, the nausea creeping up on me until I wanted to puke. I knew it was me who needed to check it; it was my job to protect Zali and shield her from anything that could hurt her. But I didn't know if I could.

This time it was too close. I was already teetering on the edge.

Zali leaned into Ezra's touch before looking up at him and forcing her lips up in a semblance of a smile. "Could you and Tris look through it first?"

My breath rushed out of me, relief like a cool breeze after a hot summer's day washing over me. But at the same time, guilt sat heavy on my chest. They shouldn't have to look through it, not when that psycho bitch Rosa could have put anything in there for Martha's staff to find.

Hearing her talk about Ash had pushed me to the limit.

I'd wanted to kill her.

I'd wanted to tear her apart.

But when she'd pulled the gun on Zali, everything changed. Instinct drove me, every fibre of my being pivoting in a complete one-eighty within a millisecond. I'd gone from wanting to attack Rosa to *needing* to protect Zali.

My body had reacted instantaneously, my mind not even registering the threat. I'd jumped, trying to shield Zali with the only thing I had—my body.

Thank fuck I had.

My collarbone had been at Zali's chest height when the bullet connected. It hit me, then ricocheted on enough of an angle that it missed her altogether. I was bloody lucky too—a fact that hadn't fully sunk in yet. Five centimetres closer to my throat or further down my chest, and I would have been a dead man.

But I wouldn't change my actions even if I could.

Even after the operation, the time I'd need to heal and all the rehab I'd have to have, it'd still be worth it.

If I hadn't put myself between them, this last twenty-four hours would have looked very different.

Our girl wouldn't have been sitting opposite me. She wouldn't have been holding Flynn's hands. She wouldn't have been asking Ezra to check what was in a grab bag handed to us in a hurry.

"Of course," Ezra murmured, kissing Zali's forehead. "We'll take it into the spare room and call you in if you need to see what's in it."

I sucked in a breath and bit my lip as I watched them take the bag into one of the bedrooms. Nerves fluttered in my belly. This could be big. It could also be nothing, but something told me it had the potential to change everything.

I wanted to be in there too, but I was paralyzed. Stuck still.

"Hey, you okay?" Zali asked me, threading her fingers through mine.

I squeezed tight and nodded with a quick jerk of my head. It was the best I could do, my body betraying me in its conflicted state.

We didn't have to wait long. Ezra walked out, his face pale and tears in his eyes. "You should come in," he said, his voice cracking.

EIGHTEEN

Zali

I walked toward the room, Ezra's hand at the small of my back. But with every step I took, it was as if my body detached further from my mind. I was hovering above myself, watching as I crossed the threshold.

I saw the items laid out on the bed. I gazed down at myself as I paused and considered them. Tris sniffed, and I saw my attention shift to him. He was crying.

He held his arms out for me, and I observed as he enveloped me in them. But I couldn't feel his warmth. I couldn't feel the safety of his hug.

I willed my body to move, to snuggle into Tristan's gentle embrace and lean against his broad chest. But I couldn't make myself lift my arms. I couldn't take comfort from him. I was stiff. Frozen still.

I watched the silent conversation pass between Tris and Flynn, the heartbreak in Tristan's eyes and the slap of rejection when I failed to lift my arms and hold him too. I fought against myself, trying to make my hands move, to lift my arms up and curl them into his shirt and draw him closer. I wanted to inhale his spicy scent. I wanted to sink into his hug.

But I couldn't. My arms remained by my sides, pinned in place by the disconnect between my mind and body.

Like watching a recording of the moment, I saw Flynn step up behind me and run his hands over my shoulders. He brushed my hair out of the way and leaned in closer, trying to interlace our fingers. But my hands were limp. Unmoving.

I was surrounded by two of my favourite people, so why was I so detached?

Flynn whispered something to me. I saw his mouth move, and I imagined the warm wash of his breath on my throat like a phantom touch.

But I didn't feel anything.

I didn't hear his words. My ears were filled with static.

The void surrounding me seemed to grow, expanding outward and pushing my psyche further away from my body. Like an out-of-focus camera lens, the edges of my sight became fuzzy. The colours were slightly off too—they were too saturated and yet dull at the same time. I blinked, trying to clear the sensation.

I observed myself pull away from Tris and Flynn, side-stepping out of their arms. Tristan's face crumpled, his tears falling afresh. He wrapped his arms around himself and sucked in a shuddery breath. Flynn reached for him, hugging Tris to his side as Ezra stepped closer and cupped Tris's face. He brushed his thumbs over Tris's cheeks and whispered something to him. I watched him kiss Tris's forehead before he gestured outside where Ry had disappeared.

I saw the hesitation and indecision cross Tris's features. I recognized the moment it turned into resignation.

Then I watched him leave, his head down and his shoulders hunched.

I looked down at myself staring at the bed. Mementos of a life cut short without notice—his shark reference book, its tabbed pages curled from constantly being read, a homemade lure, a handball, a rugby jersey—were right in front of me, spread out on the white covers.

I stared as I saw my hand reach forward and flip open the sketchbook. I turned the blank page over and blinked at the illustration before me.

I knew that place.

The pull back into myself was like that first dip on a rollercoaster, the rush making my gut swoop sickeningly.

Then the pain hit me. It sucker-punched me to the gut with the force of a freight train.

My lungs seized and my throat closed over.

My heart shattered in my chest.

Agony radiated from every pore. Every cell in my body recoiled from the sketchpad in front of me. Yet, the jagged pieces of my heart reached out, seeking to bridge the gap over time and space that yawned like a chasm between us.

My beautiful big brother had been ripped away from us, yanked forcibly from our arms. His yearning to return was so clear. This drawing, this memory he'd put onto paper, was a plea to come home. He was begging.

I could see the desperation in every stroke of his lead pencil. I could feel his tears as my own fell from my eyes. I saw them splatter onto the paper as he drew, smudging the pencil strokes.

There was no denying what Asher had drawn. The place was as familiar as my own reflection.

It was where I went when I wanted to be close to Ash, where he wanted to return to.

Jumpinpin.

Lightheaded, I gasped, my breath thready as I inhaled.

The wail that rent the air wasn't human. It was anguish, misery, and grief. It was powerlessness, regret, and a decade of missing him that came roaring back to life. It was as if I was receiving the news of his death for the first time all over again. The grief that had dulled from a gaping wound in my chest into one that I'd managed to keep discreetly behind a bandage was ripped open again, cleaving my heart and shattering my world.

My legs buckled under me, and my voice broke. Tears streamed down my face. Strong arms surrounded me, lifting me up and cradling me against a warm chest. Ezra carried me to the sofa and sat down, rocking me gently on his lap. My tears soaked through the material of his resort T-shirt within moments.

I didn't understand what he was saying, but the soft rumble of his voice soothed the jagged edges of my soul. I curled into him, trying to pull him closer, trying to climb back out of my body, away from the agony and into his.

Flynn was there too, his arms surrounding me and his chest pressing into my back. He kissed my shoulder, then my hair. He held me tight, not letting me go as I cried.

I missed Asher. I wanted him back. It was an impossible dream, a reality that I could never have. We'd both been robbed of a future together, and now all I had was a distant memory and his trinkets. Our pasts were forever inter-twined, but in this lifetime, our paths would never cross again.

It wasn't fair. I didn't want just memories. I didn't want things he'd touched or made. I wanted him. I wanted my big brother. I wanted him to be there to reach out to pet a cute dog first in case it was vicious. I wanted him to brush my knees off when I fell over after chasing him and Ry. I wanted him to tease me and tickle me until I was breathless from laughter and screaming. I wanted him to put the bait on my hook so I didn't have to touch the sandworms he'd sucked up from the water's edge, and I wanted to listen to his laughter. I wanted to see his eyes light up with excite-ment when he saw something cool. I wanted to hear his voice again and the way it dropped conspiratorially when he had a good idea he wanted to hide from Mum and Dad. I wanted to hide under his doona with him and tell him my secrets.

I wanted to hug him just one more time.

I'd do anything for just one more moment with him to tell him how much I loved him and how much I missed him.

NINETEEN

Ryder

I moved like I was wading through treacle. Getting up off the couch drained everything in me, and shuffling to the doorway took an age. It was as if my body was warning me, sirens and those railway crossing lights flashing at me.

Nothing prepared me for what was laid out on that bed. Absolutely nothing.

I couldn't look at it.

I sucked in a breath and looked anywhere but the bed. Tristan was crying, tears streaming down his face as he held out his arms for Zali. She moved slower than I did, her face blank. Utterly devoid of emotion.

I was numb.

I was being sliced open with a thousand knives.

My knees wobbled as my legs threatened to give out from under me.

Ezra's arms were around me before I knew it. His warmth, his strength seeped into me. But it wasn't enough. I couldn't do it.

He tried to guide me down onto the bed, but I resisted.

His things were right there. Mementos that were once important to Ash.

Trinkets that someone had kept for him. Was it Rosa? Did she have enough heart to keep them?

No. No, she'd killed him.

She'd murdered him. Ripped his life away from him.

That bitch didn't have a heart.

I shook off Ezra's arms and glanced at Ash's Gold Coast jersey laid out on the bed—the one we'd worn to the inaugural home game. I remembered the day we got them. I had one exactly the same.

That motherfucking bitch. I was glad she was dead. I was happy we'd left her house burning around her, the ill-gotten spoils of her theft and deceit crumbling around her as her body burned.

I tore out of there, anger as visceral as lava erupting from a volcano pouring from me. But there was nowhere to go.

The French door bounced off the wall as I shoved it open and started pacing the deck.

I kicked the sun lounger, sending it skidding across the timber platform.

But the rage still burned inside me.

I bent to pick up the coffee table, but my fucking arm stopped me from even moving it. Frustration, wrath, helplessness, and grief piled on top of each other, the combination like a nuclear bomb going off inside of me.

I roared.

My vision went red.

Blood thrashed through my veins, pounding so hard, I could hear the rushing in my ears.

I kicked the sun lounger again, toppling it. Fucking railing. I wanted to hurl the bastard over it, but I couldn't even lift it with my fucking arm in a sling.

The noise that erupted from deep inside me didn't sound human. I didn't *feel* human.

Then he was there. Tristan.

Standing in front of me, the tears still wet on his lashes, he blocked my path.

My good hand went to my hair, and I yanked, needing to feel something other than the turmoil overwhelming me. The sting helped. Or maybe it didn't. I didn't know.

"Come back to me, Ry," Tristan rasped.

I shook my head, incapable of forming any words.

"Take it out on me. I can handle it. Hit me, kick me, fuck me, whatever you need. Take it," he demanded, his voice rising to a shout. But he had no idea what he was asking for.

I wanted to inflict pain.

I wanted to excise this murderous rage boiling in my veins.

I wanted to punish her, tear her limb from limb.

I wanted to watch the life drain from her miserable eyes as she bled out.

If only I was the one who'd fired that bullet.

Tristan stepped forward, cupping my face with his rough hands. He dug his fingers into my jaw and stared at me, his own jaw clenched hard. His emerald eyes were stormy, a mix of agony and a fierce rage swirling in their depths.

He yanked me toward him, slamming his mouth against mine. I tried to tear away from him, but his grip was too strong.

He forced his tongue into my mouth, and I could taste his desperation. He needed me as much as I needed him.

I groaned and wrapped my arm around his waist, holding him in place as I sucked on his tongue, our teeth clashing together.

Demanding. Forceful. Unapologetic.

All-consuming.

My head started to spin, and my lungs burned. He pulled away, and I sucked in a breath.

"Fuck me, Ry. Take my hole."

"I thought—"

"Shove that fat cock of yours into my tight hole and rail me until I can't walk straight," he ordered, his tone leaving no room for argument.

I hesitated, and Tristan growled in frustration. "Make me feel you, Ry. Remind me how good I can feel." His voice dropped to barely a whisper when he added, "Please."

"Strip."

I ground my teeth together and watched as he shucked his buttoned shirt, revealing acres of tattooed skin and rippling muscles. The black leather chains he wore around his neck were so unassuming, so different from the suave and sophisticated man standing before me. They seemed so much more like him in that moment—on edge.

Darker too.

He toed off his shoes, then dropped his black pants to the ground and peeled his black boxer briefs down his legs. His socks were the last stitch of clothing to go, leaving him standing before me in all his naked glory. I looked my fill, staring at the taut lines and angles that were familiar but new at the same time. He was magnificent.

And he was ours.

He pulled a sachet of lube from his back pocket and kicked his clothes out of the way before shoving the packet into my hand.

Tris dropped to his knees. It was a sight to behold. His gaze never left mine. He held me enraptured. I was frozen, unable to even breathe as I watched him slide his hands over my waist and down my legs. He reversed direction, gliding his hands back up to grip my arse and pull me closer. My nostrils flared as he palmed my cock through my jeans, and my breath left me in a rush as he undid the buckle of my belt before shoving my jeans and underwear to my ankles. I kicked them away and stood before him naked from the waist down.

My cock was still soft, but the stirrings of desire were gathering in a rush. Sex had been the furthest thing from my mind, but I needed it. I wanted it. I wanted him.

Tris exhaled sharply, his heated breath teasing my sensitive skin. He nuzzled my sac with his stubbled jaw and breathed me in, burying his nose in my pubes. Sensation washed over me, the need to give him what he wanted lighting a fire inside me. My dick thickened, hardening as he ran his tongue over my length. He nipped at my glans with his lips and sucked me into the warm cavern of his mouth.

Jesus fucking Christ, he was potent.

My cry caught in my throat as Tris blew me, getting me hard in a few strokes of his talented mouth.

I carded my fingers through his hair, holding him in place as I face fucked him. With rough forward punches of my hips, I gave him no respite as I worked my way into his throat, making him gag. But he didn't protest. Instead, he gripped my thighs with his big hands, digging into the muscles there and probably leaving fingerprint-sized bruises. It sent my mind spinning and my balls readying to unload.

Need rocketed through me, and the emotional tempest swirling in me channelled into a laser-like focus.

But if he didn't slow down, if he didn't stop, I was going to come. I wrenched free from his grip, and my cock slapped against my belly after leaving his mouth with a *pop.*

"Bend over," I rasped, breathing hard. "Show me that tight hole."

Tristan was on his feet in an instant, then he was bending over the back of the couch. With his hands on his cheeks, he pulled them apart, giving me exactly what I'd asked for. His pink pucker was right there within reach.

He was offering me something he'd only ever given to one other person. The significance of that wasn't lost on me.

But I couldn't think straight.

I couldn't focus on anything other than sinking inside that tight hole and fucking him into oblivion.

After tearing the sachet of lube open with my teeth, I coated my hand in it. It dripped everywhere, but I didn't care. I needed inside him yesterday.

Slicking up my length, I bit back a groan at how close to the edge I was and focussed on Tris instead. Plunging two fingers into him, I gritted my teeth at his tight heat strangling me. I scissored my fingers, trying to stretch his hole before I lost my fucking mind.

Tris whimpered, but he shook his head. "No, no prep. Get inside me."

I pulled my fingers free and wiped the excess lube over his hole. Gripping the base of my cock, I lined it up and gritted my teeth, trying to tame the rising tide of lust pushing me to an orgasm far too quickly.

Breathing deeply, I punched my hips forward, burying my length in him to the hilt in one thrust. His slick heat was like a furnace strangling my dick. I rocketed to the edge, my orgasm barrelling down on me like a freight train.

Tris shouted out, and I groaned, fighting to get myself under control. But Tris wasn't having it. He used the couch as leverage, pulling away before fucking himself back onto my cock.

He was wild. Desperation was driving him, and I knew.

I knew what he needed and how he was feeling.

I reached around and gripped his throat, pulling him back against my chest. It changed the angle of penetration and I hissed at the tight clench.

I bit his shoulder and drove up into him over and over again until he was shaking. I tightened my grip and sucked on his skin, lashing him with my tongue.

I fucked him hard and rough, pouring every ounce of emotion into him. I let loose, not holding back at all as I unleashed.

My balls drew tight and my dick swelled.

But I needed him to come first.

I needed to deliver on what he'd asked for, to take him away from the pain and suffering.

He yanked my hand off his throat and sucked in a deep breath. He swayed on his feet, and I slid my hand down to his cock to stroke him. But Tristan was quicker.

He shoved back with his body, using his bulk to manoeuvre me. My dick slipped free, and I almost cried at the loss of the tight nirvana I'd been buried in.

Tris spun, guided me around the couch, and pushed me into the seat. He stood before me, his face strained, bruises already forming on his neck where my fingers had dug into him. His chest heaved, and his cock was limp.

He was a mess.

Horrified, I reached for him, but Tris shook his head. He straddled my hips and gripped my face, biting down on my bottom lip hard enough that I tasted the coppery tang of blood.

"Get your dick back inside me," he demanded as he lowered himself. I guided my length into him and groaned as his tight heat enveloped me once more. He rolled his hips, a sensual glide that drove me deeper.

I reached for his cock, closing my fist around him and stroking in time with his movements. He moaned, and I met his gaze, trying to communicate without words how sorry I was for hurting him. But fuck that, he needed to know.

"Tris, I'm—"

"Don't. Just kiss me."

He leaned down, and our lips met. But the fire and fury had been replaced with passion, with heat and desire. I wanted to touch him everywhere, to feel his sweat-slicked skin under my fingertips as he arched into my touch and came apart on top of me.

Our tongues tangled, and his cock leaked as I jacked him off. Swiping my thumb over his slit, I collected the bead of pre-cum forming at his cockhead. I broke our kiss and brushed my thumb over his lower lip before bringing it to my lips and licking it away. I moaned at the salty tang on my tongue and shared the taste with him.

He rocked his hips, and I nipped a line along his beard to his throat, lowering my face to kiss each of the bruises I'd left there. Tris whimpered, arching back and rolling his hips, driving me deeper. His movements became jerky, and I squeezed him tighter, rolling my thumb over his frenulum and along his slit with every upstroke.

His head fell back on a moan as I licked a stripe up his throat and sucked on his Adam's apple. "That's it, babe. Come all over me. Mark me as yours. Take what you need," I mumbled against his throat, nuzzling him as I worked him.

Tristan's channel tightened like a vice around me, and he groaned, his hips jerking as his cock hardened even more. I didn't let up; I didn't slow down. It only took one more stroke before his cock pulsed in my hand, and he shouted out in time with the first shot of cum landing on my chest. I worked him harder, faster, and he dragged me off the ledge and into the clouds with him.

My balls emptied, and I filled him with my seed, painting his inner walls with my cum. I saw stars. My chest heaved, and my pulse thrummed in my veins.

I growled, that possessive beast living inside me lighting up with the knowledge that he was carrying me within him. I lifted my hand to my lips and licked my fingers, cleaning his essence from them. I took him inside me in the same way he did me. I wanted him like that. I wanted him inside me and all around me. I wanted him to own me just like I owned him.

My body floated on a high I never wanted to come down from.

We sat there like that, Tristan's hands in my hair, him on my lap, my softening cock still inside him and my face pressed against his throat. "Are you okay?" he asked.

I huffed out a laugh that held no humour. "I should be asking you that. I'm sorry for hurting you."

"I needed it," he admitted. "Fuck, it was overwhelming seeing you and Zali going through that. She was so still. It was as if she'd completely checked out. It broke something in me. I started all this. It's all on me. But I was powerless to help. I was drowning."

"Did this help?" I asked, breathing him in. His spicy scent drove me wild, but it was a comfort too. He was safety and strength. I still couldn't quite fathom that I did that for him too.

"It did. You helped me push back the onslaught." He exhaled, then ran his hand down my back. "You caught me when I needed it. You took over and made me feel something good. Then when I was ready, you let me regain my footing."

"Good," I replied, my voice cracking. I sucked in a shuddery breath and swallowed past the lump in my throat. I didn't know why his words affected me so much, but they did. Hearing that he was struggling too was so fucking hard.

He held me tighter and pressed a kiss to my temple. "I'm sorry I put you through this. You never would have known if I didn't start digging. You would never have had to relive all this again—"

"I wouldn't change it," I mumbled against his throat. "We got justice for Asher. She'll never hurt anyone again." I clenched my jaw, breathing through my nose to steady my heartbeat thrumming in my veins. "I had the same jersey as Ash. We got them together."

"I'm so sorry you lost him," he murmured, carding his fingers through my hair gently.

"What else was in the bag?" I asked, almost too afraid to ask but needing to know at the same time.

"A half-made Lego set, a notepad with sketches...." His voice wobbled, and I held him tighter, my eyes burning with unshed tears. "He'd drawn all of you. They were good too. Lots of little details. He must have spent hours on each one. He loved you, Ry." Tris sucked in a shuddery breath, and I couldn't hold back my tears. I cried against his shoulder. "He loved you so much."

He held me tighter, our naked bodies pressed together, the sweat still cooling on our skin. Our come was smeared between us, my cock long having slipped out of his hole. My tears dripped onto him, soaking his chest.

"I loved him too," I whispered. "He was my best friend."

"There was an urn in the bag. We have his ashes. You can say goodbye to him properly."

I whimpered as my tears fell harder. We'd brought him home. We'd taken him away from that monster who'd hurt him and brought him back to where he'd be safe. We would cherish him and honour his memory. I didn't have the words to thank Tristan for everything he'd done. He'd started this journey thinking Rosa was guilty. None of us anticipated finding her alive. But by proving us all wrong, he'd given us everything—the most valuable of gifts a person could bestow. He'd given us Asher's remains.

He'd also given Ash a voice. He'd allowed us to give him justice, to avenge his death.

He'd empowered us to tell his story.

He'd given a dad, a sister, and a best friend the closure they never had before.

"Is Zali okay?" I asked when I'd finally controlled my sobs enough to speak.

"I hope so," he whispered, his voice a rough rasp. "Ez and Flynn are taking good care of her."

"Will you publish the podcast?"

"I don't know." He shook his head. "How can I make you all relive it over and over again?"

"We'll do it for Ash." I lifted my face to look properly at him. "We tell his story and make sure the world knows what she did to him."

"Zali's dad has no idea of what we've found. I can't blindside him."

"I don't want to tell him," Zali interrupted from behind Tristan. She slipped onto the couch next to us and rested her head on my good shoulder. "But he deserves to know. So does the rest of the world. I want *Tarnished Crown* published. I want them to know what a monster she was."

TWENTY

Tristan

I was in the loungeroom in Zali's yacht, pacing the luxurious space and taking it in. It was home now. Well, it was home as long as Zali, Flynn, Ezra, and Ryder were onboard. Things had been strained between us, though, and I hated it. But it was my insecurities at play, not anyone else's.

Zali handed me a coffee. "That's my job," I chastised her. "I'm supposed to be looking after you."

She perched her butt on the armrest of the couch and asked quietly, "Can we talk?"

"Of course." I sat on the coffee table opposite her and placed the steaming mug on the coaster next to me.

Zali slipped onto the sofa, sitting between my spread knees. She took my hands in hers, intertwining our fingers. "I'm sorry for hurting you—"

"Hey, you don't have to apologize—"

"I do." She nodded and gave me a small, sad smile. "You tried to comfort me, and I pushed you away. But you were hurting too. I volunteered you and Ez to sort through a duffel bag that could have had literally anything in it, and when you needed me, I couldn't even hold you. What you found was heartbreaking."

"It was," I agreed. "But I didn't lose my brother or my best friend. The mementos weren't personal to me like they were you. I thought that Ash was just a Gold Coast fan. I didn't realize he and Ry had seen their first home game together. I didn't realize it meant so much to him." I let go of her hands and cupped her face, pressing a kiss to her forehead. "I thought you loved Jumpinpin just because of how beautiful it is. I didn't realize it was somewhere that held special memories for all of you."

She nodded and whispered, "We loved it there." Her voice wobbled, and she sucked in a shuddery breath.

"I'm so sorry you lost him, kitten. So, so sorry. I'm even sorrier that you had to do what you did. I wanted to protect you from that. We all did."

"I'm sorry we lost him too," she murmured. "But knowing I brought his killer to justice is… a relief."

"I'm here if you ever want to talk about anything. Even if it's just to get your mind off things, I'm here." I ran my knuckles over her cheekbone and fingered a piece of her silky soft hair, pushing it behind her ear.

"I tried," she whispered, dipping her face down as if she couldn't look at me. "To hug you back. I tried, but it was as if I couldn't get my arms to work. Everything was staticky, and there was this disconnect between my head and the rest of me."

"Oh, love," I rumbled, getting on my knees and taking her into my arms.

She wrapped herself around me, holding on like a koala, and gripped me tight. Her breaths were ragged, and her fingers dug into my back, but she was there. She was opening up to me and we were reconnecting.

"I love you."

"I love you too," she whispered, burying her face in the crook of my neck. We sat there like that for long enough that my knees were aching. But I didn't move, not when it was what Zali needed.

"I need to find out the rest. There's still so much we don't know." She hesitated. "But honestly, I don't know if I'm strong enough to hear it right now."

"I have Martha's number. I'll call her." I smoothed my hand down her hair, then did it again, winding the length around my fist and drawing her closer. Our kiss was long and slow. It wasn't leading to anything, but I needed to reconnect with her and show her exactly how loved and cherished she was and always would be.

"Thank you."

* * * * *

I'd had to wait until it was a decent time to call Mauritius, so when the clock ticked over, I slipped into Zali's office. There were papers everywhere—taped to the walls and in neat stacks—representing her notes on the different stages of her research, to-do lists, and mind maps of connections she'd discovered. Benedict's name was circled, red permanent marker lines drawn between key points. We'd been convinced that all roads led to him. We'd been so wrong.

I still couldn't believe that it was over, that we'd found out what happened.

It seemed like a bad dream that we hadn't woken up from.

Zali hadn't stepped foot in here since we'd arrived back. I understood now, much better than I had before. She was stronger than anyone I'd ever met, but she was struggling. It was sheer self-preservation that she hadn't ventured in here. Seeing the reminder of how we'd been tricked into believing it was Benedict was too much for her right now. At least she was being gentle with herself, taking some time and space before going back to work.

Ry was itching to get back into it, but he was in no shape. As soon as we'd disembarked from the plane in Darwin, Ry had about collapsed. We'd had him rushed to a hospital to have his collarbone set and pinned in place. We stayed there in Darwin for a few days before Ry was well enough to fly. Thankfully his pilot friend had offered to pilot Zali's plane in exchange for a few days' accommodation on the beach and a flight back.

Zali was focussing her energy on Ry, making sure he was on the mend, and in turn we were fussing over the two of them. They deserved some pampering, even if it was just bringing them drinks and curling up on the couch with them to watch a movie. We were venturing off the yacht tonight for the first time since returning. We were seeing Ry's mum and Zali's dad. I was nervous to meet both, but it wasn't about me. Ry had mentioned he wanted to come out. He was starting with his mum. I just hoped she recognized that he was finally happy and supported him. I couldn't bear for him to lose anyone else. He'd suffered enough.

We were meeting Roe to walk him through everything that had happened. Zali had asked him to bring a friend with him, and he'd asked Ry's mum to be there too. I had a feeling that by the end of the night, there wouldn't be any more secrets.

With any luck, we'd get Roe's permission to proceed with the podcast and Kristy's blessing for our relationship. I was expecting the conversations to only get harder though. We had to break the news to Zali's grandparents—Rosa's parents—and from what Ezra had told me of Roe's and Zali's relationship with them, they'd see both the podcast proposal and our conclusions as a direct attack on them and their daughter. Ultimately, I didn't need their permission to proceed, but I'd rather do it with their blessing than risk a lawsuit for defamation.

But before all that, I had a phone call to make.

I flipped my phone over in my hand, unlocked the screen, then locked it again. I groaned, nerves running riot in my belly. They were swooping and spinning like a flock of birds in full flight.

If I didn't do it now, I wouldn't.

I set my digital recorder up by the phone, dialled the number, and hoped the call was answered. I didn't expect Martha's Southern-accented "Hello" after the third ring.

"Ms Holt, it's Tristan Reid," I greeted her.

"Professor Reid, I'm glad you called. Did you get home safely?"

"We did. Ry was injured, but his operation went well. The doctors are confident he'll make a full recovery with some time and TLC." I explained that I was recording the call and asked if it was okay. When I got her permission, we continued talking.

"She shot him," she surmised.

"How did you know?" I asked, both curious and concerned. Zali had scrubbed the security footage and took Rosa's computer. How did they see it?

"We heard the gunshots. I sent Eshan over to make sure you all got out safely."

"Thank you," I murmured. She really had taken care of us in the short time we'd been in the country. Her generosity and that of the staff on Langkawi were the two bright spots in our trip. I wasn't sure whether Martha's kindness was because of who she was or who we were. It was obvious that she knew who her neighbour was, but that didn't translate into knowing us. I needed answers.

"Can you start from the beginning, Martha? May I call you that?" I asked. Without giving her a chance to answer, I added, "How do you know us?"

Martha tutted. "Professor, how am I supposed to answer your questions if you don't give me time to?"

I kept my mouth shut, not wanting to interrupt her again but it also occurred to me that she was calling me professor. I'd never given her my title either.

"I was vacationing in Sydney, visiting an old friend when Rosa and Asher went missing. I'd believed the news when they announced the yacht was feared lost and its occupants drowned. It was purely a coincidence that they moved in next door. My wife, bless her soul, was at home and took an instant liking to that beautiful boy."

I smiled sadly, wishing I'd known Asher. He'd had such a profound impact on the people around him in his short life that I could only imagine what he would have achieved if he'd been alive today.

She sighed, the sound a sad one. "Val told me that Rosa was running from an abusive husband. She'd said her family had sent her here. She was hiding in a friend's house. I don't remember his full name, and I couldn't find out any information on him without asking her, but there's an actor with the same name. An English fellow."

There was only one English actor who came to mind—Benedict Cumberbatch.

"Auberon Benedict?" I asked, flabbergasted at Rosa's audacity.

"Yes, that's him," she answered triumphantly. "How do you know him?"

"Benedict was one of her staff members." I wanted to add more, to explain the link we'd found between them, but I held off. I still hadn't figured out exactly what she knew, and I needed more from Martha before I could start filling in gaps in our knowledge.

"Rosa stressed how important it was that no one knew she was there because her ex would hunt her down. She was terrified of him. Apparently, Benedict was the only person who knew where she was because she was in his house."

"I can't believe she said Roe was abusive," I muttered, horrified at what Zali would think when I told her.

"Yes. But there was something about her that didn't sit right with us. We thought it might have been because of the trauma of her abuse, so we tried to support her. But the longer she was there, the more she seemed to pull back. She pushed us away and everything Asher did upset her. She raised her voice at that boy a lot."

"What was she yelling at him for?" I asked. I couldn't fathom the change in her. She'd said that she wanted Zali and Roe with her, and yet she left them. She took her son, but then she killed him. Her actions didn't make sense even for a psychopath.

"I can only guess. But from what Asher told me—which wasn't much—she was tired of him getting in the way. He was too sad all the time. He complained too much. He was too moody. We saw him retreat into himself before our eyes."

"Their deaths were very close together, you know. My beautiful Val had a brain aneurism. It ruptured, and she died in my arms just like that." She snapped her fingers and her voice wobbled. "We didn't even know she was sick."

She paused for a long moment, just breathing. Her voice was sad when she continued, weighed down by grief.

"She was my reason for living. Her death broke something inside me. I was in a dark place for a long time afterward, and I spent years sitting alone in that darkness. When I was finally ready to come back into the world, I learned that Asher had passed too."

"I'm so sorry for your loss, Martha." Guilt weighed heavily on me. My phone call had dredged up a lot of memories for her. "I'm responsible for making a lot of people re-live their losses lately, and I'm sorry for doing that to you too."

"I had faith in you, professor. That's why I funded your research."

I sputtered, shock rendering me speechless.

"Let me finish my story and you'll understand," she continued. "Asher used to hide in the gardens along the fence, trying to surprise our staff. That poor boy just wanted someone to love him. Val had a secret gate made so he could sneak through and visit with us. He used to come nearly every day."

My smile was bittersweet. I loved the idea of him having a secret garden to play in, but he sounded miserable. "How long did he do that for?"

"It had to have been six or seven months. But then he stopped coming. Val went to visit him, but Rosa wouldn't let her see him. She said Asher had the flu. But the staff gossip, and they told us Rosa found out about his visits. She shouted at him, and he was crying. She punished him by banning him from leaving the house. He was already withdrawn, and they said he got sadder and sadder every day."

"He must have been so lonely," I murmured, my heart breaking for the little boy who'd been torn away from everything he knew and had been hurt, was probably still in pain, and all alone because of the whim of a madwoman.

"And depressed," she added grimly.

I rubbed my chest with the heel of my hand, the pain there sharp.

"It wasn't until a couple of years ago that I came back to myself, and I finally asked about him. It hadn't occurred to me that I hadn't seen him in years. I wasn't functioning much, you see," she explained. "My staff told me that they stopped seeing him when Val died. They'd asked Rosa's staff about him. She'd told them that he went him home to live with his father. They wanted to know whether he was safe, and whether she would be. She'd painted her husband as violent and unhinged." Her angry huff was filled with revulsion. "Why would she send her son home to him, especially if he could reveal her whereabouts? The woman had an answer for everything, though—she said he'd agreed to leave her alone if he got his son back. Her husband apparently loved her son and wouldn't hurt him like he did her."

"Oh my God," I breathed, disgust at the lies she'd told coursing through me. If only that's what she'd done. I could forgive her for stealing all that money. I could even excuse her faking her own death and disappearing. But I could never forgive her for taking Asher away from people who loved him, amputating his foot, then killing him in cold blood when she got sick of him.

"I didn't understand how a mother could send their only child back to live with an abusive parent, even if he supposedly loved Asher. He was safe here. But then I remembered Asher had spoken about his sister. I looked for her. I found a picture of Rosa and Zali from an old newspaper. There she was, a beautiful little girl sitting on the floor in a recording studio while her mother was the rockstar of the moment—the queen of investing. How could Rosa have left her with an abusive ex-husband?"

"Monroe wasn't abusive," I reassured her. "From what I know of him, he's a good man. He loved Rosa and Asher dearly—their deaths destroyed him—and Zali is his pride and joy."

"I know that now," she replied. I could hear the frown in her voice, the sadness permeating her tone. "I knew Monroe's name from the media reports, so I had some background checks done on him when I got suspicious. I didn't find a single thing that suggested he was anything but the doting husband and father he was."

I closed my eyes, wishing I had the power to change the past.

Martha's voice hitched, and she paused for a moment. "Val and I failed that boy. But we had no idea until it was too late. Parents fight with their children. They go through rough patches. Pre-teen kids get moody. Fleeing abuse and moving across the world would have been hard for both of them. There would have been an adjustment period. It was only when I asked about Asher years later that alarm bells started ringing. That was when I discovered her staff were all terrified of her. She'd managed to isolate them and bully them into submission. They were too scared to speak. I tried to help them. I had a solicitor give them legal advice to get out of their employment contracts, and I promised them all jobs if they left. They trusted me enough that when I asked them to do some digging, they did."

"What did they find?"

"Asher's ashes. The plastic urn was in the bottom of the cupboard in his bedroom like it'd been tossed there. The staff took them and searched his room, looking for anything that might have hinted at how he died. They found the other things in the bag hidden under the mattress."

"Why did they collect them?" I asked. "Why not telephone the authorities? Why didn't you?"

"Like I said, they were too terrified of Rosa to speak to the police. It was my first suggestion as well, but they refused."

"And you?" I persisted.

"I did. I went into the station and reported the information I had, which wasn't very much. But then nothing happened. There were no raids, no arrests, not even a single police car came to the house. I spoke with my friend, the Minister for Immigration, to make sure that Asher hadn't left the country like she said. He hadn't. I called the police again. I chased it up and was given the runaround. My complaint had disappeared."

My gut sank. Rosa had someone on the payroll high up enough in the police that they could intervene and protect her. The saying was that money was the root of all evil. In this case, it wasn't the money; it had just enabled the evil.

"No one knew what I was talking about. I went in again, spoke to the same officer, and they denied ever speaking with me. They told me I was mistaken and that I was a senile old lady. Then the station house officer came into the interview room and started making noises about me needing to be cared for. I got out of there when they threatened to have me committed."

"Jesus," I breathed, shocked and appalled by what I'd been told.

Martha continued, adding, "Rosa's staff didn't collect Asher's things at first. Rosa had shut and locked the door, leaving everything exactly as it was. When they told me, I thought it was perhaps somewhere she went to feel close to him. I still haven't moved Val's clothes out of her closet— it's where I go to feel close to her. But they said everything was covered in dust. It didn't look like it'd been touched in years. I'd told them not to touch anything until I had more information, but my second visit to the police station prompted an alternative approach."

I closed my eyes and counted backward from ten, trying to diffuse the rage and devastation her words ignited in me. How could she? Had Rosa always been a sick fuck who had managed to deceive everyone around her, or had something happened? I made a note to involve a criminal psychologist on the podcast if it ever got to the point of being recorded. One day Zali and Roe would have questions, and I wanted to be able to answer them as best we could.

"You got them to take his ashes and the mementos," I surmised.

"Yes, I asked them to go back and get what they could without it being noticed. And I did some research."

"What did you find?"

"You, Professor Reid," she said fondly. "I read one of your early papers and watched a presentation you did at a conference where you used ReimagINC as a case study. You raised some pertinent questions."

I remembered that presentation. I'd been in contact with a defamation lawyer to make sure that I didn't run the risk of being sued by Rosa's estate. Their advice was to leave off any and all names. I ignored it, going with my gut. Thankfully I had, or I might never have had this conversation.

"With a lot of digging, I found out that you'd applied for funding for the class you wanted to run as well as a podcast, and that it had been refused. I had my lawyer reach out and offer an approval with the insistence that you publish the results."

My head was spinning. Martha had come at the same problem from a different perspective, and we'd intersected. The result was the truth being uncovered. It was exactly what I'd set out to do when I'd started seeing anomalies in the way that liquidations during the GFC were carried out compared to those immediately before and after. ReimagINC had been one of the largest, yet no one batted an eyelid.

Except for me.

"What did you get out of it?" I asked, still flabbergasted that she was the one behind all of it.

"The truth—and hopefully justice for that little boy. I was holding on to his ashes, but they weren't mine to look after. He needed to be with his father."

I rubbed my eyes before dragging my hands down my face and groaning. "There are so many coincidences here, so many things that needed to fall perfectly into place to find these answers. How can I believe that they were all just that—coincidences?" I pressed my fingers to the bridge of my nose, unsure of whether I wanted her to confirm that she was behind it all or not.

"I assure you, they are purely coincidences. I had no idea you knew Rosa's daughter. I was surprised seeing her standing on my drive."

"I didn't know her until the grant was issued. She's one of my partners' researchers. When I was applying for funding, he suggested that I get approval to have non-students do the research course. He had her and her partner sign up."

Martha asked, "Has it been helpful having them on your team? I imagine that it wouldn't have been easy for Zali especially."

"It has been difficult for Zali," I agreed quietly, my chest squeezing as I thought about what our girl was going through. "She had no idea that her mother was alive—we were expecting to see Benedict—so finding her here was both a shock and incredibly painful. But Zali is strong, and she's smarter than anyone I know. She's put most of the case together—she was certainly responsible for finding all the key pieces of evidence. I never would have found half of what she did," I admitted. I left off any mention of the less-than-legal means by which she'd gathered the data—I wasn't sure Martha would want to be associated with it, and I didn't want to risk the funding being pulled now, not when we were so close.

"It was clearly meant to be," Martha confirmed.

It certainly was.

TWENTY-ONE

Flynn

I gripped Zee's hand and squeezed, needing the contact with her at the same time as reassuring her that I was there.

Seeing her mum that night was one thing. Telling her dad what had happened was a whole different level of agony, and we were all struggling.

Every time Roe sat at his kitchen table in the future, I was sure he'd picture the five of us around three sides with Zee in the middle and Ry's mum, Kristy, next to him as we delivered the results of the research and what we'd found on our trip.

Roe was ashen, pale as a ghost and shaking like a leaf. Kristy looked like she wanted to be sick. She had her arm around his shoulders, and Ez squeezed his arm. Our guy was trying to be strong; he was trying to support all of us, but he needed a hug too.

Another tear slipped free and ran down Roe's cheek. He hung his head low and heaved out a breath, curling in on himself as he absorbed blow after blow.

"Dad, I'm sorry," Zee whispered.

He shook his head and reached across the table to her. "You haven't done anything wrong at all. You did what you thought was best—"

"But you disagree."

"No. I would have wanted to prove Tristan wrong too." His lip quirked up in a half smile before it fell from his lips, and he closed his eyes, more tears falling. "I can't believe that she would do that. She stole him from us, and she ran." He sucked in a shuddery breath. "How could she have thought for a moment that I would condone her actions? Jesus Christ, she stole all that money," he whispered, the tears falling harder. "We were mourning them," he cried. "She hurt Ash. Why? How could she hurt our baby?" He buried his face in his hands and sobbed, his heart breaking before our eyes.

"I don't know," Zee replied, holding his hand tight. Her mouth was set in a hard line, anger and sadness written in the downturn of her lips and the tears in her eyes. "She was a wolf in sheep's clothing. I'm still trying to wrap my head around it. Seeing her...." Zali exhaled and shook her head.

"I'll never forgive her. Never," he hissed. "Not for hurting Ash, not for encouraging him to get up on that roof. She pushed him. She killed him." He clenched his jaw tight and closed his eyes again, more tears running down his cheeks. "She murdered my baby." He cried, his breath hitching and his shoulders shaking as the weight of his grief bore down on him.

"Dad, there's more," Zee added, sucking in a breath and bracing herself to deliver the final piece of news. Hopefully this one would help all of us to get some closure. When he looked up, she gestured to Tristan. He was the one who'd taken care of Asher since he'd been handed that bag. Ry had insisted, but he was barely keeping his head above water. Zee wasn't even managing that. She was drowning in her grief. She was mourning Asher all over again. She was struggling with the knowledge that he was murdered.

Powerlessness haunted me, and I knew Ezra felt the same. All we could do was hold Zee while she cried, listen while she screamed in agony, and clean and bandage her cut knuckles when she lost control. She and Ry were broken, but they had each other and they had us.

Tristan had stepped into a caretaker role, looking after all of us. He made sure Zee and Ry had everything they needed, and his arms were the ones Ez and I cried in when we couldn't bear the weight of Zee's and Ry's grief anymore. And he cared for Asher's urn with a tenderness that seemed to lift a weight off both their shoulders. He relieved them from carrying that burden, something I would be eternally grateful for.

Tristan had wrapped the urn in a piece of the softest leather I'd ever touched and tied it closed with a thin cord. He carried the urn to the table, setting it down in front of Zee and Ry. He opened it reverently, and Zee reached out a shaking hand, laying it on top of the non-descript, light-grey square tube. It was about half the width of a shoebox and just as long with a plug at one end. Ry closed his hand over

Zee's, the two of them dipping their heads and crying as their loss slammed into them again.

Roe choked out a cry and brought his closed fist to his mouth, his knuckles turning white with the force as he saw what it was Tris held in his hands.

"Asher, we brought you home, mate. Your dad's here," Ry murmured, pushing the plastic urn across the table to Roe. The black plastic nameplate had Asher's date of birth engraved onto it in simple script, but his date of death was missing. We'd hoped it was on there, that we'd find out precisely when it happened, but Martha was only able to give us a general timeframe of about nine to twelve months after Rosa took him.

Roe reached out with both hands and brought the box to his chest, cradling it. A sob ripped from his throat as he shattered right there in front of us.

Roe stood slowly, his chair tipping back as he straightened. We were all on our feet, Ez and Zee moving to her dad and me and Tris going to Ry. I rested my hand low on his back, rubbing the tight muscles in a circle as Tris wrapped his arm around Ry's shoulder and held him close.

"I'm so proud of you," Ry's mum whispered to him, cupping his cheeks in her hands.

He towered over her—she was barely up to his chest—but he could have been a little boy in that moment, looking at his mum with tears in his eyes and hanging on her every word. He needed to hear that she was proud of him and that she loved him. He was terrified that when he finally shared his news with her, that she'd disown him. I could see him taking it all in in case he never heard the words again.

"You never stopped loving him. You've honoured his memory, Ry. You and your friends have brought him home. He's finally back with all the people who love him." Ry nodded, blinking back a fresh stream of tears. We let him go, and he hugged his mum tightly. "You can all say goodbye to him properly now."

"It's like losing him all over again," he whispered, his shoulders shaking as his mum comforted him. I wiped my eyes and leaned my forehead against his good shoulder, giving him a half hug. I wanted to wrap him in my arms, to comfort him the way I knew he needed, but he wasn't out. Neither Kristy nor Roe had any idea that we were all together, and I wouldn't betray Ry's confidence by doing anything to force him out.

I shouldn't have worried.

Ry let go of his mum and reached for me, hugging me to his side and pressing his forehead against mine. "I don't want to wait anymore. Life is too fucking short."

I nodded, my smile bittersweet.

He sucked in a shuddery breath, tears still clinging to his eyelashes, and nuzzled our noses together. Our faces were so close, I could reach up and kiss him, and the temptation to do it was overwhelming.

Ry murmured, "I haven't said it to you before, but I'm in love with you, Flynn. You're all everything I've ever wanted."

His mum gasped, but I couldn't bring myself to look at her. I couldn't risk his happiness or my own by seeing disappointment in her gaze. My heart was filled with effervescent bubbles bursting in my chest, and I gripped his shirt harder, trying to stop myself from climbing him like a tree and clinging to him. Now that we had him, there was no way we were letting go of him. "I love you too," I whispered.

I grinned, happiness radiating out of me like those bubbles were fireworks. Butterflies swooped in my belly, and I touched his cheek with my thumb, in awe of his bravery.

Ry was risking everything for us. He was coming out so that we could be open, so that he could share his truth. But his mum….

"Can I kiss you?" He grinned, and it was a sight to behold. He was beautiful when he was broody, but when he was happy, he was utterly breathtaking.

I basked in his adoration, unable to tear my gaze away from him.

Kristy made a noise that sounded oddly like a squeak. I didn't know whether it was out of disgust or happiness.

Ry stilled, his smile turning forced. I pressed my hand to his cheek, keeping his face turned my way, and he gripped me tighter, holding onto me with shaking hands. With my heart in my throat, I looked at her.

She stood there, wide-eyed with a broad smile on her face, her gaze darting between us. She looked equal parts delighted and surprised, and I laughed, giddy at the way she'd clasped her hands together and was shifting her weight from side to side as if she couldn't contain her excitement.

"My boy's in love," she squealed. There was a commotion behind her, but Ry had captured my chin and lifted my face to his. I saw the tension drain out of him, the worry lines creasing his brow smoothing out. His shoulders relaxed too. But in place of the fear, an intensity that drew me in like a magnet flared in his eyes.

I nodded, ensnared in those hazels. He pressed his lips to mine, his hand on my chin controlling my movements, and I heard Roe say quietly, "Holy shit."

"Four quarters, mate," Ez said.

Ry pulled back, then brought me in again for a chaste, lingering press of our lips together. It was an innocent kiss, but there was no doubt he was claiming me in front of everyone, and I loved him for that even more.

Breathless, we finally pulled apart, and Ry's cheeks flushed a pretty pink. He rubbed his nape with his good hand and huffed out an embarrassed laugh as he drew me to his side. "So yeah, that was me coming out."

"I didn't see this coming at all," Kristy gushed. "But I'm so happy. I thought you were crazy about Zali, but the three of you are always together. Maybe that was just me projecting though," she apologized.

Ry blew out a breath, and I squeezed his waist, lending him my strength. He knew he had our support no matter what he decided. He didn't have to say anything more—he didn't even have to come out to her at all—if he chose not to. None of us wanted him to lose the little family he had, and although the risk of her freaking out was lower given her reaction, it wasn't out of the realm of possibility.

"Shit, this is harder than I thought it would be." He huffed and ran his fingers through his hair, stalling for a moment longer.

"Ryder," his mum said, capturing his attention. Her happiness had evaporated, worry in its place. "You can tell me anything, hon. What is it?"

"I'm proud of you," Tris praised. "You don't have to say anything more."

Kristy nodded. "You don't. But you can. I love you, Ry. I will always love you. You aren't afraid of that changing, are you?"

He closed his eyes and nodded.

"Oh honey," she soothed. "It doesn't matter to me who you love as long as you treat each other right. Flynn has grown up to be a beautiful man. He's kind and caring and he clearly loves you. I'm thrilled for you."

She hugged both of us, squeezing me tight. "You never have to be afraid to tell me anything."

That was when I knew, without any doubt, that Kristy would be there for Ry no matter what.

She pulled away, and I looked over her shoulder at Zee, Tristan, and Ezra. They all wore matching heart-eye stares and shy smiles—just like me—and I cuddled into Ry's side, shuffling closer and laying my head on his chest.

"Thank you," Ry responded quietly. He squared his shoulders and inhaled as if he was sucking up some courage. "Mum, I'm not just with Flynn. We're all together." He gestured between the five of us and swallowed hard, waiting for her reaction.

"All of you," she repeated, looking between us. "As in, the five of you together."

He nodded, a sharp dip of his head. Tension vibrated off him, his muscles taut and his breaths coming quicker.

"Wow, um. Okay." Kristy laughed and shook her head. "Sorry, Ry, I'm shocked."

He paled and seemed to shrink into himself. I stepped in front of him, shielding him with my body as Tris, Ez, and Zali rushed to his side.

Kristy reached out and cupped his face gently, tears in her eyes and her smile back as she flicked her gaze between each of us. "I just gained a daughter and three new sons."

I nodded, and her smile grew.

"Ry, you surprise me every day, but this…. This is the best surprise I could have asked for. It's unconventional, and I have no idea how you'll make it work, but judging by that reaction—" She gestured to indicate the way we were gathered around him, Ry in our centre protected from all ends. "—you're already doing a great job of it. I don't know a more deserving group of people." She covered her mouth and laugh-sobbed. "Oh hell, you've got me blubbering now."

Still hugging the urn, Roe reached for her and wrapped his arm around her shoulders, giving her the same comfort she'd given him a few moments ago. The afternoon's emotions were like a rollercoaster—up and down and twisting and turning. I was dizzy with it. I could only imagine what

Roe was going through, and yet he was still there for his friend. They had a completely platonic love, like siblings, and it made me smile seeing them together.

"We're both thrilled for you," Roe said with a warm smile that was still a little sad. "Thank God we've got some happy news to celebrate."

I looked between Zee and my guys, and they nodded. "There is something else," I added. "We're moving in together. We already spend most of our time on the Noble Steed, but we're thinking of getting a house."

"We're looking at one this weekend," Zee added. "It's ten minutes away, private, on the water, and has a deep-water berth off a jetty. It's also got a recording studio." She left the rest unsaid, but Roe swallowed and nodded.

"It'll be perfect to record your podcast in, Tristan—"

"Martha Holt, my backer, has agreed to amend my funding terms to make the requirement to publish conditional upon your consent. We've done what we set out to do. We found a money trail and followed it. More importantly, we've gotten justice for Asher. Nothing more needs to happen."

Roe bit down on his lip and nodded slowly. "I appreciate that. But the narrative I helped spin was false. I want it corrected." Roe lifted his chin defiantly. "I want the world to know what she did. I want them to hear what a monster she was. Her suicide was the best thing we could have asked for. I'm sorry you had to witness it, but the world is a better place without her in it." He exhaled sharply and forced a smile.

It was the one lie we'd told him, and it was as much to protect Zee as it was for his sake. He didn't need to know that his daughter had fired the fatal shots. I suspected that he'd be proud, but I wouldn't dare risk it. Our decision to withhold that piece of information was unanimous. Even Zee preferred that he never found out. We'd explained the fire that consumed her house as her attempt to harm us.

Martha had kept us in the loop, explaining that the police had accepted Rosa's staff members' account of the evening. They'd told them they heard her screaming, hurling insults at her visitors. She'd thrown the bottle of booze at us and then threw a candle at it. While it burned, she'd pulled the gun and shot at us, hitting Ry before turning it on herself. The story wouldn't stand up if an autopsy or a coroner's investigation were carried out, but her staff's eyewitness accounts had avoided the need for it. The death certificate was issued with suicide by gunshot wound as the cause of death.

Zee had already been in contact with the Grande Banque Unie to have her accounts closed down and the funds donated to a charity she planned to set up in her brother's name. She'd asked Ez for help with it, and together they were going to start drawing up the mission statement. She wanted to help victims of parental kidnapping—children in Asher's position—to reach out and seek help. Zee would provide the resources necessary to back up operations to get them home. I was so freaking proud of her.

Roe interrupted my musing, adding, "But enough of her. Let's talk more about this house you're looking at."

TWENTY-TWO

Zali

The afternoon was full of highs and lows. I was so fucking proud of Dad for the way he handled himself. He was so strong, and even through his grief, he'd thought about everyone but himself. He'd been so happy for us, and after pulling Ezra aside, he'd asked Ry outside to sit down and talk. Ry thought he was in for a lecture, but Dad had offered to listen to him if he ever needed to talk.

They were out there for over an hour, sitting together on the couch I'd sat on many times before, talking. Ry was happy when he'd walked back inside—lighter too. Just like he'd done with Tristan, Ry opened up to Dad. I didn't know what they'd spoken about, but Dad had assured me when we left that we were all going to be okay. That was all that mattered to me.

I flopped onto the bed, exhausted. I was completely drained, emotionally spent and empty. I didn't know what I needed, but my guys were a good start. Not for sex. I didn't know if I could even get into it, but I needed to be in their arms.

As if he could read my thoughts, Flynn crawled up over me, straddling my hips and leaning down to kiss me. The kiss he'd shared with Ry at Dad's was so intimate, so loving, yet so innocent at the same time. I wanted that. I think I needed it too.

He wrapped himself around me, crushing me into the bed and holding me tight. Ez was next to us a minute later, kissing my forehead and hugging me tight. Tris squeezed in behind him and brushed my hair off my forehead before running his hand down Flynn's back. Flynn shivered above me, arching into Tristan's touch, and it was as if he'd touched me. I hummed and snuggled into their embrace, but I was missing my other guy.

"Where's Ry?" I asked.

"Right here, baby girl," he said from the doorway. Leaning against the frame, he wore only a loose pair of basketball shorts that sat low on his hips. The top of the V framing his cock was visible, and I sighed happily. He was tanned and gorgeous. They all were.

"We want to make you feel good, love," Tris rumbled in his deep voice.

"I'm sorry." I groaned. "I'm not sure I'm up for anything."

"Who said anything about sex?" Flynn asked, sliding off me to lie opposite Ez and Tris. "We're talking ice cream."

"A manicure," Ez supplied, bringing my fingers to his lips, nipping the pads of my fingers affectionately.

"A romcom," Ry added, and I snorted out a laugh. I couldn't see any of them, except Flynn, wanting to sit through that.

"Or we could make ourselves scarce and you could ask Cara over. Have a girl's night," Tris suggested.

"You'd do that for me?" I asked. "Any of it, all of it?"

"Baby girl, we'd do anything for you."

"Without hesitation," Ez added. "Call Cara, sweetheart. She's your friend—let her help you get through this." I nodded. I loved my guys. I wanted to be with them, but a little girl time with Cara sounded perfect. She was a ray of sunshine, and I needed that desperately.

* * * * *

Barely an hour had passed, and Ry had pulled together a mountain of snacks, Tris had come back to the yacht with enough Baileys and butterscotch schnapps to sink it, and Ezra and Flynn had gone to pick up Cara. I was sitting on the couch in the sun, looking out over the crowded marina, yearning for quiet.

We'd looked at the house online, and it seemed perfect. I wanted to see it. My yacht was my safe space. It was a retreat as well as my home, but we needed something different now. I wouldn't ask Tris to give up his career, especially not now, so that meant he needed to be able to commute to the university each day. Flynn was there too, finishing his degree, and Ez and I had a charity to set up. Ry would need a lot of physio in the short term, and moving forward, I wanted him to be able to choose whether he would stay on, doing the things he did, or move on to something else. All of that meant we'd constantly needed to be moored, and frankly, there were too many people around. The threat was gone, but I didn't want to be around anyone I didn't have to.

And we needed a bigger bed.

Movement caught my eye, and I jumped up, rushing across the gangway and hugging my friend. "Thank you for coming," I whispered, my voice wobbling as she squeezed me tight. I hated being an emotional wreck, but today had been hard. Good too. But also hard.

"I can't wait to have a sleepover." She giggled, the messy bun on top of her head jiggling with her movement. She was effortlessly happy, and my mood lifted, a smile instantly pulling my lips up as Cara handed me a bag and hooked her arm through mine.

"Up here." I gestured to the gangway and added, "Hold on as you're crossing."

"This is gorgeous," she gushed. "Wow."

"What have you brought?" I asked, surprised at the weight of the bag I'd taken off her.

She grinned and knocked my hip with hers. "You needed cheering up."

Ez set down the plastic tub that was the size of a box of A4 paper and asked, "Where should I put this?"

Cara blushed, suddenly shy, and bit her lip. "Um, somewhere inside? Do you have a kitchen table we can sit at? Maybe in a loungeroom if there's no carpet."

I asked him to pop it on the coffee table, and when Flynn asked about what he was carrying, Cara told him it was all for the freezer.

"It's all the essentials," she explained. "Ice-cream, cupcakes, and my pampering box—mani-pedis, facials, and a movie."

"I've never done this before," I admitted. "Obviously I've gone to day spas and that sort of thing, but I've never had a girlfriend to do it with."

"Neither have I," she admitted. "Mum and I do it though."

"I wish I knew what that was like." I sighed. It was one of the things I'd thought about a lot over the years. I'd wished I had my mum around so that we could do the girly things together, but it was never meant to be. I was angry that she'd robbed me of that, but grateful I managed to escape from her when she'd left.

"Turns out my mum was a piece of work. She stole a shit ton of money, faked her own death, kidnapped my brother, and murdered him." My anger bubbled over, and tears stung my eyes. I was so fucking sick of crying. "I'm sorry," I apologized, shaking my head as my voice wobbled. "I didn't mean to yell at you."

I didn't want to take my anger or heartbreak out on Cara. She was my friend. She didn't deserve my ire, especially not when she'd defended Rosa in class, thinking she was doing the right thing. I exhaled and forced a smile, hating the way she'd paled. "You'd better sit down," I added. "I have a few things to tell you."

I laid it all bare, told her everything except the truth of how Rosa died. Cara didn't interrupt. She didn't ask questions. But she held my hand, and she hugged me tight when I cried for Ash. She did too.

The emptiness inside me grew, everything draining out of me. I slumped against the seat and sighed. "It's all completely fucked up."

"I'll say. Are you okay? It's a lot to get your head around."

"I... I don't know." I shrugged, not knowing what else to say. I thought I was coming to terms with what had happened, then I'd close my eyes and see her face again. I'd think about Ash and what he went through, and I was back at square one. I knew from experience that the pain of losing them would eventually fade to something that was bearable, but I still couldn't fathom the horrors inflicted on my big brother. "I'll get there, but it's going to take a while, I think."

"I'm here for you anytime you need me. Don't ever hesitate to call me. I'll be on your case too—this is the first of our sleepovers and girls' nights, okay?"

I nodded and managed a small smile, grateful beyond measure for Cara's friendship. "Thank you."

"Anytime." She squeezed my hand. "Is Ryder okay?"

"He will be, but he's wearing a sling and has months of physio to do to get back movement and strength. He might never fully recover. I'm worried about the damage the bullet did."

"Poor thing." She rubbed my arm, and I wasn't sure who she meant. It didn't really matter. "All of you deserved so much better than her."

"Yeah, we did."

Ry and the others walked out, and he sat on the armrest of the couch next to me. Running his hand through my hair, he smiled down at me. "You okay, baby girl?"

"I will be."

"We've set up the coffee table with some snacks. Everything is covered, so there's no rush for you to go inside. Drinks are on the buffet, and Cara's movie is already set up to go when you're ready. I've also popped some popcorn for you. It's on the counter in the lounge."

"Thank you."

Ez stepped up beside him and explained, "We're gonna go out for a while. Message us if you want us to come back. If we don't hear from you, we'll crash at Flynn's place."

"Okay. But you can stay here if you want. You don't have to leave."

"Spend time with Cara," Tris encouraged, wrapping his arms around Ezra's waist from behind and leaning his chin on Ez's shoulder. "We'll come straight back if you want us to."

"We're only a phone call away," Flynn added, bending to press a kiss to my lips. "We can be here in ten minutes tops if you need us." That was why they were staying at

Flynn's apartment. He'd barely been back there for weeks, but it was the closest to the marina.

I watched them leave, and Cara watched me. "They're so nice. I thought Ezra was a bit of a dick—" She clapped her hand over her mouth, and her eyes widened. I snorted out a laugh. He had been a dick that night. "Oh my goodness, I'm doing it again. He's your boss and your friend, and I keep insulting him. I didn't mean…. I hope you're not offended. He seems really nice now," she backtracked, her voice still panicked.

I held my hand up and shook my head, still laughing. "It's okay. He *was* being a dick that night. He had some stuff going on, but he's sorted it out. He's… kinda wonderful now." My cheeks grew hot, and Cara tilted her head, considering me more closely.

"They're all protective of you."

I looked down as my smile turned embarrassed. If I looked at her, she'd know exactly what we had, if she hadn't already guessed. "I'm protective of them too."

"Hmmm," she agreed. "You know, my offer to be there for you also includes you talking to me about anything. I'm a good listener." She paused for a moment and added, "And I'm insanely jealous. I was jealous when I thought your only boyfriend was Flynn, but having Ry too? He's… lovely."

I snapped my head up and opened my mouth to speak, but nothing came out.

She laughed. "Were you trying to hide it?"

"No, not that," I waved her off. "You said he's lovely. I agree; he's one of the best men I know, but he's not everyone's cup of tea."

"He followed the boy I thought was cute to the bar, ready to be my wingman. But when he overheard him being mean to the bartender, he was honest and told me what he'd said. Then he kept me company all night. He didn't try to hit on me—not that a man as gorgeous as him would—"

"What?" I asked. "You're beautiful. You're smart and sweet, and you're so much fun—"

"I'm a big girl, Zali. I'm the one who's not everyone's cup of tea," she said matter-of-factly.

"Then they're fucking idiots. Any guy would be lucky to have you on his arm," I countered. "I hate people sometimes."

"And I love you for it." She waggled her finger at me and grinned. "You didn't deny it either."

"No, I didn't." I bit my lip and grinned shamelessly. "We're together too."

"Urgh, you're so lucky," she huffed. "I just want one nice guy." She gestured inside and said, "I want to know everything while I'm giving you a mani-pedi and a facial. Do you have champagne?"

"I've got better than that—we're drinking cock-sucking cowboys."

Cara choked on her breath and blinked.

Backtracking, I added, "But I do have champagne."

"I haven't had a cowboy before. I want to try one." Cara's excited grin was infectious.

I hopped up, reaching out for her. Hand in hand, we dashed inside, and I poured our drinks while Cara got set up. I bloody loved the guys for suggesting this. It was exactly what I needed. I was like a kid in a candy store, looking at all the nail polish Cara was laying out. I had no idea which one to pick. She started on the bottles soon after that, laying out cleansers, toners, exfoliators, face masks and a bunch of different treatments. She had a container of cucumber wipes and the fluffiest of towels. It was like our very own DIY spa. I couldn't wait to get started.

Excitement and happiness pulsed through me, and I thought about Ash. This time my smile didn't slip. I had no proof and there was no logic behind it, but I chose to believe that he was the one who'd made our paths cross at the university. He knew Cara would be exactly who I'd need. I hoped I'd one day be able to do the same for her.

I poured half a dozen shots, trying not to mix the Baileys into the schnapps, and carried the tray over to the table.

"Oooh, yum," Cara exclaimed. "To girls' nights."

"And the best girlfriend I could ask for." We clinked our glasses, and I tipped mine back, drinking the shot. It was creamy and sweet and packed a punch. The three each I'd poured for us would be plenty to have me tipsy for half the night—exactly what I wanted.

"We need music," Cara added, pulling her phone out of her pocket.

I waved her off, turning on my sound system and upping the volume once we'd chosen a feel-good girl-power playlist.

We spent hours talking and giggling, doing countless treatments on our faces and drinking round after round of shots. The world had a hazy tinge to it, and my yacht was rocking a little more than usual, but I was light. I was happy.

"First kiss?" Cara asked.

"Don't remember his name. He was cute though. I was in my first year of high school. I'd gone to primary school with this guy, and I found out he lived near me. Flynn couldn't come out that night."

I remembered the night like it was yesterday. He'd been trying to get me to hang out without Flynn for weeks. He was annoyed that we were always together. He was jealous that I was always with my best friend rather than spending time with him. I'd wanted Flynn with me, but it was his brother's birthday, and he knew better than to go out—he was never included in any of his family gatherings, but if he wasn't there at all, he'd get in trouble, and the punishments would last for weeks.

"We hung out at his school's disco, but he bad-mouthed Flynn. So I kissed his best friend to piss him off and rang my dad to come and get me early. What about you?"

"Oh, um...." She pressed her lips together and scrunched up her nose adorably, her face flushing red. "I kissed a boy once, but he didn't want to do anything else. I haven't really even pashed anyone before."

"That's okay." I shrugged. "There's no timeline. It's important that you feel comfortable. It's okay if you don't want to do anything like that either."

She sighed and threw her arm over her eyes. "No, I do. I really do. But I'm not exactly popular, and I get nervous around people." She lifted her arm and peeked at me from under it. "I wish I had your confidence."

The truth was, Cara didn't need my confidence. She was enough all on her own, and I hated that she didn't think that. She had confidence in spades when it mattered. It was a fierceness and loyalty that was rare to find. The way she'd stood up to Ezra when he'd spoken to me at the bar the night we'd all gone out was incredible. She just needed to realize it.

"I don't think you should change a thing about yourself. You're so great, and you will find your perfect guy. And you do have confidence. Remember when you went off at Ez? That was fierce."

She flushed a pretty pink and giggled. "He was being nasty to you, but it was fun to tell him off."

She picked up a nude polish that was delicate and a little sparkly. "You should use this one. It's you," she suggested. It was feminine and sweet and the total opposite of any colour I would pick to represent me, but I agreed. I liked that Cara thought the colour fit me.

Cara smiled wistfully. "I'd love to be brave enough to be able to walk up to a boy and ask him out. But I don't think I could. Maybe I just have unrealistic expectations. My ideal guys all seem to be written by women."

"Book boyfriends are the best."

"They are. Where are my guys to rescue me when I get in every embarrassing situation? Guys in books are always, like, a pro-footballer or hockey player. You know the type—strong and silent and grumpy toward everyone except his girl. Then there are the hot silver foxes. They're in need of a second chance at love. They've been burned and are wary. Our book boyfriends fall for the heroine and one another, and their group is always a perfect match."

She'd suggested before that I sleep with both Flynn and Ry and even now hadn't batted an eyelid when I told her I was with both of them. My sweet friend may have been a virgin, but she knew exactly what she wanted, and without even realizing it, she'd come out to me as being polyam. I didn't give a fuck what society said and whether it thought I was a cock slut, but having a friend whose sexuality was like mine was an incredible feeling.

"Real life needs to imitate art more often," I sympathized.

"You can talk." She laughed. "Two of the hottest guys on the planet are madly in love with you. I need what you have, but with a couple of guys who love curvy girls."

"Cheers to that." I handed her a shot glass and raised my own. We clinked and drank back the creamy liquid, and I grabbed a handful of blueberries off the charcuterie board Ry had set up for us. We'd demolished most of it and downed half the bottles too. I would have a monster hangover tomorrow.

"I'm so drunk, I can't paint my nails straight." Cara giggled.

"Let's eat popcorn and watch the movie instead," I suggested. We'd done our toes already and I loved the pale colour on mine. I'd chosen a vibrant light purple for Cara, the same colour as the Jacaranda blooms. She insisted on something much paler but like the colour she'd picked for me, I wanted the perfect colour for her too. She was bright and sunshiny and so pretty too.

With *Legally Blonde* playing in the background, we swapped to water and popcorn, and the next minute, I was being roused by Tris gently shaking me. I pulled him down and kissed his cheek, rubbing my face against his stubble like a cat wanting to be fed. I did. I'd missed him; I'd missed all of them. I wanted to stretch out naked on cool sheets and have them feast on me.

"Morning," he rumbled, his voice rough with desire.

I peeled my tongue off the roof of my mouth and grimaced. It felt like I'd swallowed cotton wool and didn't taste good at all. I also desperately needed to pee. But at least I didn't have much of a headache.

"Oh my goodness," Cara gasped from next to me. "I knew it!"

"Huh?" I asked.

"That's why you're all so sweet to each other. You're with Professor Reid and Ezra too."

I blinked and looked at Tris, but before I could say anything, Cara added, "You can't be so obvious at uni, or you'll get in trouble. No one will ever hear anything from me, but you need to tone down... all that. The sexual tension is off the charts." She fanned herself and mouthed to me, "Oh my God... so hot."

I couldn't help but giggle, my sides hurting from how much we'd already laughed during the night.

Tris grinned, his eyes full of affection as he perched awkwardly on the armrest and played with my hair. "Thank you, Cara," he replied. "We've all found more than just the solution to this case this summer. My being with Zali is an issue, but because she's not technically a student of the university, it's not career ending. But my relationship with Flynn is. I don't want to put you in an awkward position, but I'd appreciate it if you didn't report us."

"You don't need to ask me to keep this a secret. I'd never hurt anyone like that unless I thought you were taking advantage of Zali and Flynn." She paused for a moment and narrowed her eyes. "Are you?"

Tris laughed and shook his head. "God no. I'm wrapped around my girl's little finger, and as for Flynn, he knows how to handle me."

I groaned, shifting in my seat to get a bit of friction on my clit. He was a bloody tease. He knew I loved to watch them together.

"Breakfast's ready," Ry called from the doorway. "Come on up whenever you're ready."

TWENTY-THREE

Zali

I waved Cara off as the rideshare we'd ordered for her drove out of the marina car park. With Ezra's arm around my waist and Flynn's hand in mine, we walked back to my yacht. The day was already hot, and I was itching to go for a swim at Jumpinpin. I wanted to be naked in the water, to feel it run over my skin. Our appointment to meet the realtor was at lunchtime, so we still had a few more hours before we could go there.

That meant one thing.

Stepping over the gangway, I tugged on the string of my bikini top and slipped it off, dropping it on the floor. Ez was behind me in a flash, tugging me back against his chest as Flynn came around in front of me. "We don't want to do this outside. We don't want to share you today, beautiful," Ez growled. "Get in your bedroom and get the lube ready. We're gonna need a lot."

I moaned, and Flynn flicked open the button on my shorts, tugging the zipper down. "Take these off so we can watch you shimmy that cute butt of yours away while we get Ry and Tris."

I kicked them off and stepped out of them, leaving my slides on the deck where my shorts fell. I was naked and they were fully dressed. My nipples peaked and my cunt clenched at the way they eyed me like a meal. "How about we just yell out to the others and get the party started while we wait," I countered, sliding my fingers down my belly. I was already wet, already needy.

"Love it when you're demanding," Ez murmured. "I want in your sexy arse." He palmed me, brushing his fingers over my pucker.

"Tris, Ry," I shouted. "Need you in the bedroom. Now."

I gripped Ez by his belt loop and Flynn by his linen shirt, taking them with me, my juices slicking up my thighs as I led the way.

My bed was perfectly made. Even one-handed, Ry still insisted on doing nearly everything on board. It helped distract him, giving him a sense of normalcy after everything we'd gone through.

Flynn yanked off the covers, sending the mound of white pillows flying. Ez pushed me over arse up and face first into the sheets, and I moaned, my tight nipples grazing the silky material.

"So beautiful," Ez murmured. "So strong and sexy."

Hands landed on my arse, kneading my cheeks before they slid down to my knees. Ezra. A wash of his warm breath blew across my cunt, and I shivered, anticipation thrumming through me. He brushed his soft stubble against my thigh as Flynn crawled on the bed in front of me. I lifted my face to look, and he was working his hard cock, jacking off as he watched Ez work his way to my core, teasing me with gentle kisses along my inner thighs.

Flynn threaded his fingers through my hair and pointed his dick at my mouth. I opened, greedily lapping at the salty essence pooling in a drop at his slit. I moaned and begged, "Face fuck me."

He inched forward just as Ez licked a swipe across my cunt lips. Flynn thrust a little deeper with each pass, and Ez devoured me. Pre-cum coated my tastebuds, and I soaked Ezra with my own juices. Flynn's piercings slid over my lip and tongue. I moaned, desperate and needy for more.

I wanted to be filled.

Every hole stretched and used until I was sated.

I wanted to feel their cum inside me, dripping out of me when I walked. I wanted them to cover me in it like one of those splatter paintings.

I wanted to be owned and claimed.

Ez added his fingers, and I cried out, arching into his touch. My back was a deep curve as I strained to get closer to Flynn.

"Now that's a beautiful sight," Tris purred as he and Ry walked in.

I preened, the knowledge that they liked what they were watching turning me on and driving me higher.

The flick of a lube cap had my cunt clenching, and Ezra hummed. "You like that, don't you, jailbird. Want us to fuck you all over."

"Everywhere," I breathed after popping off Flynn's cock.

"Good," Ry growled. "Because I want that pretty mouth of yours around my dick just like you're doing to Flynn." Fingers were at my arse, prodding my hole in counterpoint to Ezra's in my cunt.

"Do it, Ry. Put those fingers in our girl's hole," Flynn gasped as I took him deeper, his cockhead hitting the back of my throat. I gagged, and he angled my head back, rising up higher on his knees. "Take it, Zee," he grunted.

That was their cue. I was stuffed full with fingers in my arse and cunt, both moving hard and fast. I didn't have time to get used to them before Flynn thrust forward again and forced himself as deep as he could go. My throat closed around his cockhead, and his piercings massaged me as he pressed deeper. He wasn't manhandling me hard, but it was enough that I spaced out, dropping into a zone where I was their toy. Their fuck doll. I couldn't breathe around his length, and he held it there, his cock throbbing as two fingers inside me turned to three, Ez and Ry stretching me to the point of pain.

I fucking loved it.

Flynn pulled back, and I gasped in a breath, tears leaking from my eyes as my throat stung.

I needed Tristan. My professor. I wanted his dick too. I threw my hand out sideways and caught his hip. Blindly reaching for his cock, I fisted his slick length, but he batted it away. "You're ours to fuck today, kitten, and I want your tits. So come like the pretty little slut you are, and we'll all take what we want off you. We'll use you until you can't stand. Everyone will know how much you love cock. They'll all want a piece of you. Your arse, your pussy, and even your mouth."

Oh fuck, his words.

The rushing inside me built higher and higher, and Ez hummed. The vibration went straight to my clit. I cried out, hissing when Ry added another finger. I didn't know what he was up to, but the stretch was like he had his whole hand up my arse, fisting me.

Memories slammed into me of the way he'd obliterated my senses when he'd fisted my cunt, and I cried out, my channel tightening as I rode the edge.

Flynn punched his hips forward again, pressing into my throat, and Ez bit my clit.

I shattered, my body convulsing and ecstasy washing over me like a cool breeze on a hot summer day.

Flynn was gone out of my mouth before I could stop him. I cried out in protest, blinking my eyes open so I could bring him back to me. His cock was an angry red as he gripped its base and tugged his balls away from his body. He was on the edge too, and I watched him avidly trying to fight against his body's basic instinct to fuck.

Cold lube drizzled down my crack, and Ry withdrew before pumping back in and twisting his hand at the same time. I shouted out, the sensation overwhelming.

"She's gonna come again. I can feel it," Ez murmured against my lips.

"Bite me," I begged, and he didn't hesitate, closing his teeth over my clit again. The sharp sting set me on fire, igniting my nerve endings until I was a shaking, sweaty mess.

Then they were gone, and I was being manoeuvred like a rag doll, spun around and draped over Flynn's hard body. He brought his fingers to my nipples, twisting and pinching them as his cock nudged my cunt. I moaned, begging him to take me.

But he didn't. He waited, and I whimpered, begging, "Fuck me, please."

"We're here, beautiful," Ez promised from between my legs, his hands closing around my hips. "We've got you."

He pressed his cockhead against my hole, both their dicks prodding me. I wiggled my hips, trying to get closer, but Ezra's grip tightened, holding me still.

They stretched out the wait, stringing me on for an eternity until I arched back and demanded impatiently, "Fuck me already."

Ry chuckled softly, a dark sound that to any sane person would have signalled impending doom. But for me it amped up the excitement.

Flynn and Ez timed their thrusts perfectly, each slamming into me with the force of a freight train and splitting me open even though I'd been stretched. I cried out, the burn stealing my breath. My mouth open, I sucked in a lungful of air and Ry's cock at the same time.

Gagging, I opened my eyes and saw him grit his teeth. "Gonna fuck this pretty mouth, baby girl, and you're gonna swallow every drop of my cum. You aren't going to waste a drop, are you."

My eyes closed in acquiescence, and he fisted my hair, pumping his hips forward in a steady rhythm. Flynn and Ez started moving too, this time in counterpoint, each time pressing against the thin wall between my holes. I cried out.

The weight on the mattress shifted, and Tristan draped himself over me, lying across my body. He stole my breath, pressing me hard against Flynn. His cock prodded my side, slipping under my tit into the tight squeeze between Flynn's and my chests.

He thrust in, using my body to get himself off the way they were all doing.

I floated, my body climbing and need and desire spiralling through me.

Another orgasm hit me, and my guys rode it out, bucking into me and prolonging it until I was breathless. Panting, Ry let me come down for a moment before he gripped my hair tight and thrust forward, sinking into my throat.

Their grunts and groans were like a symphony, every noise they made driving me higher and higher.

Their movements turned jerky, the thrusts getting harder and more desperate as my cunt clenched and released around them. Over and over, they fucked me, slowing down only to speed up again when I started the climb and tossing me over with so much skill, I lost count of how many times I shattered in their arms.

My head was hazy, the room spinning behind my closed eyelids. Breathless, my throat ached, my arse was raw, my cunt was tender, and my ribs bruised from the force of Tristan's thrusts. I came again, my cunt throbbing long and hard.

Ez shouted out, the hot spray of his cum on my inner walls like a drug to an addict. I floated, riding the high of the pulse inside me just as Ry pulled back, his corona pressing against my lips. He roared and filled my mouth with his seed, flooding me until I was forced to swallow.

But more came.

Ry pulled back, his cock pulling out of my mouth with an audible pop as Flynn let go of my nipple and brought my lips to his. We shared Ry's cum, passing it between us on our tongues as he kissed me until I was breathless. I drank in his cry as he filled me.

The flood of warmth between our bodies and Tristan's groan was hot as fucking hell, and my body tightened once more.

"Oh yeah. Again," Ez ordered, pumping his softening cock into me. Flynn did the same, and his piercings massaging my oversensitive inner walls set me off again.

I cried out, the force of my orgasm side swiping me. Darkness closed in around the edges of my vision, and my body went loose, floating in a cloud of ecstasy.

TWENTY-FOUR

Zali

FOURTEEN MONTHS LATER (MARCH)

We'd nicknamed the house our castle, and it certainly was. All it needed was a moat, but we'd decided being surrounded on three sides by water was good enough. We owned the entire chunk of land on the U-shaped bend in the river. There was a deep water mooring for the Noble Steed, and at the opposite end, our beach was private and had the most crystal-clear water I'd ever seen.

A sub-tropical forest sheltered the front of the estate from the road, a pair of gates at the entrance the only hint that there was even a house on it. It was the only change we'd made to the property after receiving a few visits from people wanting to fish or swim along the river and not realizing the property was privately owned.

It was peaceful, perfectly quiet, and full of wildlife. Home to a mob of wallabies and at least a couple of koalas, we also had a pair of wedge-tailed eagles nesting on one of the highest trees, and I'd seen a wombat toddle across the gardens bordering the helipad a few weeks earlier.

Yes, the helipad.

The house had everything you could possibly dream of—swimming pool with a pavilion to die for, gym, sauna, sixteen-seat theatre, recording studio, wine cellar, separate office building, library with one of those roller ladders and floor-to-ceiling shelves filled with books, caretaker's cottage, helipad, garage specifically for toys next to the office building, seven extra bedrooms, eleven bathrooms, and most importantly, a main bedroom big enough for an Alaskan king bed that we could all fit comfortably on with enough walk-in closet space to fit all our clothes.

We'd been sold on the house before we saw the bedroom, but walking into it was one of those moments. We'd spun in a circle, took one look at the one-hundred-and-eighty-degree view of the water and the balcony that faced it, and decided on the spot.

We needed it.

Tris and Ez insisted on selling their apartments and giving me the money from them. Ry gave me his savings. Flynn insisted too, but I wouldn't let him, not when he was still studying and barely earned anything from his job—when they gave him shifts. I didn't need them to give me anything, and I hated accepting the transfers, but this was our place, not mine. I didn't want to refuse their contribution and have them call it my house.

Today wasn't the first celebration we'd had, but it was one of the most important. It was the launch date for *Tarnished Crown*—the irony of my mother's nickname and my own wasn't lost on me, but I'd come to believe my guys. Our nicknames were where the similarities between us ended.

It was also Asher's birthday. He would have been twenty-six. He'd been gone for as long as he was alive, and that fact broke my heart. We'd scattered his ashes on the winter solstice. It had been an unseasonably warm day. The sky was a brilliant blue and the waters glassy. I'd asked Dad to let me know when he was ready so we could do it together. He'd picked the solstice, and although the weather was forecast to be awful, it had turned out picture-perfect. It was almost like Ash was telling us he approved of picking a day that symbolized new beginnings.

There were always dolphins at Jumpinpin, but that day it was as if all the sea life had turned out to say goodbye. There was a herd of dugong hanging out, eating seagrass and flashes of silver bait fish and bigger jewfish and tailor darting under the runabout. A pod of what had to be twenty dolphins had followed us, exiting the mouth of the river right as we were removing the mooring ropes from the runabout. They'd stayed with us until we'd stopped at the mouth of the bar.

We'd all said something, sharing our memories and saying our goodbyes to Asher before Dad, Ry, and I spread his ashes.

Now we were getting together again to commemorate his life by launching the series that would tell the world his tragic story. But it wasn't a sad day. We were all determined to make it a good one.

As usual, we were gathered around the pool and the outdoor kitchen that abutted the pavilion. We spent most of our afternoons and evenings here except for a few weeks during the coldest part of winter when we were wrapped up in front of the fireplace.

"Zee, get in with us," Flynn called from his perch in Ry's arms. The bullet wound had scarred Ry, leaving a gouge in his trapezius muscle. Plastic surgery had improved the look of it, but Ry wore the scar proudly—it was his daily reminder that we'd gotten justice for Ash. Seeing it gave him peace.

"In a minute," I agreed. "I'm just waiting for Cara to get here."

Kristy handed me a drink, and I asked, "How are things with you, Mum?"

She beamed. She loved it when I called her that. She and Cara had been my rocks in those first few months after finding out the truth of what happened. I hadn't realized it until then, but Kristy had been a mother figure to me for years already.

She'd been there for both Dad and me. I couldn't say the same about my own egg donor, the evil bitch that she turned out to be.

But as much as I said that she deserved to die, I wasn't completely heartless. My guys had held me while I cried when I thought about the life I'd taken.

I was privileged that they were helping celebrate Asher's life with us. They'd helped us mourn his loss all over again, but now it was time to honour him.

It hadn't been an easy road to this point. The nightmares were the worst, and I wasn't the only one of us who had them. I had a recurring dream of Rosa's shot landing lower, killing Ry. There was another one where I watched her push Ash from that rooftop, and no matter how fast I ran, I never reached him in time. I could never catch him.

We relied on each other during those dark nights. My guys could always pull me out of the misery I was left with after a rough dream. But it wasn't only them. Dad and I had become closer, and I had Kristy and Cara now too. They were always up for a gossip or to have a girls' night—handy when all my guys cleared out to watch whatever sport was playing at Dad's house.

"I'm good. Happy." Kristy smiled, and I caught the flush staining her cheeks. "I had a date last night. He was lovely."

"Good. He'd better treat you right."

She laughed and wrapped her arm around my shoulders, hugging me tight for a moment. "Of all the children I gained when Ry came out to me, I love that you're the most intimidating of all."

"Me? I'm a delight." I cut her a look, and she snorted another laugh. My grin probably looked more like a dog baring its teeth. "See? Happy."

She raised a brow and shook her head, biting back another laugh. "If that's what you call this—" She gestured at me, pointing at my tanned body and the smile that now seemed to radiate from my very soul when I was with my men and my family. "—then happiness looks good on all of you."

She flicked her gaze to Ry, and her smile turned soft. He was laughing with Flynn, their arms wrapped around each other as he sank under the surface with him. Flynn was better in the water now. The two of them had spent so many hours together in the pool and at our beach that Flynn's confidence had blossomed.

But Ry was stealing the show at that moment. The smile he wore was beautiful. He'd come so far and was a better man for it. His uncle and his dad's best friend had been shitty about his sexuality, but he'd stood up to them and held his head high. While their relationship was unlikely to ever be repaired, Ry no longer had to listen to their toxic rhetoric on how to be a man.

He'd turned a corner since we'd returned from Mauritius—we all had—and we were all focussing on looking forward rather than back. We were all determined to enjoy every moment our short lives on this planet afforded us.

Together.

I looked across at Dad joking with Ez and Tris. They'd become fast friends, Dad and Tris developing a special bond that warmed my heart every time I witnessed it. The three of them looked ridiculous in Hawaiian shirts, Tristan insisting on a black-and-white one rather than loud colours like the others. Beers in hand, they laughed at something Dad said, and like they could feel eyes on them, Ez and Tris turned to look at me, their smiles growing when I blew them a kiss.

I couldn't believe that this was my life now. We were happy. Ridiculously so. We argued over petty shit like all people in a relationship did. I complained when the toilet seat was left up, Tris's pet hate was someone leaving the nearly empty bottle of milk in the refrigerator rather than tipping it out, and Ry lost his shit over one of us throwing the wrong kind of plastic in the recycling bin or rubbish. But all in all, the problems we dealt with between us were minor.

It wasn't all sunshine and roses otherwise though. Ry losing his uncle and family friend had hit him harder than he cared to admit. The stubborn infection that had buried itself into his shoulder added months to his recovery.

He'd turned into a bear, growling at everything and everyone until he managed to kick it and start healing again.

Flynn had walked away from his family too. They'd tried to blame a supposed break-in at their house on him. We could only guess their motivation, but their demand for cash in exchange for dropping the charges was a decent clue. The case was weak at best, but his parents had been backed up by his siblings in accusing Flynn of stealing cash and some jewellery. They'd reported seeing him sneaking out of the house with his old school backpack in his hands. In actual fact, he hadn't been there in over a year, and we'd vouched for his whereabouts that night. His alibi was locked down so tight that the police had arrested his parents on charges of making false police reports as well as fraud. We'd taken out a restraining order against them.

But Flynn's initial arrest had rocked him to his core.

Ez had walked away from the force, but it hadn't been easy for him either. Inspector Puglisi had referred him to Ethics, and the investigation had threatened Ezra's reputation. But he had good representation, and both the union and his private lawyer had thrown out every claim. He was now working for me in our fledgling charity.

Ry had come on board with us too, looking after logistics and generally organizing everything for us. He still insisted on doing all the cooking, but I'd managed to talk him into letting someone else to take over the cleaning and landscaping. He hated lawn mowing, and with land as vast as ours, it was a full-time job. I didn't want him waiting on me hand and foot anymore anyway—we were equals, not employer/employee anymore.

Tris was drowning in work, but he was seeing the rewards too. He'd hired Cara and another guy from our class, Jude, to help with preparation of the podcast for production and a team of media students to look after editing. He'd delayed the launch to help build media attention for it, and allowing the anticipation to build was his best move yet.

I couldn't believe that the time had finally come for the first season to drop. Ten episodes of the life and lies of Rosa Weatherall were locked in to go to air—one each week from now until the beginning of May. Season two—the truths we discovered—would run from mid-June.

Tarnished Crown was going to turn Tris into a rockstar, and his proteges—Cara and Jude—were already fielding job offers. No one but us knew Tris had signed movie rights for an Amazon exclusive movie and that Cara and Flynn were helping with the screenplay.

"I wonder where Cara is," I mused, pulling my phone from the back pocket of my jean shorts to call her. I wasn't used to wearing clothes at home, but the pockets did come in handy.

"Right here," Cara said as she dropped her beach bag on the cabana with a weighted sigh.

Her smile was strained, but she still looked adorable wearing a floaty-looking floral dress, broad-brimmed hat, and Chucks.

"Hi. Sorry I'm late," Cara apologized as she came over to hug me, holding on to me extra tight for a moment.

"Better late than never," Dad murmured quietly, a reverence in his voice I hadn't heard before. He was staring at Cara wide-eyed, his mouth open and the pulse point on his throat going wild. He slicked his bottom lip with his tongue, wiped his hand on his shorts, and held it out to her. "Monroe Stevens. I don't believe I've had the pleasure of meeting you before."

"Cara Delaware," she breathed, a flush staining her cheeks and a nervous giggle erupting from her. She slotted her hand in Dad's, and they shook, holding on to each other for a fraction longer than necessary. Their gazes held.

Ez slipped in behind me and wrapped his arm around my waist. I relaxed back against him, and he murmured, "Maybe today is the beginning of something else apart from the podcast."

"I hope so," I breathed. Dad deserved to find the happiness I'd discovered and experience what true love was like. He'd lost so much, and if I could dream of anything, it would be that Dad found his great love.

* * * * *

"What's this, Zali?" Dad asked, picking up the gift box I'd placed next to him. We were still outside, the sun having long since set, a quiet descending on the estate. The moon reflected off the water, and stars glittered across the sky. Ry had lit the firepit, and we were gathered around it, toasting marshmallows. Strings of fairy lights hung from the branches of the massive Moreton Bay fig that towered over us.

I swallowed. This was it. I wasn't sure what his reaction would be, but I'd soon find out.

"Open it, Dad," I said, sitting down beside him.

He lifted the lid and sucked in a sharp breath. It was the last photograph we think had ever been taken of Asher.

Martha's wife had snapped it only a couple of weeks before she'd died. Ash was sitting on the sand, looking out over the ocean, sketchbook in his lap. The sun was high in the sky on a bright blue day with a perfect ocean in front of him. I could only see his profile, but the longing in his gaze was obvious even from a distance.

He'd changed so much in the months after that bitch had taken him. He looked older, more mature. His shoulders had started to fill out, and his legs were even longer. We could only see the toes of his prosthetic foot, but I'd been overcome with relief when I'd seen it. The thought that Rosa could have been lying about giving him one had crossed my mind, and, for once, I was glad to have been proven wrong.

But it was the hunch in his shoulders that broke my heart, the sadness that hung over him like a spectre that haunted me.

When Martha had emailed the photo to me a few weeks ago, I'd stared at it for a long time, not knowing whether to delete the email so we'd never see it again, or to print it.

"I.... Thank you," Dad whispered, tears in his eyes. He sniffed and wiped his face with the back of his hand before letting out a huff of breath.

"You all brought him back to me. You gave me a chance to say a proper goodbye to my baby. You found his killer. Now you've given me this too." With the frame still in his hand, he hugged me tight to him, holding on to me like a lifeline. "I love you, Zali," he whispered. "Thank you."

I pulled back and opened my mouth to respond, but he shook his head. "I know you're protecting me from something, and that woman was a coward." He paused for a moment and added, "Put it this way, if she didn't kill herself when you confronted her, I'd be okay with that. So, thank you for righting the wrongs she committed."

I was speechless. I had no idea what to say to that or even if I should say anything. I looked at Ez, Tris, and Flynn standing on one side of Dad, but their carefully blank faces spoke volumes—it was my decision. When I turned to Ry, his face was set in a hard glare, hatred burning from him. He lifted his chin and nodded slightly, squaring his shoulders and sitting straighter. Dad noticed the subtle movements and smiled, satisfaction lighting him up.

When we pulled apart, Dad added to the group, "The first episode is about to hit. I'm here if any of you ever need to talk, and I acquired a punching bag that's quite therapeutic." His knuckles were showing it too. It didn't matter that he had boxing gloves—he preferred hitting it bare.

Dad looked at the photo again and sighed. "I'd give anything for us to have one more moment with him, but I'm so grateful for the memories. I took them for granted until I couldn't make any more. Now they're all I have. I want to cherish even the smallest things. Moments with all of you are my favourite."

He reached for Ezra, who was sitting on the log next to him, and squeezed his shoulder, still hugging me close. "I'm sorry for the way I reacted when you two told me you were together. I said some awful things, and I didn't understand how you could possibly love more than one person. But I see it with all of you. It's obvious just how much you love one another. I'm so happy that you have that love in your life."

Dad was right. We would do anything for one another.

They were it for me.

My great love story.

My family.

In a world filled with eight billion people, I'd found the four men who made my soul sing. They lit me up. They lifted me and made me a better person. Just like I did for them.

They made me want to live every day to its fullest. They gave me their love unconditionally, and I loved them unendingly.

We weren't perfect—no one was—but they were perfect for me.

They were perfect for one another too.

I'd once thought that Queen was my shield that had also trapped me. I'd become a hardened loner, my circle consisting only of the handful of people who wouldn't let me walk away.

I was the infamous hacker. A queen by name and status. I was untouchable. Uncatchable. Unstoppable. I'd committed more crimes than I could count.

I'd done far worse since beginning this case.

Boundaries didn't contain me the way they corralled the rest of the world. Like the chess piece, I went anywhere I desired. I lived by my own rules and my own moral code. If I wanted something, I took it.

But I'd changed. Softened. I was no longer trapped. I wasn't a loner either.

I'd learned just how fragile life was. I may have been untouchable behind a computer, but I wanted to experience every touch by my men possible.

Societal boundaries were still bullshit, but our party of five, and the bond I shared with my guys, was immutable.

I still took whatever I wanted, whenever I wanted it.

Just like I had last night.

Every one of the dreams I'd never dared to have had come true fourfold. I had the love of these incredible men—my best friend, my professor, my once boss, and my alpha. We'd built a home together. We'd gone through hell, and now we were surrounded by love and happiness. I wanted this life, this love, and these orgasms, forever.

One lifetime with them would never be enough.

*****

Haven't had enough of Zali and her men?
Download the alternate ending here:
https://bookhip.com/TBRFRRR

Want to find out if Cara gets her happily ever after?
Pre-order Sweet as Puck now:
https://books2read.com/SweetasPuck

Two men who need a second chance. Could she be the sunshine who lights their dark days?

I've never been kissed.

I'm not exactly everyone's cup of tea.

I'm shy.

I'm a fumbling mess most of the time.

And my curves turn boys off.

Until Monroe and Alec.

But they're not boys. They're... *sigh.*

Monroe is my best friend's father.

He's the sexiest silver fox I've ever seen, and I melt with his praise and gentle guidance.

But he's wary—the loss of his wife and son left him broken hearted. I want to be his second chance.

Alec is so different. He's the bad boy of the NHL—getting caught pucking around with his teammate's wife destroyed his reputation.

He's grumpy, arrogant, and the best pro-hockey player our league has ever seen.

I shouldn't fall for either one, never mind both. It has epic disaster written all over it.

But we can't seem to stay away from one another.

If only we weren't doomed from the start.

Sweet as Puck is a steamy bi-awakening, age gap, why choose MMF romance. It features a disgraced hockey star seeking redemption, a widower learning to open his heart to love again and the inexperienced curvy girl who finally finds two men who treat her like the goddess she is.

Pre-order Sweet as Puck now:
https://books2read.com/SweetasPuck

I appreciate your help in spreading the word, including telling a friend. Reviews help readers find books! Please leave a review on your fave review site.

About Ann Grech

By day Ann Grech used to live in the corporate world and could be found sitting behind a desk typing away at reports and papers or lecturing to a room full of students. She graduated with a PhD in 2016 and is now an over-qualified nerd. But the grind got old, and the voices got louder. She still has the librarian look nailed, but she's a little freer to be herself now.

She's never entirely fit in and loves escaping into a book—whether it's reading or writing one. But she's found her tribe and loves her book world family. She dislikes cooking, but loves eating, can't figure out technology, but is addicted to it, and her guilty pleasure is Byron Bay Cookies. Oh and shoes. And lingerie. And maybe handbags too. Well, if we're being honest, we'd probably have to add her library too given the state of her credit card every month (what can she say, she's a bookworm at heart)!

In 2019 she was an Award-Winning Finalist in the Fiction: LGBTQ category of the 2019 Best Book Awards sponsored by American Book Fest for her story In Safe Arms.

She also publishes her raunchier short stories under her pen name, Olive Hiscock.

Ann loves chatting to people online, so if you'd like to keep up with what she's got going on:

Join her newsletter (you'll get two free books!):
https://landing.mailerlite.com/webforms/landing/d8m4r2

Follow her on Instagram:
@anngrechauthor

Follow her on TikTok:
@authoranngrech

Like her on Facebook:
https://www.facebook.com/pages/Ann-
Grech/458420227655212

Join her reader group:
https://www.facebook.com/groups/1871698189780535/

Follow her on Goodreads:
https://www.goodreads.com/author/show/7536397.Ann_
Grech

Follow her on BookBub:
https://www.bookbub.com/authors/ann-grech

Follow her on Amazon:
https://www.amazon.com/~/e/B00IJPO3EM

Visit her website for her current booklist:
http://www.anngrech.com/

She'd love to hear from you directly, too. Please feel free to e-mail her at ann@anngrech.com or check out her website for updates.

ANN GRECH'S BOOKS

BILLIONAIRE BOSS GIRL

Professorhole (why choose/Polyamorous – MMMMF)
Bosshole (why choose/Polyamorous – MMMMF)
Alphahole (why choose/Polyamorous – MMMMF)

SPINOFF FROM BILLIONAIRE BOSS GIRL

Sweet as Puck (MMF)

RULE OF THREE

Three Hearts (MMF) (Also available in audio)
Yes, Captain (MM)
Triple Beat (MMF)
Threepeat (MMF)
Third Time's A Charm (MMF)
Triple Threat (MMF)

PEARCE STATION DUET

Outback Treasure I (MM)
Outback Treasure II (MM)

SPINOFF FROM PEARCE STATION

Three of Us (MMF)

UNEXPECTED

Whiteout (MM)
White Noise (MM)
Whitewash (MM)
White Wedding (available in the series omnibus,
White Winter)

MY TRUTH

All He Needs (MMM)
In Safe Arms (MM)

STANDALONES

Home For Christmas (MM)
The Gift (FMMM - free for newsletter subscribers)
Take Two (MM – free for newsletter subscribers)

M/F TITLES

One night in Daytona
Ink'd

GERMAN TRANSLATIONS

Outback Treasure I
Outback Treasure II

www.ingramcontent.com/pod-product-compliance
Lightning Source LLC
Chambersburg PA
CBHW030519120726

47904CB00005B/1530